WRITING
HOME

WRITING

HOME

AWARD-WINNING

LITERATURE

from the

NEW WEST

Edited by Brian Bouldrey
Foreword by James D. Houston

Heyday Books ✦ Berkeley, California

For Jill Olson and Owen Bly, New Westerners

—B.B.

© 1999 by The San Francisco Foundation

Library of Congress Cataloging in Publication Data:

Writing home: award-winning literature from the New West / edited by Brian Bouldrey ; foreword by James D. Houston.
    p.   cm.
  ISBN 1-890771-22-8 (pbk.)
    1. American literature—West (U.S.) 2. American literature—20th century. 3. West (U.S.) Literary collections. I. Bouldrey, Brian.
PS561.W77   1999
810.8'0978'09045—dc21

                                                              99-40589
                                                                   CIP

Cover Art: "Bright City," 1993, by Wayne Thiebaud, collection of the
    San Francisco Museum of Modern Art, courtesy of the Campbell-
    Thiebaud Gallery, San Francisco, CA
Cover Design: David Bullen Design, Albany, CA
Interior Design: Rebecca LeGates
Printing and Binding: Publishers Press, Salt Lake City, UT

Orders, inquiries, and correspondence should be addressed to:
Heyday Books
P.O. Box 9145
Berkeley, CA 94709
510/549-3564; Fax 510/549-1889
heyday@heydaybooks.com

Printed in the United States of America

10 9 8 7 6 5 4 3 2 1

Contents

Memoir and Personal Essay

Fiction

Poetry

Acknowledgments

Very special thanks to Cedric Brown, whose idea this book was, Malcolm Margolin, Julianna Fleming, Wayne Thiebaud, James D. Houston, Wendy Lesser, the Bancroft Library, and The San Francisco Foundation.

—B.B.

Foreword

James D. Houston

The stories and essays and poems gathered in this volume all speak for themselves. But something needs to be said about these two awards, which have given so many of us an early boost and have, for decades now, nourished California's thriving literary life. The Jackson. The Phelan. We refer to them as entities with lives of their own. But how did they get here? And why?

When you're starting out as a writer, you don't think much about such matters or about where the money may be coming from. You just hope that sooner or later some of it will come your way. The first check I ever received for a piece of writing happened to have James D. Phelan's name on it. In those long-ago days—my undergraduate days in San Jose—I knew nothing about this fellow, whether he was an alumnus or the former chair of a department, whether he was alive or dead. I only knew that every spring something called the "Phelan Awards" were given out for stories and plays and poems by campus writers. For a while I was trying my hand at sonnets. They had a special category for sonnets, and eventually I submitted one I thought might be a contender. I came in third. Since I had never applied for anything or come close to winning anything, I was very happy to take third place in the sonnet contest at San Jose State. At the awards ceremony I got to hang out with other aspiring writers. And thanks to James D. Phelan—whoever he might be—I walked away with a check for ten dollars, which was a serious piece of money back then. I was sitting on top of the world. "Ten dollars for fourteen lines," I was thinking, "that's over seventy cents a line!"

Two decades would pass before I fully understood how that check had found its way into my pocket and where it fit with Phelan's numerous efforts to encourage the work of the creative imagination. The campus awards, by the way, were somewhat different from the award being celebrated here. The intent was similar, the source was the same, but those were local rather than statewide. Phelan had never attended San Jose State. He simply wanted to recognize younger writers in the valley where he'd enjoyed his final years.

In the late 1970s I had the good fortune to spend two months as writer-in-residence at Villa Montalvo, his palatial spread outside Saratoga, in the foothills west of Santa Clara Valley. While there I learned that his father had come to California during the gold rush and made a fortune in banking and real estate. Born in San Francisco in 1861, Phelan had served as the city's mayor, elected on a reform ticket in 1897. A Democrat in a predominately Republican state, he later spent a term in the U.S. Senate, where he made some friends and made some enemies, as politicians usually do.

I have to confess that his political career has not interested me nearly so much as the fact that he named his villa for a novelist. Has anyone else done this? Towns and cities sometimes do. Oakland has Jack London Square. But who else has named his own residence after a writer of any type? It has always seemed to me to be a key to Phelan's passions and preferences, particularly since this novelist was one that few people had heard of back in 1912, when the villa was completed.

An ardent Californian, he felt a special kinship with the fellow who had coined the name of his home state. It appears for the first time in *The Adventures of Esplandian,* a novel by Garci Ordoñez de Montalvo. Little is known about Montalvo, except that he wrote this sixteenth-century romance, a tale of preposterous adventures carried out by a bold Spanish knight whose exploits take him to "an island called California, very close to the side of the Terrestrial Paradise...." The word is not Spanish. It is a Spanish-*sounding* word, an invented word, a science-fiction name for a fantastical place. Montalvo's novel was published in Seville in 1510, twenty-five years before the earliest explorers, sent out by Hernando Cortez, sighted and named what is now the tip of lower or Baja California.

An estate with a legacy both literary and regional: this is in perfect keeping with Phelan's tastes. Born to wealth, shrewd in business, he was also a voracious reader, an essayist too, a sometime poet who traded manuscripts with friends, and a student of European history. An exceptionally cultivated man, he was very much at ease in the company of writers, painters, and sculptors. Before becoming mayor, he had served as President of the San Francisco Art Association. His circle included some of the most eminent creative people of his day, among them landscape painter William Keith; architect Arthur Page Brown, who designed the Ferry Building; poets George Sterling and Edwin Markham; and his longtime friend and confidante, novelist Gertrude Atherton. To this day one of the villa's apartments is named for her.

He passed away in 1930. A bachelor all his life, with no immediate heirs, he bequeathed his Saratoga property to the people of California, with the grounds to be maintained as a public park, and the buildings "to be used as far as possible for the development of art, literature, and architecture...." In keeping with his will, The Montalvo Center for the Arts now offers a year-round program of plays, concerts, gallery shows, readings, and residencies. It's an Italianate villa, with columns and balustrades, surrounded by 175 acres of gardens and forested slopes. By the time I first checked in, it had already served as an elegant oasis for hundreds of writers, painters, sculptors, and composers.

He also left money to the San Francisco Public Library, the Art Association, and the Palace of The Legion of Honor. He funded the awards contest at the San Jose campus. And he set aside an endowment to "be used annually for awards in literature and art, to bring about a further developing of native talent in California." Launched in 1935, the James D. Phelan Award was the first of its kind on the West Coast, reflecting his longtime belief in the creative spirit of his home region. Seven decades later we are all the richer for it.

Joseph Henry Jackson was another kind of benefactor. He too was an ardent Californian, though not by birth. He did not have Phelan's kind of money, but he had a legendary energy that made him a spokesman for the West and for the West Coast. In his day he was one of the most highly regarded and influential literary voices in the country.

He was born in New Jersey in 1894. When we entered World War I, he left college to organize an ambulance unit and later served as an infantry lieutenant. After the war, at age twenty-five, he headed for California, settling in Berkeley. He went to work for *Sunset* magazine in 1920, rising to editor-in-chief. In 1930 he took over as literary editor for the *San Francisco Chronicle* and remained there for the rest of his career.

For twenty-five years he composed a daily column, "Bookman's Notebook." He also edited a Sunday book page for the "This World" section. In addition, he launched a weekly radio show called "Bookman's Guide," which ran for eighteen years. Broadcast first over KGO, it was later carried by the Pacific Coast Network and eventually aired coast-to-coast via NBC. His columns, which were reprinted in the *Los Angeles Times,* together with his radio show and occasional pieces for the *New York Times* and the *Saturday Review,* gave Jackson a national voice. Fair-minded and even-tempered, he was surely the most listened to literary commentator west of Chicago.

His influence was felt in another way, as a frequent judge of contests, both local and nationwide. During his quarter century with the *Chronicle,* Jackson served at various times as judge for The Phelan Award, the Commonwealth Club Medals, the O. Henry Memorial Awards, The Atlantic Prize, The Harper Prize Novel, and the Pulitzer.

For most of us, this would have added up to a full-time job. But somehow he found time to author books of his own, more than a dozen titles, most having to do with the history, culture, or literary life of his adopted region. The best known today is *Anybody's Gold: The Story of California's Mining Towns* (1941), recently included by the *San Francisco Chronicle* on its list of the twentieth century's 100 best nonfiction books by writers west of the Rockies. Many years before the gold rush had been rediscovered as a key to California's past and present, Jackson had given us this pioneering work.

In 1944, he edited the first significant anthology of West Coast literature: *Continent's End: A Collection of California Writing.* An early champion of writers such as John Steinbeck and William Saroyan, he believed in California as a literary region with its own unique vitality and promise. It is impressive now to note the poets and storytellers he had recognized and brought together into a single volume almost sixty years ago. Among them we find, in addition to Saroyan and Steinbeck, Hildegarde Flanner, Kenneth Rexroth, Josephine Miles, John Fante, M. F. K. Fisher, James M. Cain, Budd Shulberg, George R. Stewart, Gertrude Atherton (still based in San Francisco then, and still writing), and Robinson Jeffers, whose famous poem had given the collection its evocative title.

Soon after Jackson's death in 1955, some friends began searching for a way to remember him and his legacy. This group was led by novelist and historian George Stewart and by James D. Hart, who would later become Director of the Bancroft Library and who for many years served as Secretary to the Jackson Award.

In his eloquent introduction to the 1970 re-issue of *Anybody's Gold*, Wallace Stegner remembered those meetings: "From the beginning it was clear what his most fitting monument would be; he had helped so many writers that he ought to be remembered through a fellowship to a young writer of promise. Prose or poetry, it didn't matter; Joe had a history of liking and assisting both. But the geographical territory from which those fellows should be drawn did matter, and the committee of his friends had some discussion about it before they made up their minds."

While Jackson's audience was national, his passions were closer to home. In an effort to be true to his life and work, they settled at last on Northern California and Nevada, the parts of the world he had inhabited and roamed and written about and come to love. They raised some seed money to get it launched. Two years later the first Joseph Henry Jackson Award went, fittingly, to Salinas Valley writer Dennis Murphy, for his taut and compelling short novel, *The Sergeant*.

In *The Paris Review* interview series, "Writers at Work," Katherine Anne Porter speaks of her apprenticeship. "I spent fifteen years," she says, "learning to trust myself: that's what it comes to."

Every writer talks about the time required to find one's way. She was the first I'd heard describe the task as learning to trust oneself on the page. It immediately struck me as an essential truth. And years of disciplined practice, as she details elsewhere in the interview, is the way to get there. But this particular type of trust can sometimes be nudged along by other means.

Back in 1967 the manuscript I submitted was a new departure for me, not new for literature perhaps, but a kind of storytelling I hadn't tried before. I had not yet published any long fiction. I wasn't at all sure I could bring this off. A short novel called *Gig,* it concerned one night in a piano bar, told by the piano player. Customers gather at the lid of his grand, and it becomes a little theatre-in-the-round, arranged not in acts but in "sets," as a musician would conceive his evening of music, with an emphasis on the lyrics of the songs he plays, a kind of guiding scripture.

The Jackson judges that year were all writers I admired. Their recognition increased by a huge measure my belief in what I had attempted, as well as my commitment to the writer's path. The money, of course, was very gratifying, as was the author's luncheon and the press release that followed. But what these awards are really about, in my experience, is faith. The Phelan, The Jackson—aimed at younger writers—offer you that next increment of faith in your own imagination, what it has given you so far, what it has yet to give.

Santa Cruz, California
June 1999

Introduction

Brian Bouldrey

"Please give me your pens," the man said, holding out his hand.

It was hard for me to give them up, especially when surrounded by so many books and documents. I was standing in the outer lobby to the University of California-Berkeley's wondrous Bancroft Library, the repository for thousands of rare books, texts, diaries, and records.

It did seem ironic to put away my pens in this scholarly place, as ironic as the strict order and rigorous referential caretaking that goes on in the Bancroft in Berkeley, a city that often prides itself on chaos and casualness. After relinquishing the ink, I was offered any number of soft-lead pencils (providing their own sensual experience: the elementary school aroma of wood shavings; the lacquered yellow, the color of a knee-jerk test-taking alarm; the little nubbin of snapped-off lead rolling under the fingertips). And, to protect the rare things that I would pore over with my grubby, oily hands, they gave me cheap white cotton gloves, the kind handed out to us in high school marching band. I decided that this visit to Bancroft was some sort of nostalgia trip.

Nostalgia: both personal and general, for while I was drawn into my own past by a simple pencil and a pair of white gloves, I had no idea what sort of history I was in for when the librarian brought out two storage boxes full of manuscripts, the complete record of the winners of the James Duval Phelan Award and the Joseph Henry Jackson Award, sponsored by The San Francisco Foundation.

A Californian named James Duval Phelan served as a United States senator and civic leader in San Francisco in the late nineteenth and early twentieth centuries. During his lifetime, Phelan encouraged and financially assisted California-born writers, artists, and musicians; he also provided very generously for them through his will, after his death in 1930.

Similarly, Joseph Henry Jackson was the literary editor of the *San Francisco Chronicle* and a noted author and editor, presiding over many awards, including the Pulitzer Prize. He was always interested in discovering and encouraging new writers as they came into Northern California and Nevada. After his death in 1955, his friends established an award in his name for writers living in those places.

(Both of these figures are further described in James D. Houston's foreword to this collection.)

Each year, hundreds of hopeful young writers submit their work. Between these two awards, some of the most prominent names in literature have been nurtured—writers like Ernest J. Gaines *(The Autobiography of Miss Jane Pittman, A Lesson Before Dying)*, Paul Fussell *(The Great War and Modern Memory)*, poet/filmmaker James Broughton, poet Philip Levine, editor Wendy Lesser, Leonard Gardner, Jane Hirshfield, Sallie Tisdale, Dagoberto Gilb, and David Shields—and many others have also emerged, thanks in part to this recognition.

In 1998, at the cusp of "too late"—for recipients of the prizes must be no older than thirty-five—I received a "special" award given sporadically to writers of nonfiction. At the ceremony, awards administrator Cedric Brown approached me about a possible project: could I assemble a worthy collection of work by past winners of the prizes as a way of introducing a third award? I said I'd see. That's how I found myself plumeless and mittened in the Bancroft Library, rummaging through the prize-winning works. It was an eerie and thrilling experience. For I got to touch—or rather my gloves got to touch—the original manuscripts of many now-famous texts, including Leonard Gardner's complete manuscript for *Fat City*, David Shields's *Dead Languages* (then called *Emile Coue's Likely Cure*), and poems revised on the page by Jane Hirshfield.

As I pawed through these archives, it became apparent that the awards have changed over the years. Sometimes the prizes were given to artists. For a time, composers were eligible, and thick accordioned piles of sheet music filled the folders. Plays have won, as has scholarly criticism. But whether Jackson or Phelan intended it or not, the award-winning writers over the decades have returned again and again to a single theme: what it means to be a writer from the West.

Wallace Stegner, arguably the quintessential California writer, created in his novel *Angle of Repose* the turn-of-the-century East Coast transplant Susan Ward Burling. She is an artist by talent, but within her first year of living in the West, she begins writing dispatches for *Scribner's* and *The Atlantic Monthly:* "Willingly or unwillingly, she collected experience and wrote it back East in letters. Perhaps she wrote so fully because she wanted to divert [her abandoned friend's] depression. Perhaps she was only indulging her own starved desire for talk."

Having read my share of writing of the West, both between the covers of books and in grotty manuscript, I have a funny little theory about what may be the only commonality all of the work shares: they can all be read as if they were letters to folks at home. Whether the writers are among the early visitors to the West—John Muir, Bret Harte, Mark Twain—or the ones who moved here last week, the sense of "here" and "there" never quite disappears. And no matter how many people have gone to the West, they write as if they were the first to stumble upon El Capitan in Yosemite or that great burrito stand in San Francisco's Mission District. Sometimes these writers are from the West, but they, too, seem to know that this extraordinary place requires explanation and interpretation—even among fellow natives. They describe these places with a travel guide's detail, with a biblical zeal to convert nonbelievers, and with the ardor of a romantic—as if no human had ever encountered this place before. Like Susan Ward Burling, willingly or unwillingly, they all collect experience and write it back home in letters.

The writers collected in this book speak to us across the years as well as the distances, and they speak of the experience of coming into the West, either as the children of immigrants or as immigrants themselves. Their personal voices defy the stereotypes of cowboys out on the range—Dagoberto Gilb describes his working-class Latino upbringing; Fenton Johnson reminisces about being a Southern man finding a home in the far West; and Wendy Lesser tells us how Northern California shaped her life. All of them faced disappointments, challenges, dashed hopes—but somehow, those busted-up dreams became inseparable from the joy and romance of their successes.

The librarian tapped me lightly on the shoulder. "We're closing soon." I had been so deeply drawn into the stories, poems, and memoirs filling these boxes that I hadn't noticed the time. I felt slightly naughty, as if I'd been caught reading someone's diary—or a hundred people's diaries. My personal nostalgia had mingled with other people's nostalgia.

I handed the librarian my pencil, now slightly gnawed upon, and asked him to hold the materials for me. I would send a memo to Cedric at The San Francisco Foundation: yes, there is definitely something here worth writing home about.

In choosing the selections for this book, I wondered whether I could construct an anthology that would reveal something large and perhaps even universal about the West. Letter writing is what I came up with. Other than that, the range is fantastic. The West is the practice behind the theory of multicultural diversity—and the winners of Jackson and Phelan prizes reflect that diversity. And the West is not a melting pot. Our systems of values and ethics rub up against each other and create an interesting friction, sometimes painful, sometimes exciting.

This book is not a melting pot either, but a confederacy of voices. Sometimes they sing harmoniously, sometimes they clash with each other (James Broughton's memories of counterculture life aren't quite in step with Lisa Michaels's childhood among radicals; Sallie Tisdale's ideas of wide open space are challenged by Wendy Lesser's), but always, they return to the ambiguities and contradictions of living counter to and harmoniously with this mythic land.

So how do you organize a book that celebrates the chaos of the West? How do you let a quiet poem about a wedding on Mount Tamalpais peacefully resonate with a noisy slice of life served up by Anne Finger? Here at the continent's end, all the loose strands of shared and unshared values must be left to dangle—unevenly, untied. To link them together or trim them for evenness would defeat the purpose. For that reason, I've chosen the most rudimentary and straightforward architecture for this book, dividing the work into nonfiction, fiction, and poetry. Look for patterns elsewhere.

The journey to this imperfect and untidy view of the Golden West is not one of disappointment. Fiercely individual, the works in this book explore, defy, and ultimately reshape the myth of the West. I hope you will be just as excited as I was to find that the complex reality is far more interesting and beautiful than the myth.

San Francisco
August 1999

Memoir and Personal Essay

Notes of an Emigrant Son

Fenton Johnson

I grew up in the Kentucky Knobs, steep Catholic-ridden ridges that form a ragged barrier between the gentleman-farmer Episcopalians of the rolling Bluegrass (to the north) and the dirt-poor Pentecostals of the lumpy Pennyroyal (to the south and west). For nearly two centuries the Catholics of the Knobs have made whiskey, legal and illegal, for sale to all buyers. When your living is tied to sin, you tend toward a liberal view on the subject, a fact our Protestant neighbors appreciated. Over the years my town became an ecumenical melting pot, where (according to my father) you could tell a man's religion by his weapon, or lack of one: Catholics carried guns, Baptists carried knives, Episcopalians stayed in their cars and used the drive-up window, invented, at my family's tavern, anyway, to service the demands of their propriety. In our innocence we thought we were a part of the world of human events, as much a part of it as all people, anywhere; and then television arrived, and we discovered that we were not a part of the world, deep in the Kentucky Knobs; not very much a part of it at all.

Fenton Johnson was born and raised in rural Kentucky. He is the author of two novels, Crossing the River *and* Scissors, Paper, Rock, *and a memoir,* The Geography of the Heart, *which focuses on the loss of his partner to AIDS. In addition to the 1987 Jackson Award, he has received numerous awards and honors for his work, including a Wallace Stegner Fellowship in fiction and a National Endowment for the Arts Fellowship in literature. He now teaches at the University of Arizona in Tucson and is working on a book about the contemplative life in America.*

The rugged hills kept the law and television at bay, until around 1960, when the town hired its first police force and its families bought their first TVs. Eventually, the town bought off the police; television proved less tractable. With everyone (literally) watching, California came to the Knobs, hand-in-hand with the 1960s, courtesy of television the first decade to reach us more or less on schedule.

My family owned a black-and-white hand-me-down in a fake woodgrain case. On clear nights the signal was lost to the universe, but on overcast nights it bounced off the clouds, into our wide valley, and we picked up fuzzy versions of NBC and CBS. But they were enough—NBC carried Walt Disney, and even in this two-hundred-year-old town of eight hundred people, buried in the Kentucky Knobs, he had his impact: it would be a cloudy Sunday evening, and the fields that stretched along the east side of the Jackson Highway would be swarming with kids, playing fox and hounds and kick the can, and then it would be 7:30 and we would disappear all at once, to our houses, or to the houses of neighbors lucky enough to own televisions, to watch Walt Disney's *Wonderful World of Color*, in black and white.

Dwellers of the hinterlands, we came to think of television and California as synonymous, however Walter Cronkite might broadcast from New York. We watched and saw surfers, city dwellers, streets lined with orange trees and washed eternally with sunshine. (Where did those trees get water?) We saw palm trees, whose pointy fronds hinted at moonlit nights on the beach, unimaginable acts in the sand. We saw images of a bucolic countryside where city boys speaking high English led adventurous lives with heroic pets, where smart city folks brought enlightenment and progress to ignorant farmers. We watched *Beverly Hillbillies* and *Green Acres* and saw ourselves, or at least how the world saw us. We watched and went outside and saw our knobs in a new light: swarming with mosquitoes and smartweed, peopled with yokels, demanding everlasting labor to produce, not oranges and melons and nuts, but demon booze and tobacco, that evil weed. We watched and compared and, through television, came to know both shame and envy.

California! I dreamed of it on my school bus, kids packed three to a seat and in the aisles. The route wound through hills populated by white people whose surnames relegated them from birth to tin-roofed shacks of peeling clapboard. The kids from these hollers had no hot water and around February the bus got rank; across March I cultivated the habit of taking a deep breath before climbing aboard. Once in the county seat, black children were crammed onto an already overcrowded bus, adding racial tension to the overburdened air. Kids who lived in brick houses with shingle roofs and indoor plumbing—we prayed for a window seat and looked steadfastly out, dreaming, in my case, anyway, of a place where there were no race wars, no poverty, hot water for all and no sweat after a day's work; dreaming, in a word, of California.

We lived under the largest and longest of the knobs, Muldraugh's Hill, a forested limestone outcrop that stretches in a lumpy green hundred-mile arc around central Kentucky's Bluegrass. Behind it lay Fort Knox, headquarters not for any gold—by the 1960s all the gold had left for New York, or Europe—but for the United States Army Armored Divisions, whose commanders liked Muldraugh's Hill and the Kentucky Knobs because the terrain was so very similar to Vietnam.

On summer nights, we adjourned to our backyard, to watch their practice wars, reflected from the clouds more brilliant than sunset until long after sunset, flaming red and orange from the bombs and tracer flares and tank maneuvers at Fort Knox.

Later in the 1960s we moved inside, to watch the *CBS Evening News:* the war in Vietnam and the war at home—demonstrations and riots, first in Watts and Harlem, then Detroit, then Louisville, growing always closer, or so it seemed to the white men of my town. With all those men my father kept a pistol handy, ready to protect his family from the enemy beyond Muldraugh's Hill.

All that time the enemy was among us, tendered hospitality in our living room, through the medium of the fake woodgrain box, that brought us images not only of the war's ugliness but of its unpopularity, at home and abroad. While my father kept an anxious eye turned outward, his family split from within: his oldest son to the Air Force, to be shot and nearly killed in Thailand; his second son with a wife and child, grateful for his sole-support deferment; his third son to the Marines; his fourth son, myself, a contentious rebel, determined, even in high school, to avoid the draft.

My older brothers gone, my father and I were left at home, to watch Walter Cronkite together. Riots, demonstrations, hippies in

San Francisco: my father and I watched together, and saw differently. My father watched and saw the Southern Democratic party machine and the comfortable white paternalism of his childhood discarded flat-out, in exchange (as he saw it) for madness and anarchy. I watched and saw a world breaking chains of racism and old-boy politics, in an exhilarating dash for freedom and justice.

We were both wrong, of course, but no matter: our differences were not ones of politics but of generations, the old, bloody struggle of fathers and sons. As Vietnam escalated so did the heat of our quarrels, until only the women of the family, my mother and four sisters, preserved an uneasy truce, a delicate exercise in Southern manners, where the art lay in saying as much as possible about anything, nothing, so long as it wasn't Vietnam, or race.

When at the height of these conflicts Joseph E. Seagram, my father's employer, awarded me a scholarship, I didn't give the East Coast a thought. This was my ticket to California, a place as far from and as different from the family and the old country as any American place could be. My father's friends and the parish priest warned against letting me go—"he'll come back a hippie," they said, careful to say their pieces in my presence. My father knew nothing of California but what I knew, what we had seen on the news, and that must have worried him, but he knew also that I had earned this freedom, and he did not stand in my way.

And so I went to school in California. At Christmas vacation I returned, with shoulder-length hair and the announcement that I was applying as a conscientious objector, the only person in my home county to receive a C.O. across the Vietnam years. The following summer my father and I fought to a brittle silence, forged in front of the *CBS Evening News*.

In sixteen more years we broke that silence only once. On the day of my father's last bout with chemotherapy, I drove him home, through an autumn rain. Sugar maples and dogwood and sumac flamed against the limestone cliffs, scarlet leaves and bone-white rock both brightened by the wet, as water brightens seashells. On that last trip from the hospital, my father asked that I drive him down the side roads and lanes of his childhood: along the river, across the one-lane, oak-planked, cable-and-girder bridges, past deer camp, past the red brick church where he had married. In that wordless hour we touched the tender edges of this sixteen-year-old wound, cut into our lives by the *CBS Evening News,* enlarged by our own stubbornness and pride. We touched and drew back—the nearness of his death could not change this—but unspeaking, we acknowledged the bloody ties, larger than politics, larger than television, larger, in their way, than my departure for California. Now, long after the fact of his death, I am torn between remorse, that this moment was so short, and gratefulness, that it happened at all.

In my eagerness to flee Kentucky I jumped the gun, leaving in June to participate in the National Forensics Tournament, held (coincidentally) at Stanford, my college of choice.

The day before I left, a high school girlfriend took me out to drive and drink beer, and after two Falls Cities she said, "Watch out for the soup." "The soup?" I asked. "They put drugs in your soup," she said. "I saw it on Walter Cronkite," and probably she had. I did not order soup, my first day in San Francisco, but this was only because I was waiting for someone to offer me marijuana, which I had decided to accept. The next day, a blonde debater from Beverly Hills sidled up to me and said, "You want to get stoned?" and I knew that yes, I had arrived; I was in California.

Speaking on labor relations, I was eliminated in the tournament's first round, the judge noting for my benefit that "steel" was pronounced with one syllable, "oil" with two. My speech teacher flew back to Kentucky, leaving me, a seventeen-year-old from the Kentucky Knobs, alone in San Francisco, with almost no money. I was supposed to get to Los Angeles, where I had a sister waiting for me, where I was expected to spend the summer. No doubt I had told my chaperone that I had this plan, and sensitive to the fact of my poverty I no doubt told him that all had been arranged, yes, sure, I would be fine, it would all be O.K. But alone on Market Street, the question hit me: how to get to Los Angeles? Did you take a plane or a bus? How did you catch a plane or a bus? I had never done any of this, except to get myself to San Francisco, and that had been arranged for me. I was alone, with enough money to make a phone call. Maybe. How much did it cost to make a long-distance phone call? How did you *make* a long-distance phone call?

I walked for hours. I knew I ought to look for the bus station, but I was afraid to ask directions, not afraid of the people but afraid of looking ignorant, looking country, in this city, so much more vast and overwhelming than it had seemed when defined by the confines of the television.

I wanted to call my sister but I did not know if I had enough change. Finally I dialed an operator, to find out what I would need to call Los Angeles. "How much does it cost to call Los Angeles for three minutes?" I asked.

Deus ex machina; proof, that this was California; proof, maybe, of *Deus* Himself. "You can have it free," the operator said, and placed the call, and I talked to my sister in Los Angeles for a half-hour, expecting all the while for the operator to interrupt and demand more money than I had, more money than I'd ever seen. But I finished the call uninterrupted, and my sister volunteered to buy a ticket for me. I was to get myself to the airport, where all would be arranged.

Reared with manners, I was ashamed at having neglected to thank my benefactor. I was ignorant of the impossible odds against reaching the same operator, I was ignorant of most everything except the things that in Kentucky I had learned from birth: Don't talk religion or politics; don't wear plaids with stripes; thank those who do you favors. So I put my dime in the phone and called the operator, and asked again, "How much does it cost to call Los Angeles for three minutes?"

And of course I reached the same operator: "You want to call somewhere else?" she asked, and I said no, no, I just wanted to say thanks.

"Well, Ma Bell is a pig company that rips off the proletariat, and you sounded young and poor and like you were in trouble," she said. This was California; this was San Francisco, in 1971, a peculiar window in time and geography where such things happened.

She kept me on the phone for a half-hour more. She lectured me on religion ("This Catholic bullshit is for the birds. Have you heard of the Buddha?") *and* politics ("Capitalist pigs send their kids to Stanford. Why aren't you going to Berkeley?"). I—who knew nothing of either college and had chosen Stanford only because it was expensive, and Seagram was paying the bill, and I figured I should take my benefactors for what they were worth, and because it was in California, so very far away from Kentucky, and because of Walt Disney's *Wonderful World of Color* on those cloudy Sunday nights, because I came to Stanford for all those reasons—I could think of no reply to her monologue. I had never heard a liberal, a *radical*, so impassioned about politics, I had never talked to a phone operator who was impassioned about anything, and I knew then that I had arrived at the place where for seventeen years I had been going; I had arrived, a young Southern liberal, unchained in the promised land.

I hung up and flew south, to a miserable, smoggy summer in Los Angeles. I returned to Stanford in the fall, to have my country accent and ways mocked, much to my surprise and disillusionment. After all, I reasoned, as children I and these Californians had watched the same *Wonderful World of Color,* the same *CBS Evening News.* I counted myself as one of them—I rebelled, grew my hair, burned my bridges—only to find that they did not share my sense of our connection. Instead they saw me as I was, a Southern country boy, no matter how vigorously I protested the contrary: "But I'm not from the South. I'm from Kentucky!" I'd say; "We went with the North!" Only now can I hear how funny this must have sounded to these Californians.

From those first years in California I have been engaged in a battle to reform that belief, acquired during adolescence from television, that city dwellers differ from rural folks, Californians differ from Kentuckians, only in the nearness of their houses one to another, and in the species of trees that populate our front yards. Courtesy of television, it's a point of view that's grown more popular with time. And no wonder: the dollar is as negotiable in New York as in Iowa; television must sell the same detergent, with the same script, in Los Angeles and in Louisville. And so the medium delivers the unequivocal message, that I absorbed so thoroughly as a youth: in America, one place is pretty much like the next, and moving among them is a matter of calling the Mayflower man and filing a forwarding address with the Postal Service.

My experience offers, to put it mildly, abundant evidence to the contrary. My life has been one of encountering and learning to assimilate (or deciding to reject) regional differences that are subtle, yes, but avoidable only by someone whose eyes are fixed so firmly on the dollar sign that he is unable to comprehend the evidence that presents itself to the senses, and to the heart.

I take note of an easy trap here, all the easier for the thousands of miles between California and the hometown I have left behind. "It is the rule," writes Kentucky farmer and author Wendell Berry, "that we often romanticize what we first despise," and I understand what he means: it is as if from guilt at my ready acquiescence with my loss, and from longing for its recovery, I have created a vision of a place that never existed, at least not in the form in which I imagine it.

And yet the two places, California and Kentucky, *are* different, wonderfully, maddeningly so. Perhaps because I am suspended between them, I observe those differences at every turn: differences in culture, in manners, and in language—less in the words themselves than the ends to which they are put. Recently, in the middle of one of my meandering anecdotes, a California acquaintance made an abrupt gesture of interruption: "So get to the point!" he said, an imperative that may never have been spoken in the history of the Commonwealth of Kentucky. There speakers and listeners understand that the point of a story lies not in getting to its point—to its end—but lies instead in the journey, in covering the distance from here to there. In this way each story encompasses a miniature life, whose point lies not in its conclusion, but in the territories covered along the way.

And California: a place where language is a medium not so much of storytelling and social intercourse as a means of transacting business. This is the place where it is possible to Get Things Done, whether building a computer empire or making a movie. Largely freed from the intricate burdens of political, racial, class, and genealogical structures, Californians proceed quite comfortably about their affairs, unencumbered by social burdens and responsibilities, considerations that in Kentucky constitute the fabric of social intercourse.

This is not by way of saying that one place is better than another; it is to say that they are different, and to note that difference, and to remark on our obligation to observe it and to exercise our judgment in passing it on.

In *Losing Battles*, Eudora Welty writes, "There is only one way of depriving the ones you love—taking your living presence away from theirs—no one alive has ever deserved such punishment, although maybe the dead do; and no one alive can ever in honor forgive that wrong, which outshines shame and is not to be forgiven until it has been righted."

And yet this is our shared experience, in America, a nation of immigrants turned emigrants: the experience of leaving behind the people and places we love. Only Americans, conditioned by mass culture, could believe that it is possible to break cleanly away from such ties, from home, from family, from place; any place.

My peculiar circumstances involve me more intimately in that dilemma than most. When my family's home is sold, as will likely happen, its sale will mark the end of my immediate family's presence in these knobs: two hundred years on my mother's side, one hundred twenty-five on my father's. In one generation we have ceased to be tied to one place, instead to become itinerants: three children in California, one in Tennessee, three scattered to the small cities of Kentucky, one rural dweller in the northern counties of the state.

This is profoundly unsettling, to myself, to Kentucky-born writers as a whole, a slew of whom have followed their fortunes to California, only to return, back to the Bluegrass, back home. There are many reasons I could offer as to why this nostalgia afflicts Kentuckians, and Southerners in general, but they are less relevant here than the fact that I see the same phenomenon, less intense but quite noticeable, among my California friends and acquaintances. Once here, they have tended to stay put; once settled, they have in the most determined way set about establishing roots.

I like to conjecture that the current preoccupation with individual and family history and genealogy bespeaks a growing sophistication in our perceptions of the gap between how television presents us to each other, and how we really are. As an adjunct to that, I like to think that as a nation we are on the verge of learning to settle down; learning that hardest-won lesson, that the grass on the other side of the fence is probably no greener and is certainly a great deal harder to get to.

This is idle speculation, of course, born most likely of the luxury of belonging neither to Kentucky nor California and so being capable of imagining each in my own image. And yet I'm hardly the first to observe that as a nation we have exhausted our frontiers. For a nation which has spent its lifetime pushing westward, looking outward, perhaps the time has arrived to look inward and look back.

When I think about it, which is too often, I compare this small green apple and this large navel orange: Kentucky and California. I compare their virtues: Kentucky, with its abiding sense of belonging and sense of place; and California, with its sheer opportunity to do and see and have. As a writer, as an American, it is my good fortune, and my quandary, to be caught between the two, in a dilemma as old as this pilgrim nation: neither Kentuckian nor Californian, fox nor hound, divided east from west and always somewhere in-between.

The Mimbres

Sharman Apt Russell

Three years before my husband and I bought land on the Mimbres River, an unusual amount of winter snow and spring rain prompted what locals authoritatively called a "hundred-year flood." That left us ninety-seven years. We were also reassured by the large dikes built by the Army Corps of Engineers between our agricultural field and the riverbed. These dense gray mounds of gravel, contained improbably with heavy mesh wire, were ten feet high, twenty-five feet at the base, and ugly. They efficiently blocked our view of the river which, at that time, was not much of a loss. Although things were to change quickly, when we came to southwestern New Mexico, the price of copper stood high, unemployment was low, and—through our land—the Mimbres River stretched bone-dry.

Like many country dwellers not born in the country, we find it hard to believe we were once so naive. We actually sought out river

Sharman Apt Russell is currently completing a new book, The Blind Voyeur: Essays on Flowers, *and teaches at Western New Mexico University and Antioch College. She has published both fiction and nonfiction books, including* When the Land was Young: Reflections on American Archeology; Kill the Cowboy: A Battle of Mythology in the New West; Songs of the Fluteplayer: Seasons of Life in the Southwest *(a part of which won her a Jackson Special Award in Nonfiction);* The Humpbacked Fluteplayer *(a children's book);* Frederick Douglas; *and* Built to Last: An Architectural History of Silver City, New Mexico. *She has received a Writers At Work Fellowship in nonfiction, a Pushcart Prize, the 1992 Mountains and Plains Booksellers Award, and the 1992 New Mexico Presswomen's Zia Award. "The Jackson Award came in 1989, and it was really a wonderful encouragement and an important push and perhaps meant something to Addison-Wesley, who went on to publish three of my books."*

bottom land. We didn't think in terms of rusted wheel bearings, smashed foot bridges, soil erosion, or property damage. We didn't think of rivers at all in terms of property: rivers were above real estate. They were gifts in the desert. They were frail blue lines that disappeared on the map. In the arid Southwest, rivers—even inter-mittent rivers—were to be coveted.

In the coming years, we came to know the Mimbres River bet-ter. On my part, it was not an idyllic relationship. The only road to our house is a rough and rutted trail of packed dirt that goes over the stream bed. When the river does run, about seven months of the year, water seeps into our car bearings and the brakes freeze at night. When the river runs too high, we stall in midstream and must be hauled out by a neighbor's four-wheel drive. Those of us on the wrong side of the Mimbres, a collection of seven families, tried to deal with the conflict of road and river. We got together for workdays and animated discussions in which we all pretended to be engineers. We built an elegant wood and rope "swinging bridge" for pedestrians and at the gravelly bottom of the stream installed cement culverts—only to have both swept away by spring run-off and heavy rains. On the occasion of such rains, the Mimbres became impassable by any vehicle. Whenever this seemed imminent, my husband and I parked our car on the side of the river that led to town: fifty miles to Deming, New Mexico, for his teaching job and thirty miles to Silver City for mine. The next day, we would get up painfully early, walk a half mile to the crossing, and wade.

The cold water didn't bother my husband; the problems of this part-time river only intrigued him. In the early 1970s, New Mexico's Soil and Conservation Service had experimented with our section of the Mimbres by cutting down all the cottonwoods. At that time they believed eliminating these great trees, some more than a hundred years old, would mean more grass for cattle. Today, it seems as inspired an act as putting cans on a cat's tail. Without the cotton-woods to hold the soil with their roots and break the impact of water, subsequent small floods swept over the denuded ground like efficient mowing machines. When the channel was dry again, the eroded result could only charitably be called a river. My husband's dream was to bring the old Mimbres back. To this end, he planted branch after branch of cottonwood in the hope they would miraculously grow. Miraculously, they did. He charted the re-vegetation of willows, chamiza, and walnut. He personally scattered the fluff of cattails. In a meditative silence, he walked the gray dikes built by the Army Corps of Engineers and saw a greener future.

On the morning of the second "hundred-year flood," we woke to a triumphant roar and strangely clear view. Below our house, what had last night been a field of winter rye was a mass of brown water lapping at the goat's pen. Something important seemed to be missing. It took us longer than seems reasonable to realize what that was. The ugly gravel dikes were gone. A strange, dark, churning river had taken their place, a river that also included part of our land, much of our topsoil, and our entire car.

We didn't learn the fate of the Volkswagen until later that morning. Excited and impressed, my husband dressed and went down to inspect the situation. I stayed in the house with our two-month-old daughter. Everyone in the neighborhood was out inspecting, and those who had gotten up early had the chance to see our car—parked on the "town" side of the river—slowly lifted up and carried along in the force of the flood. The little Bug was in good company, with giant cottonwoods torn from their roots and the debris of upstream bridges and irrigation pipe. When my husband returned to confirm the destruction of our single and uninsured vehicle, his face showed a kind of pleasure. Looking out over the changed, aquatic world, his eyes gleamed. He almost laughed. This was a big flood. This was bigger than the last one-hundred-year flood, six years ago. This was a *river.*

Our neighborhood was once a small ranch now divided into forty, ten, and five-acre parcels, with a restriction that no one can further subdivide. This restriction, as well as the property's irrigated land, was part of our reason for being here. We also liked the people who had come before us. As the limited number of house sites sold, a sense of community emerged which resulted in a name: El Otro Lado (The Other Side). For our private street sign, Jack and Roberta Greene, among the first to buy, painted this in informal and cock-eyed calligraphy on a wooden board they posted at the highway. Divorced, in his early fifties, Jack had once posted a want ad for a companion in the *Mother Earth News* and thus met the also divorced, forty-eight-year-old Roberta. This slightly comic, slightly suspicious background proved misleading, for the Greenes became our role models, the sanest couple we knew. Neighbors in a rural community, we were all bound by mutual needs. We borrowed hand saws and drill bits from each other's tool box. We shared the maintenance of a Rototiller, and if a friend went out of town, we fed their horses, goats, chickens, dogs, and cats. Inevitably, we were all building passive-solar adobe homes and had much to say to each other about green-houses and R values. Despite ages that ranged from thirty to sixty, we became close and comfortable and gathered almost every Sunday night—movie night!—around Jack and Roberta's new VCR.

Now, with the flood, we were not alarmed at being cut off and isolated together. Phone lines had been washed away, and the power pole rocked precariously in the middle of the rushing brown water. Huddled in sweaters, we converged as a group to note its sway. Our main fear was that without electricity we could not use the VCR to watch Roberta's copy of a Lina Wertmuller film. The pole held, and a potluck was arranged where, over four different salads, we discussed the river, the weather, and our fields—three words for the same thing.

That easily, the flood became another community event, another movie, another bond.

Upstream, a friend almost lost his life when he tried to cross the water in his new jeep. All night, his pregnant wife walked the crumbling bank and called his name. In the morning he was found clinging to a log, much chastened. His was not the only four-wheeler to go down the river. A small family-owned sawmill contributed some equipment; a rancher lost his prize tractor. The best news, according to everyone, was the loss of the dikes. As it turned out, they had channeled the Mimbres in such a way as to increase its force and power. One landowner threatened to shoot any engineer who tried to re-erect them. This did not prove necessary since the state labeled the entire area a floodplain, a belated nod to nature that prevented further interference.

On our property, the water scoured the river bed as the channel shifted to carve out chunks of irrigated field. When the flood subsided, a matter of days, it left a muddy battleground strewn with logs, misshapen debris, and two rubber tires ten feet in diameter and three feet thick. The small, laboriously planted cottonwoods did not survive. In fact, not a blade of grass remained. Elsewhere on the Mimbres, where the ground had been protected by trees, the torrent overflowed the banks and took down a few of the older cottonwoods. In less than a month, that part of the river was green again.

In southwestern New Mexico, the Mimbres River winds from the pine-covered Gila National Forest, down to the scrub oak and juniper of our land, south to the high plains of the Chihuahuan Desert. In its sixty-mile length, the river drops 4,500 feet and covers four life zones. Narrow, intimate, made lush with irrigation, this area has a long history. I found my first pottery while digging a squash bed in the garden. Since then I have found many bits of clay, their edges irregular, like pieces of a jigsaw puzzle scattered in the dirt. As sometimes happens, the first one was the best: a palm-sized shard of black-on-white ware, its painted lines straight and elegantly thin. Such lines mean that the original pot was made between A.D. 1000 and 1100, the "Classic Period" of the Mimbreno Indians.

In their hundreds of years here, this branch of the Mogollon culture farmed, hunted, gathered, and painted pots that are world-famous today. The designs are often fantastical: southwestern versions of the griffon and the unicorn. Many are natural drawings of animals and insects. Some are quite bawdy—penises as long as your arm! Some resemble Escher paintings with their mirrored images and field reversals. In all, they present an extraordinarily talented culture. Over six thousand Mimbres pots are stored across the world in museums like the Smithsonian; you can also find Mimbres ware for sale, discreetly advertised in the back pages of such magazines as *The New Yorker*. Apparently, once the artistic fervor hit them, these Indians made a lot of pots. Most are found in the burial sites beneath the homes and villages that the Indians abandoned around the thirteenth century. Most have a "kill hole" at the bottom of the bowl, which may have allowed the spirit of the dead to escape. And some scientists theorize that the pots were made exclusively by women, with certain artists or prehistoric celebrities producing on a regular basis.

Modern Mimbrenos are proud of their heritage and exploit it ruthlessly. Designs crafted a thousand years ago can be seen on locally made earrings, T-shirts, stationery, calendars, aprons, towels, and coffee cups. An ancient picture of a bighorn sheep, now extinct in the valley, might pop up on an advertisement for farm equipment or a recruiting poster for the nearby university. While such theft is easily sanctioned, the commercial value of the actual pots is controversial. A Mimbres bowl can be worth as much as $25,000, and pot hunters regularly bulldoze sites that an archeologist might take years to uncover. Pot hunting, of course, is illegal on state or federal land, which most of the valley is not. Although archeologists wax indignant, they are considered by some natives to be just another breed of pot hunters, ones who take their loot to be stored in far-off museums.

In truth, we are all pot hunters here. How could it be otherwise, when the glamour of the past combines with profit? We perk up our ears when we hear that someone down the valley found seventy-two pots in her front yard. Seventy-two! Closer to home—a quarter mile from my doorstep—a doctor and his wife inadvertently destroyed a Mimbres bowl when dozing a building pad for their new house. On the hill above us, an ancient burial is found complete with human body and turquoise beads.

Such stories confirm that the qualities of a good home site have not changed much in a thousand years. In digging the foundations for our adobe, my husband uncovered a large grinding stone or *metate* buried three feet deep. After that, we watched each shovelful, but no pot emerged that would pay off our land mortgage. Mimbres pots may still be under the forsythia or kitchen floor, but it offends our aesthetics to run about with a backhoe digging arbitrary holes. We remain pleased with the *metate* and, conventionally, keep it outside our doorstep with an associated collection of *manos:* fist-sized, hand-held rocks worn smooth with grinding. Like most people who live in the valley, we count continuum as a return on our money.

Mimbres pottery is glamorous for its age and beauty. But it is only part of a small museum scattered over our twelve acres. A band of Apaches called the *Tci-he-nde* or Red Paint people left their arrowheads, as well as a four-inch spearpoint now on a shelf of knickknacks. Named for a stripe of paint across the warrior's face, this tribe probably entered the area long after the Mimbrenos' exit. They continued the tradition of farming. At least, they tended their crops between times on the warpath, first with the Spanish and later with the Mexicans and Americans. In the nineteenth century, chiefs like Mangas Coloradas and Victorio found it increasingly hard to hold off the growing horde of gold-hungry, silver-hungry, copper-hungry, even meerschaum-hungry miners. Where miners went, forts and soldiers followed. And by the late 1860s, Mexican and Anglo farmers had also settled the Mimbres and would supply the boom town of Silver City with bumper crops of potatoes. Such early entrepreneurs dry-farmed pinto beans where my front yard yields grama grass. In

1869, they established the irrigation system that waters my garden. Over the years, these men and women dropped their own momentos of baling wire, lavender glass, and bone white china. Most recently, I found in our field a perfect 6 1/2 ounce Coke bottle. Its thick shape, patterned with raised letters, dated from the 1940s—seemingly an emblem of the modern world, until we compared the heavy diminutive bottle with an aluminum can red-flagged NutraSweet.

The Mimbrenos, the Apaches, the dry farmers are all gone—and not just because they died. The sudden disappearance of the Mimbrenos, along with Indian groups like the Anasazi to the north, is still a mystery. In their ruins is a sense of calm which seems to preclude war or pestilence. Their dead are properly buried, their kitchen utensils neatly stored. In contrast, the Apaches were clearly driven out. At one point, an Indian agent promised them a reservation on their homeland, but the citizens of Silver City objected, and nothing came of it. In 1886, the famed year that Geronimo surrendered, the entire Red Paint people were put on boxcars and shipped to Florida and permanent exile. For the dry farmers, the weather simply changed, and it began to rain less. The river itself was no longer that "rapid, dashing stream, about fifteen feet wide and three feet deep" described in 1846 by an American soldier.

Oddly, or perhaps not, such disappearances continue today. They are a part of the valley's heritage. In the ten years we have lived here, we have seen most of our friends and many of our acquaintances leave. Most obviously, a failing local economy is to blame. The Mimbres Valley is in Grant County, one of New Mexico's richest mineralized areas. Twelve miles to the east, the Santa Rita Mines began producing copper as early as 1804, and for most of the twentieth century that yellow metal—not quite so yellow as gold but more abundant—was excavated from a hole that eventually swallowed the entire town of Santa Rita, including its hospital and schoolhouse. Mining is an extractive industry. In the 1980s, the Kennicott Mining Company declared that only forty years' worth of low-grade ore existed at the strip mine they advertised as "the world's prettiest copper pit." Many smaller operations in nearby Hanover and Pinos Altos had already played out, and the other major company in the area, Phelps Dodge, also began to count the years. No one employed by the mines paid much attention. No one even mentioned it to new-comers like us, and we didn't ask. As it turned out, forty was not the magic and seemingly far-off number. For it wasn't the amount of copper that caught Grant County by surprise, but the price per pound. By the time that price fell to under fifty-eight cents in 1982, the layoffs had already begun.

Still, that is only part of the story. Most of our friends did not leave the Mimbres Valley because they could not find a job here but because they could not find the job they expected of life. They and we came to this area for the small-town ambiance and rural lifestyle. Not surprisingly, neither the small town nor the surrounding rural area required many editors, landscape architects, graphic designers, psychologists, or political lobbyists. More surprisingly, some of us discovered that we needed to be these things. We had embraced a concept of happiness that required escape from the contaminated, stressful cities. For love of land—for love of beauty, for love of the valley—we could adjust to a lower standard of living. We could not adjust (at least not all of us) to being high school teachers or car mechanics.

Our closest neighbor is the car mechanic. His real interest is solar energy systems, and he wonders why his back hurts and why he spends his time under the hoods of cars as old as himself. Another friend would like to build houses but the economy here is too depressed and he lives, instead, on odd carpentry jobs. For five years, my husband was the high school teacher. Because of the long drive, he left for work at six in the morning and returned from work when it was too dark to see the land he was working to pay for. Increasingly, he became frustrated by conditions in his job which prevented him from doing it well. He was angered by the blatant cul-tural contempt for teachers, even as he recognized in himself echoes of that contempt. As one close relative told him, public school teach-ing is a "deviant career choice." Even the school administrators seemed to agree. Finally, for a number of reasons, none of which had to do with low salary or discipline problems, my husband left Deming High.

It hardly needs to be said that he does not want to leave the Mimbres Valley. For now he pursues part-time work which includes free-lance photography and outfitting in the Gila Wilderness. Together with my salary, this income does not add up to what we have discovered—another surprise—we would like to have. Still, in the privacy of the valley, we can pick and choose our conveniences. We have an outhouse; we also have a word processor. Social identity, not economics, is perhaps the more real dilemma. What is a man with a patchwork of jobs as insecure as our river? Will my husband be happy at the age of fifty-five?

We don't know the answers to these questions, and in the willful charting of our lives, we wonder what turns we are taking and what roads we irrevocably pass. We wonder if we will ever regret our choice to step outside what we were taught to consider the mainstream. Perhaps we should wonder why we feel that it was a choice, as though how and why we came here was a conscious navigation, as though we are not, all of us, riding logs down a river.

In the theme of departure, there are variations. Jack and Roberta Greene retired here to build a home, garden, and become potters. Together, that first year, they made enough forty-pound adobe bricks for a small, liveable studio. They would need another two thousand for their one-bedroom house. Meanwhile they planted an orchard of peaches, plums, apples, cherries, and walnuts. A master gardener, Roberta also grew lavish rows of strawberries, chilies, tomatoes, lettuce, peas, eggplant, cucumbers, onions, leeks, radishes, potatoes, and corn. Their raspberry crops were famous. It was far more food than they could eat, and in the summer they took the surplus to Silver City's Farmer's Market. In their second year, the two thousand adobe bricks lay neatly stacked in lines that spilled over into Jack's vineyard. Enthusiastically, they began to lay up the walls. Jack studied wiring, and they did most of the work themselves, including a compost toilet and solar hot-water system. By the time they had been in the valley five years, they had a beautiful Santa Fe-style home, an established orchard, a shed of useful tools, and the acceptable identity of a retired couple. As part of the grand plan, Jack began a kiln for their pottery work.

We profited greatly from the Greenes' knowledge, as well as from their tool shed. But by the time we began to lay up our own walls, Jack and Roberta were showing signs of restlessness. Before his "radicalization" and divorce, Jack had owned a chain of liquor stores in California. Twenty years later, with a beard and a wife from *Mother*

Earth News, he was still the businessman, still a driver. The dream house was built. Now he couldn't quite see truck gardening for minimum wage or making pots for less than that. One day he and Roberta bought a video store in Silver City. At that time, it was the only video store in town and contained less than fifty movies. With Jack's retailing expertise and the labor Roberta once spent on her garden, the business grew quickly. For a while, the Greenes tried to straddle two worlds. But inevitably the "simple life" (burning and hauling trash, commuting to town, crossing the river, chasing cows from the garden, fixing a broken windmill, canning tomatoes) proved too burdensome. Some time after the second hundred-year flood, they bought a furnished house in town and put the Mimbres adobe up for sale.

In the nineteenth century, the French visitor Alexis de Tocqueville observed, "An American will build a house in which to pass his old age and sell it before the roof is on; he will plant a garden and rent it just as the trees are bearing; he will clear a field and leave others to reap the harvest; he will take up a profession and leave it, settle in one place and soon go off elsewhere with his changing desires."

My husband used to quote this in wonderment. Now we see how easily it could apply to us. When Jack and Roberta left, taking with them our Sunday night movies, the disintegration of our community began. The car mechanic opened up a bicycle shop in Silver City, and it is only a matter of time before he moves there too. The wife of one couple is in law school in Albuquerque. Another neighbor job hunts in Santa Fe. As we count the number of friends who have left the valley, as well as El Otro Lado, we are surprised at their number. Suddenly, we are no longer newcomers, we are the ones who are left.

On the river bank, my husband has planted more cottonwoods. With the dikes gone, he hopes this batch will survive the next flood. Many cottonwoods have already started up on their own, for this, after all, is the work of flooding—to tear down dying trees and carry seeds to new parts of the river. The chamiza is returning too and small patches of willow. Although it has only been a few years, the flood seems to have happened long ago, to much younger people. These days, my husband broods over the increase of mobile homes in the valley: the tiny aluminum squares that mar his view of rolling hills and the fang of Cooke's Peak. Insistent against a backdrop of mesas, these trailers represent a different vision of the country, a vision we had not foreseen as overnight they pop up on the treeless tracts of land a son is carving from his father's pasture. The valley, like the river, cannot be predicted.

In the marital urge for balance, we switch sides often now. This week it is I who grow depressed at the thought of leaving the Mimbres Valley. It is not only the green fields that hold me, but the loss of my naivete. I am not sure I want to spend another ten years learning new lessons. Here, at least, we know our enemies. In this mood, I tell my husband that mobile homes are democratic. I tell him that new friends will come. I tell him that he will find the right job or find he doesn't need to. I tell him that the next flood will be a hundred years away and, in the meantime, his cottonwoods will grow tall. Let's stay, I say this week. Let's stay.

In Washington Square

Wendy Lesser

Some places are points in a landscape and others are places in the mind. Tucson, for instance, is the former, Hell the latter (though even Tucson, when I cite it this way in the pages of a book, momentarily shifts out of the landscape and into your mind). Many places are both—that is, an actual geographical location with an overlay, or underbelly, of fictional, imagined, spiritual existence. This double life is especially characteristic of large cities. World capitals like New York, London, Paris, and Rome belong not only to their citizens and their tourists, but also to the novelists, poets, painters, architects, journalists, playwrights, and filmmakers who have inhabited and borrowed them. A Henry James character, remarking on his "latent preparedness" for a visit to London, recalls: "I had seen the coffee-room of the Red Lion years ago, at home—at Saragossa, Illinois—in books, in visions, in dreams, in Dickens, in Smollett, in Boswell."

Perhaps best known as publisher of the preeminent journal, The Threepenny Review, *Wendy Lesser is, in her own right, an incisive author of five books, including* Pictures at an Execution; A Director Calls; His Other Half: Men Looking at Women Through Art; The Life Below the Ground; *and, most recently,* The Amateur, *a memoir. Some chapters from* The Amateur *won Lesser a Jackson Special Award in Nonfiction in 1988. In* The Amateur, *she writes, "I have tried for most of my life not to be identified with California....It is always possible that I am deluding myself; we Californians have made a specialty of self-delusion. But we have also specialized in certain forms of clarity and directness. The clarity and the self-delusion go hand in hand, support each other, make each other necessary. And I am the child of both traditions."*

Cities hold onto the events that have taken place in them and the novels that have been written about them. Each urban crevice stores up this radioactive material and gradually leaks it out to successive generations. Especially if you live in an old city, you will be conscious not only of the many other lives led alongside your own, but also of the past and future lives crowding in. Far from diluting the effect of your own experience, this crowded history will strengthen each present event: the cracked sidewalks and porous building materials will store up and give forth your own life to you in a way that the smooth walls of a New Town or a planned city never could. For people who live in older cities, the distinction between a place in the landscape and a place in the mind becomes impossible to make.

You are lucky—or, let us say, your life will more easily make sense to you—if the place in which you live and the language you speak have some inherent connection to each other. I do not just mean that it is hard to be an exile, though in a broader sense perhaps that is exactly what I do mean. America, for instance, is a country full of exiles. Its language was developed in a small, closely knit society, with words that applied to the everyday features of a circumscribed island life; and this language, transplanted from Britain, was then supposed to be adequate to describe a vast continent filled with strange geographies and peopled by numerous different strands of humanity. The language couldn't really do this: it had to stretch, and sometimes break, to cover its new ground. The result is that American literature tends to be quite abstract in comparison to the concreteness of English literature. Think of our nineteenth-century Transcendentalists and Britain's social novelists, our serious-minded experimenters and their witty explorers of the "conventional" and the "real." Think of Moby Dick and Middlemarch.

For an American living west of the Mississippi, this alienation from the sources of the language becomes still more extreme. Our town names, like Los Angeles architecture, seem mere parodies of themselves: Albany, California, is not even Albany, New York, much less the original Duke's Albany or his even more ancient country, Albion. The names we Californians give our things and places are echoes, and these imaginative echoes all seem to come from two removes elsewhere. Thus "Gloucester" is merely a cheese I can buy at the local foodstore; it has no concrete connection to a town in England or even Massachusetts.

This kind of displacement will often lead to an elevation of the imaginative connections over the real. When I buy my Gloucester cheese in Berkeley, I think neither of the place in England where it originated nor the town in New England that borrows the name, but the Earl who fathered Edgar and Edmund in King Lear. My cheese skips its geographical heritage and goes straight to the literary sources that have become, ex post facto, its ancestors. One is likely, under such circumstances, to forget about the chronological trans- mission of culture and believe instead in a kind of all-encompassing literary unconscious. The problem is similar to the one described by Emerson in relation to architecture. "The American who has been confined, in his own country, to the sight of buildings designed after foreign models," he says, "is surprised on entering York Minster or St. Peter's at Rome by the feeling that these structures are imitations also—faint copies of an invisible archetype."

A further sense of removal from the sources of meaning afflicts those who, like myself, were brought up in the suburbs. Our literary memories, in English, are most those of urban places: primarily London, secondarily New York and Boston. In America, one also has a back-up set of memories provided by the pioneer or rural literature of James Fenimore Cooper, Mark Twain, Willa Cather, and others. But for the child of the suburbs there is no imaginative echo sur- rounding real places, no literary ancestry infusing the objects of everyday life. Especially for the California suburbanite, there is a dis- tinct separation between the real and the fictional—between the swimming pools, shopping centers, cyclone fences, and one-story ranch-style houses that constitute existence, and the "bleak houses," "New Grub Streets," and "Bostonians" that constitute literature.

As a denizen of the California suburbs, I grew up feeling the absence of something, knowing that a deeper layer of significance ought to lie behind the flatness of my surroundings. My first response to this longing was to immerse myself in science fiction, which made up the bulk of my reading from age ten to age sixteen. This, if it did not give me literary echoes, at least gave me the sense that hidden meanings enriched everyday objects. The reason much science fiction seems banal is that it is so obviously a search for significance. It projects our daily life or our current technologies onto an unknown future or an alien planet, and thereby asks for ultimate causes, ultimate meanings. Science fiction is the opiate of the atheists.

It gives those who believe in rationality the assurance that something larger than randomness or human ineptness is at the root of our existence. Coincidence rationalized into pattern is the essence of science fiction; we who can find no rational connections in our disjunctive daily lives are thereby persuaded that understanding is simply a matter of seeking out the missing pieces.

I should say a word about how I started reading science fiction. My parents were divorced when I was six. My father, who until then had worked in the San Jose office of IBM, took a job with the New York branch and moved east; my mother, my younger sister, and I stayed in the three-bedroom, linoleum-tiled, flat-roofed Palo Alto tract house my parents had bought when I was three. (Tract house perhaps conveys the wrong impression: these redwood-frame houses, called "Eichlers" after their designer and builder, were manufactured en masse in the 1950s as starter homes for aspiring young suburbanites, but they were—and still are—considered nice properties, and the one my parents bought in the Greenmeadow subdivision for $20,000 in 1955 would today sell for about $500,000.) When my father moved out, he left behind in the two-car garage a mass of assorted possessions that he apparently could not bring himself either to dispose of or to take with him. Among these were five copies of a magazine called *Unknown Worlds,* vintage 1942.

I can still remember the crackly feel of the old paper and the monochrome look—olive green, I think—of the black-printed covers. I discovered these magazines the summer I was ten, and I spent a large portion of that summer avidly reading and re-reading them. Some of the stories were by Fritz Leiber, Theodore Sturgeon, and other people who went on to science fiction fame; several, amazingly, were written by L. Ron Hubbard (though I didn't know enough then to be amazed); my particular favorites tended to be by someone with the unlikely name of L. Sprague de Camp. I would lie on my bed on a hot summer afternoon and read *Unknown Worlds* until I was too terrified to be alone any longer. Then, dazed with the effort of getting up too suddenly, I would wander out onto the sunlit, grass-lined, clean, new streets of nearly identical Eichlers, and even the shadowless world of Greenmeadow, populated by my friends and neighbors, would seem to emanate some of the lurid uncanniness I had absorbed from my reading. When my father came on one of his semiannual visits, I asked him whether the magazine still existed, and if so, whether I could have a subscription. But *Unknown Worlds* had long since gone out of business, so he bought me instead a five-year subscription (one year at a time: my father is generous but never extravagant) to a monthly called *Fantasy and Science Fiction*.

Two things broke me of science fiction. The possibility of drawing together the imaginary and the real, of finding places in the mind that were also places on earth, was first shown to me by "real" novels and by cities. And because I was a suburban child, the city itself was a novel to me: a place where miraculously diverse characters acted out their unknown and therefore fascinating fates on a seemingly limitless stage.

My first city was San Francisco. However young and small it may seem by comparison to European or East Coast capitals, it was more than enough of a city for me. I remember the zeal with which I decided I would learn the city—by observing where the Number 30 bus went, by figuring out the order and direction of Clay, Washington, Jackson, Pacific, and most of all by walking everywhere. Instead of attending classes during my last semester of high school, I persuaded the school authorities to let me take an unpaid job in San Francisco. (Since the job was for a firm of city planners, my employment was deemed sufficiently educational to replace my lost semester, but my father couldn't get over the fact that I was working for no pay. In a way, he was right to worry: it was to become a lifelong bad habit.) I spent most of my lunch hours, and quite a few of my supposed work hours, walking through San Francisco's various neighborhoods. Each house I passed became my house, each view my own private discovery. My first sense of the city was therefore intimately linked with a feeling of possession.

Yet a city only really becomes your own when you let go of it a little. The special quality of both cities and novels is that they are enriched by previous use, handed to you by others, made intimate by your awareness of their vastness. Both the novel and the city live by projection: immersing yourself in a crowd of characters or citizens, you become defined in relation to them; you lose yourself to find yourself. The city was not something I could take home, like a product in a suburban shopping mall. It was only mine as long as I left it in place. And so the owner had to give way to the observer.

Meanwhile, a similar thing was happening to my novel-reading. I began by demanding identification, by wanting to be the characters or have them be me. I didn't like novels about alien personalities. Emma Woodhouse was a pill, Sonia Marmeladov a pathetic martyr, Adam Bede a stuffed shirt, and Esther Summerson was too smirkingly self-effacing to be borne. Every novel, then, was judged by how strongly it made me sympathize with its central characters. Since I was sixteen years old and had spent my entire childhood in redwood-framed suburban comfort, this didn't leave much to identify with.

But as I gained the city by beginning to let go of it, I also began to give literature a longer rein. It was not that I grew to like Esther Summerson (does anyone?), but rather that I came to understand the value of not liking her. That a world could be alien to me and still mine—that empathy was a hardwon claim and not an easy virtue— was something that both novels and cities could teach me.

And finally they were also able to teach me their own limits. Eventually I learned that San Francisco was not the only city, and that its Washington Square—the broad expanse of bench-lined lawn in front of Saints Peter and Paul Church in North Beach—was a mere shadow of the "real" Washington Square, the one in Greenwich Village. And even this New York Washington Square was by now a faded reality beside the fictions it had generated: the beatnik hangout, the playground for Grace Paley's mothers and children, the locus of Thirties intellectual strolls, and most of all the title of a Henry James novel.

Washington Square is the type of Henry James novel I would have hated when I was sixteen. The heroine, Catherine Sloper, is a frumpy, somewhat slow, exceedingly sweet-tempered girl who is caught between a stern father and a sleazy beau, neither of whom really loves her. She is not the kind of character one would want to identify with in the first place, and the likelihood of identification is made even smaller by the poor little fate she ends up with in this novel. If the novel is supposed to be about sympathy, it is maudlin; if it is about irony, it is cruel. Yet *Washington Square* is finally neither maudlin nor cruel, and one must therefore conclude that the novel, like the city from which it draws its name, gains its meaning from something other than the easy substitution of one human being for another. In fact, the best novels, like cities, emphasize the impossibility of such substitutions: they reveal the difficulty of feeling empathy in the face of the strongest demands for it. *Washington Square* is about the severe limits on one person's ability to feel for and judge on behalf of another—and it is also about our innate desire to see others as mere projections of ourselves.

Nowhere in the novel is this conflict exhibited more strongly than in James's description of the Square itself. "I know not whether it is owing to the tenderness of early associations," he says, "but this portion of New York appears to many persons the most delectable. It has the kind of established repose which is not of frequent occurrence in other quarters of the long, shrill city; it has a riper, richer, more honourable look than any of the upper ramifications of the great longitudinal thoroughfare—the look of having had something of a social history. It was here, as you might have been informed on good authority, that you had come into a world which appeared to offer a variety of sources of interest; it was here that your grandmother lived, in venerable solitude, and dispensed a hospitality which commended itself alike to the infant imagination and the infant palate; it was here that you took your first walks abroad, following the nursery-maid with unequal step, and sniffing up the strange odour of the ailanthus-trees which at that time formed the principal umbrage of the Square, and diffused an aroma that you were not yet critical enough to dislike as it deserved; it was here, finally, that your first school, kept by a broad-bosomed, broadbased old lady with a ferule, who was always having tea in a blue cup, with a saucer that didn't match, enlarged the circle both of your observations and your sensations."

And by this time we have literally become Henry James. The twentieth-century child of the California suburbs is expected to "remember" this childhood of nursery maids and blue teacups. The process of projection is seemingly complete and apparently unthinking: "you" the reader have quite naturally evolved into the author, whose own "early assocations" were precisely those of the upperclass Washington Square existence. Yet the transformation is neither complete nor unthinking, for just as you have begun to take possession of this fictional childhood memory, Henry James interrupts you with the final line of his description: "It was here, at any rate, that my heroine spent many years of her life; which is my excuse for this topographical parenthesis." The vividly remembered Washington Square has become a mere "topographical parenthesis" in a novel, the "heroine" of which is precisely not the sort of person into whom one can comfortably project oneself. The illusion of projection, in other words, has been shattered by a reminder that we aren't all the same person, and that novels aren't life.

If this is a sad reminder, it is also a relief. Henry James would be the first to admit that novels can limit life as much as they can enrich it. And sometimes the sober realizations that novels impose on us, such as the awareness that people can never truly identify with each other, or that life is a matter of alienation, isolation, and false projection, get temporarily wiped out by an unexpected urban event. I am thinking in particular of something that happened once in Washington Square—my Washington Square, the one in San Francisco.

It was a warm Sunday afternoon during the month of June. I was passing by the Square during one of my habitual walks through the city, and the usual assortment of ancient Asian couples, Italian families, aging flower children, and miscellaneous San Franciscans were disporting themselves on the grass. As I glanced over the park, I noticed that two raggedly dressed, heavy-set men, apparently drunk, had begun to fight each other. Actually, it was hardly a fight, but rather a case of the tougher man picking on the weaker one, in the manner of a playground bully. The tough guy pulled off the weak one's shirt and strolled away with it, leaving his victim looking helpless and pathetic (as one does when violently deprived of clothing in a public place). And then, just as I had decided the whole disturbing incident was over, a man in a knit cap—a longshoreman, from the looks of him—who had been standing with an entirely different group in the park, left his friends and headed toward the tough guy. Now, I thought, they'll start to fight. But the longshoreman just took the shirt away, walked over to the weaker drunk, and handed it back to him—an act of pure and gratuitous kindness, following from nothing and leading nowhere. The longshoreman went back to his friends and I continued on my walk, pleased that for once the city had violated my novelistic notions of causality, projection, motive, and pattern.

Pidgin Contest Along I-5

Frank Chin

The air war Operation Desert Shield has started. I am in Portland, on the road with my five-year-old son for an adventure during the Chinese New Year's season, when the TV tells me the ground forces of Operation Desert Storm are moving fast. One wants to start the new year right, home with the family. My home is the road. Interstate 5. So, while Mom works teaching school in California, and before Sam himself starts school, I strap our son into the tiny red '77 Honda and get a move on my home again.

The road's changed. America's changed. At first I don't take offense at people sticking their T-shirts in my face when I sit down with Sam after stacking our plates at the salad bar at the truck stops. I have gone from truck stop to truck stop for years after discovering they, of all the roadside cafés, take chicken-fried steak and the salad bar as serious American art for the stomach. Till this moment I'd found American truck stops to be road-opera idealizations of the naturally democratic old west out of a Sergio Leone spaghetti western.

"America doesn't want us as a visible native minority," writes Frank Chin in "Confessions of a Chinatown Cowboy," an essay in Bulletproof Buddhists. *"They want us to keep our place as Americanized foreigners ruled by immigrant loyalty. But never having been anything else but born here, I've never been foreign and resent having foreigners telling me my place in America and America telling me I'm foreign." Along with plays, essays, and short stories, he is the author of the novels* Donald Duk *and* Gunga Din Highway, *and a collection of stories,* The Chinaman and Frisco R. R. Co., *which won the American Book Award. A Berkeley native, he won the Jackson Award in 1965 and the Phelan Award in 1966. He now lives in Seattle.*

Check your guns, your drugs, your prejudices, and your grudges at the door. All shootouts and fistfights off the premises. No exceptions.

The T-shirt hand silkscreened on 100 percent cotton with an American flag over a map of Saudi Arabia, Iraq, and Kuwait, with the words "THESE COLORS DON'T RUN!" in my face, doesn't bother me. It is the look on the man's face that goes along with the T-shirt that bothers me. I've been the only yellow in roadside restaurants before. I am often the only yellow for miles around. I'm used to it. I'm used to being mistaken for other yellows and other races. It never messes up my enjoyment of the local salad bar and search for the best chicken-fried steak in America.

No one has ever picked a fight with me with a T-shirt before. And all the eyes in the truck stop have never been hard on me, making a big deal of me before. "These colors don't run!" I read out loud. "Amen to that, brother. Where can I get one these righteous T-shirts?"

In a truck stop near Medford I look up from my salad bar and sirloin into an American flag, red, white, and blue, on a black T-shirt and, in belligerent red across the chest the legend "Try Burning This One, Asshole!"

I have an urge to introduce myself as an Iraqi cabdriver on vacation from New York but chicken out and say, "Boss T-shirt, brah! You think they got T-shirts like that in my son's size? Oooh, make my boy look sharp!"

We are admiring the hollow bronze man with an umbrella in Pioneer Courthouse Square in Portland. Sam has discovered sculpted animals, beavers and ducks in the planter boxes. Now he counts the nails in the heel of the bronze man's shoe. I look forward to stopping in the coffee hut on the corner for a cappuccino. Portland is a beautiful little city. Off the road. Out of the world. Then a kid in a black leather jacket, earrings, and no hair walks by and grumbles something.

"What did he say?" Sam asks.

"I don't know," I say. I have to think. "He said *foreigners*," I say. "Poor kid doesn't know how to cuss." Then I see we are surrounded by these funny-looking white kids who mean, mean, mean to be offensive, don't know how to cuss. As with the college kid who'd sneered "Literary conservative!" at me for saying texts do not change and the Marxist who'd meant "Cultural nationalist!" to wither me with contempt, I want to take the fuzz-headed boy aside and teach him how to swear. You want to rile me, kid, you call me a *Chink!* or you might call me a *Jap!* I'm not a Jap, but I'll know what you mean. But *foreigner!* Come on! That's too intellectual to really get me on the proper emotional level.

Then I see we are surrounded by these Clairol kids in black leather. I forget about the cappuccino and say, "Let's walk on out of here, Sam."

I see this need to teach our young how to properly cuss and offend with the specificity of a smart bomb as the first step toward full literacy and I-5 civility. You read to get the knowledge you need to win a fight, or, in this case, pick a fight, and avoid a fight.

On campus I seem to hear something else. I hear white kids on campus bitching about courses that teach nothing but hatred of whites and other kids talking PC. "Political correctness."

It's a shame white kids are sheltered by lingering white supremacy from the real world till they get to college. Nonwhite kids grow up in America despised by whites from birth, from history, from folklore, from their best friend the TV set. By the time they get to college they've learned to deal with it as a childhood disease. Either that, or it's fried their brains and turned them into gibbering Gunga Dins anxious to bugle the charge of white supremacy to white out their race and culture. Owooooo! Hear that wolf?

A multicultural America, a multicultural I-5, doesn't mean whites have to give up Christianity or hate themselves. It doesn't mean an orgy of mutual hostility either. Nor does it mean racial and cultural exclusivity. One thing it does mean—and I think PC is an attempt toward achieving this—is American standard English, the language all of us have to use to do business with each other, will be the one language reserved for civility, the one language we can speak without provoking each other. The American standard English of the newspapers and TV news, the language of the marketplace, will become more and more a pidgin, like pidgin in Hawai'i.

In pidgin Hawaiians, whites, Christians, pagans, Chinese, Japanese, Portuguese, did business with each other without giving up their identities, or their cultural integrity, or selling their children to monsters.

Political correctness seems to be a too serious and fascist, demagogic way of saying *civil language*. Of course, when civility is not our purpose, there are other languages and vocabularies available to us. With the need for a language of civility and doing business with strangers without betraying our secrets or slashing our wrists or starting a war in mind, I suggest PC stand for *pidgin contest*.

Civil language and tolerant behavior can't be imposed from the top without exercising heavy police-state censorship and driving everyone with a discouraging word underground. But in the bustling, competitive, passionate marketplace atmosphere of a port city or corner store, civil language and tolerant behavior are invented, or you go broke, brah.

In *The Movie about Me* there are pidgin contests held to encourage the use of the language to trade culture and lit. Pidgin is a live, up-front, face-to-face, present-tense language. The contestants tell heroic classics—*Chushingura, The Oath in the Peach Garden, Robin Hood, The Three Musketeers*—live. They compete with pidgin tellings of the fairy tales "Jack and the Beanstalk" and "Momotaro, the Peach Boy." On the way back home, driving I-5 South, Sam likes the idea. Yeah, it's better than punching somebody in the mouth and craving a many-fronted race war.

Then we walk back into the real world, a crowded resort restaurant around Lake Mount Shasta in Northern California, to get out of the nasty wind and rain.

"Did you tell them we're closed?" a middle-aged, crinkled-up woman bleats to another, taller, less crinkled-up white woman.

"We're closed," the taller woman says. For an instant I don't believe my ears. This has not happened to me since the South in the early sixties. Never in California.

"We're closed," the taller woman says again, and I can see she sees from the look in my eye I don't believe they are closed at all. I am not about to punch either of these old white ladies in the face. I look around for a customer to catch my eye and punch him in the face, and none does. Then I remember Sam, my five-year-old boy about to start school, is with me.

"They're closed, Sam," I say, take his hand, walk out, and wonder what I am teaching my kid letting skinheads and sixties-style white racists in California run us out of town. The winning of the Gulf War seems to have released an ugly brand of American patriotism that expresses itself as righteous white supremacy such as I have never seen before along the road between Seattle and LA I've called home for thirty years. I would have thought a nice cathartic victory would have released more winning sentiments on the road. What has happened to I-5?

Hello, America, This is LA

There are signs the times are freaking out. All over LA, wherever I drive, from Echo Park and Silver Lake to Hollywood to downtown and J-Town and Chinatown, I see magpies harassing hawks all over the sky. There are other signs of good times. There is an oriole, bright yellow and stark black on the wings and throat, in our weird tree flowering red fingers the morning of the day my friend the TV goes crazy with bad, bad news.

I pick up Sam from the school bus a little before three. He buckles himself in the backseat, and we're on our way to Chinatown for our usual after-school noodles when the news of the verdict acquitting the cops who'd beaten Rodney King comes between country songs and an appropriately remote broadcast from Hawai'i hyping travel over the LA FM country music station. "It's a bad day to be a cop or black man," I say.

My seven-year-old son knows Rodney King is the black man he'd seen beaten by LA cops on TV last March just after we're back home from a trip up and down I-5 to Seattle, through the Gulf War, and back down a road bristling a new, more blatant white racism. Skinheads in Portland. A resort restaurant in Northern California saying, "We're closed," when they were full of white people stuffing all manner of breakfast in their faces. And home to see Rodney King shot twice with a laser gun and beaten and beaten and beaten.

Between then and now black dislike for Koreans in little mom-and-pop groceries grows. The Korean groceries and liquor stores have all been broken into and/or robbed, and Mom and Pop have the same prejudice about blacks as the white Americans who taught it to them.

It might have helped if the blacks understood Korean manners and Korean culture have been toughened by a long history of being kicked around by the Chinese and the Japanese and a wartime society riddled with vicious spies, where being inquisitive about your neighbors and their personal lives is not necessarily a friendly gesture.

The tension breaks when a Korean grocer shoots a black teenage girl in the back and kills her. The grocer believed the girl was stealing a bottle of orange juice. The store's security camera that recorded the whole event on videotape shows the girl approaching the counter with money in her open hand as the grocer rages and screams at her.

The grocer is found guilty of voluntary manslaughter and given a suspended sentence. Blacks are outraged and are even now demanding the recall of the judge who let a Korean woman kill a black teenager without jailtime.

In response to the anger the Korean mom-and-pop grocers stop making change and throwing it at their customers and learn to smile and make Ozzie-and-Harriet Hollywood TV commercial small talk. I find it a little disconcerting. Smiling and small talk as a Korean martial art. The effort the Korean mom-and-pop stores are making to get along with the surrounding community is obvious all over LA. No doubt about it, they're willing to work at getting along. And the standard of getting along is hard-style Disneyland.

After our noodles in Chinatown we drive home past Dodger Stadium, see a hawk flap its wings over a line of palm trees, and see it's being run off by a pair of nagging magpies, see the same thing across the street from our house across our view of the HOLLYWOOD sign, and turn on our friend the TV set and see it is a bad day to be anybody in LA.

Korean mom-and-pops and generic LA minimalls are looter and pyro bait.

On the English-language LA channels some newspeople disconnect major sections of their brains. The pretty faces and trained voices who think they can do the news till the cows come home don't see the cows are home. One reporter has no idea the guns she was describing appearing in the hands of people are real guns, and when the police shove her out of the way, she reacts, not to the gunfire, but to the cop's rude shove.

Back in the newsroom a million-dollar anchorman asks a pie-eyed, panic-stricken ninny chattering his teeth in the mike if most of the looters don't look like "illegal aliens."

The pretty face frozen on hold grabs the anchorman's question like a lifesaver and says, "Yes, most of the looters look like illegal aliens." To these fools, I would look like an illegal alien. They're so fried in their insight that if white-haired Barbara Bush, the president's wife, should be pushing a shopping cart, she'd look like an illegal alien.

Reporting the looting and burning of Korean stores working into Korea Town proper, the reporters for the English-language news run from pompous to melodramatic to thumbsucking gibberers. It isn't until the newscopter sees the wave of looters charge in and out of Fedco, a huge warehouse discount store for government and state employees, that the newsies lose complete control. Mr. Purple Prose of the newschoppers gives up the morally loaded philosophical lingo and says it all in his voice going up and down out of breath as he blurts in amazement and moral outrage, "They're looting Fedco!" as if Fedco is a church or an orphanage.

My neighbors aren't among the looters. College educated. Liberal. Mixed marriages. Middle class. Still they act strange. As the smoke from the fires stuffs the air with the smell of burning rubber and electrical insulation and feathery black leaves of the ash fall on our houses and grass, I see some neighbors come out of their house with a portable TV, turn it on, and get into their outdoor Jacuzzi to what? Work off the tension of the day? Others start barbecuing in their backyard at sunset and invite friends, as if the curfew doesn't include them and the gunfire we hear clearly, a block or a mile away we can't tell, won't come any closer, and the smoke from burning LA won't flavor their meat.

The verdict from Simi Valley tells us all in LA there is no law. The looters don't read the news in the paper. They get it off the TV and the radio, their best friend, their storyteller. The looters are the children of the children who never had a childhood. Kids of kids who grew up alone, who never had a story told them by a live body, who grew up with TV as their storyteller. The black, white, Asian, and Latino kids and families out looting together are just acting like society on their TV acts when there is no law.

Had they a sense of myth that began with a live storyteller telling stories their people have valued through history, and if not those, then stories any people value—Greek myths, Bible stories, Br'er Rabbit, Hans Christian Andersen, the Peach Boy, the Boy born of Lotus—more people might look on themselves as more than the moral equivalent of consumer goods and stay away from the mob.

Then on TV there is a fake Spanish California mission-style minimall with a guard from a private Korean security outfit on the roof with an Uzi, a jumpsuit, a flak jacket, a baseball cap, and dark glasses.

The call had gone out on the channel that airs Korean programming for all good men to come to the aid of their Korea Town at the minimall, and they show up with shotguns, pistols of all kinds, Uzis, and AK-47s. The Alamo in Korea Town is a minimall.

In the race war that's started we're all going to choose up sides and appear at the appropriate minimall to man the barricades? The combined TV of LA with its two Spanish-language channels, and hours of Chinese, Japanese, Korean, Vietnamese, Farsi, and on and on programming, and visions of the action on the streets, is a vision of LA beyond *Bladerunner,* and not real, I think. It's all grotesque exaggeration. And it's impossible to choose up sides. The racially and culturally specific parts of towns, the barrios, the Chinatowns, Li'l Tokyo, Hollywood, Fairfax, blacks, Jews, white Christians, and even the dreamers and movie stars of LA, all are too interwoven into each other's business and loyalties to simply drop everything and Alamo up at our minimall behind barricades of rice sacks and shopping carts. We cannot blast and shoot each other into oneness. But we call agree on a common standard and language of civility. For a long time now, people on all sides, high and low, have and have not seemed to have accepted *business* as a synonym for *life.* Now we seem to agree the fire department is a good thing. It's a start. Whole civilizations have been started with less.

No school. Good. Sam's school is less than a mile from the downtown collection of courthouses and Parker Center Police Headquarters the TV news expects to go up in flames any second now. I take Sam out in the daylight, just down the hill to the Chinese bakery to order a cake for Dana's birthday. We pull open the door and walk in. The bakery is open. Still Mom and Pop the bakers freeze, and their eyes swirl and their breath gets short at the sight of me. "Hi," I say. "We'd like a cake."

They don't understand. They wait for me and my six-year-old son to stick 'em up, or loot 'em or trash the joint. "We want to buy a cake," I say.

They don't move.

"We'd like it to say, 'Happy Birthday Mom,'" I say.

Poppa Chinese baker opens his mouth, and nothing comes out.

"Are you open?" I ask.

He nods his head. I start again. They understand.

While Mom and Pop are steaming the medium-sized two-layer cake into being for me, the door opens behind me. I turn and see a young Chinese woman in the doorway. She jumps back. "Are you open?" she asks.

"Yeah, come on in," I say.

"Mom, Dad? You okay?" she asks, and goes behind the counter. She's the daughter. This is her bakery, and she asks me if we're open? Is the young man in the car outside a cop? Welcome to Paranoid City.

We get the cake in a box and take it home.

Then George Bush declares war on LA, sounding as frustrated and pained as Alberto Fujimori ruling by mandate in Peru.

Sunday, the family cocooned up snug with our best friend the TV set, I drive to Chinatown along deserted streets in broad daylight. The streets are empty. I take a walk around the places I like to eat and walk into one. Empty. The Mexican kitchen help and the Chinese cooks in their kitchen whites and waiters sit and stand around a table where the owner sits and holds his head in his hands. It's around three in the afternoon. The sun shines outside. In here they don't know if they're opening or closing. Some of the tables are still stacked. Some of the tables on the floor have no tablecloths, no place mats with the lunar zodiac around the edges, no red napkin, fork, spoon, and wrapped chopsticks, no teacup and water glass. The kitchen is cold. No one notices me.

"Are you open?" I ask.

The owner looks up; everyone looks up. The owner recognizes me as a frequent customer, tries to smile, and looks like he's going to cry. "First the riots. Now the curfew's killing us. We haven't had even one customer in two days till you walked in." Martial law seems to have worked.

On the way back I hear over the radio news of a huge peace rally in Korea Town. People are praying for forgiveness of the looters and peace in LA. Whole families show up. Others stop and join. Estimates range from 30,000 to a high of 100,000. It seems like good news, as I drive past stuff from the looting binge appearing for sale at yard sales. This is the America where reading is only good for reading signs and price tags. There is no story, no myth, no history, no art. Only TV. And now that the U.S. Marines and the army have had a taste of treating American streets like Panama and Grenada, I wonder if they can go home again.

Sam is down to sleep to be up early off to school in the morning tomorrow.

Police State

Every day after school, I pick Sam up at the bus and drive through Elysian Park, past the Dodger Stadium parking lot and the Marine Corps Naval Reserve Training Station, into Chinatown or Little Tokyo for noodles or sushi. Salmon egg sushi was Sam's first solid food. He doesn't like meat. Doesn't like veggies. He likes sushi, rice, and fish. Salmon eggs. Sea eel, softshell crab. Mackerel pike. Broiled smelt exploding with eggs. I tell Sam of trying to teach his half-sister, Betsy, how to drive in that parking lot and how she managed to drive into the only tree in this huge parking lot. True, it's a pitiful excuse for a tree, next to that pitiful little block house of a ticket office. Sam laughs every time he sees the tree and thinks of Betsy bumping into it.

This is a nice drive between our house and Chinatown and J-Town. We often see hawks perched in the tops of the trees of Elysian Park or cruising over the soft cliffs of Chavez Ravine, across the street from the Dodger Stadium parking lot.

It's a nice time of day. I break from staring at the blank page and screaming screen, do my mailing at the Chinatown or Little Tokyo contract postal station, walk around the town talking about life with Sam, watch the afternoon light reflect off glass walls of one building onto the textured concrete slab of another, snack, and shop for dinner. In Chinatown we walk by the square ponds full of fake rocks painted in fake colors, topped with the statues of Kwan Yin and the gods of wealth, happiness, and long life long ago broken off at the ankles. We look into the waters of one pond for the turtles and usually count more than a dozen basking on rocks and each other, swimming in the shallow water over pennies, and beaking at the puffy body of a dead goldfish. There are feeders grown large in these ponds. One has a golden carp. The other pond has crawdads.

In Little Tokyo there are the big granite boulders in Little Tokyo Village Sam likes to climb. There is the Amerasia Bookstore, where Irene, one of a group of Asian American UCLA students who call themselves Aisarema (Amerasia spelled backward) and are dedicated to saving the Amerasia Bookstore from closing, stands behind the cash register and folds little origami things for Sam. And all the sushi chefs at Frying Fish know Sam and call his name when we step inside.

One day, walking to sushi, we see National Guard Humvees parked all over the Honda Plaza parking lot. The Humvees are too big to fit in the marked parking spaces. They don't even try. Inside a J-Town fast-noodle shop we see the boys of the National Guard in their battle fatigues and flak jackets sitting down working chopsticks and noodles, with their M-16s leaning against the little tables. Sam and I are the only living things on the street. We look on the woman who runs the sushi bar and the chefs who call Sam by name as friends. We all cheer each other up, and I get my appetite back enough to eat.

Chinatown and Little Tokyo are dead. For days, for weeks after the riots, and waiting for the trials of the people arrested in the riots and the trials of the cops who beat up Rodney King to start, Sam and I are the only customers in our favorite J-Town sushi bar. Everyone else who walks in is a cop acting casual. Big guys in suits with guns under their jackets. They crouch over the pictures of the sushi and take a long time reading, looking, and choosing.

One day on our way home on the road past the Marine Corps and Naval Reserve Training Station, we see the cops have set up a satellite dish, telephone lines, a couple of mobile booking stations, a fleet of unmarked pickup trucks in different colors, a fleet of motor-cycles, a fleet of black-and-whites, a trailer serving as an on-site office, a phalanx of portable toilets. A command post. A base.

Two new, washed, gray or brown, nondescript four-door American-made Chevies waving several wire antennae like porcupine spines out of the trunks pass us on the inside bumper to bumper doing about sixty. Each car is full of four big men in dark glasses who don't give a thought to the likes of us in this flimsy little toy of a car. They know me before I know they're there. They know my every move before I make it, which is why it's easy for them to sneer their pursuit packages past me. "The Feds, Sam," I say. The two cars race by me bumper to bumper, at the next intersection two more cars swoop in front of the first two, and all continue racing at sixty in a kind of FBI automobile drill team. Sun Tzu the strategist says, Do not fuck with these guys. Even if he didn't say that, he should have, and I treat them like natural wildlife in the park.

For the next several days, we seem to drive home from sushi or noodles just when several pairs of motorcycle cops gurgle their machines toward us through Elysian Park and into the command post and the teams of Feds and local cops practice teaming up to trap cars in traffic and shove them over to the curb. Damn, it's a pretty sight. All these big new cars full of big square-jawed, uptight, muscular Americanismo diving and swooping as one out of Dodger Stadium parking lot, past the spiny green baobab trees by Barlow Respiratory Hospital, into shadows of impossibly tall and spindly palm trees in Elysian Park.

Sam enters his softshell crab phase. Every day he orders salmon eggs and a softshell crab appetizer. Miso soup with no tofu, no seaweed, no green onions, just soup. Coke to drink. He also likes the broiled mayonnaise sauce that tops the broiled New Zealand green mussels I order.

I see smoke rising from the corner of the Marine Corps Naval Reserve Training Center parking lot where the cops have set up a command post. "Oh, no, there's a fire at the command post," I say, and wonder how long ago it started. Is there anything about it on the radio? What happened? Has it started again?

As I roll past I see flames and smoke in the corner and cops in uniform, in their helmets and black leather jackets. They look like the bandits who threaten the village in Kurosawa's *The Seven Samurai*, but with paper plates instead of long weapons in their hands. It's a barbecue, not a bombing.

"It's a barbecue!" I say. "They're having a barbecue. They're roasting steaks and chicken and hot dogs on a barbecue. Whew." I laugh. Sam asks why I'm laughing. "I hope the cops have a fine long evening of barbecue. I never thought I'd ever say that before now." Owooooo! Hear that wolf?

from Split

Lisa Michaels

In 1969, my father was arrested for his part in an antiwar protest in Boston and was sentenced to a two-year prison term. (He and my mother had split up several years earlier, but they had remained close, sharing the child-rearing duties and trying to forge a new kind of divorce, one that was in keeping with their progressive politics.) He began serving his time at Billerica not long after his twenty-eighth birthday. I was a little over three years old. Once he was settled, my mother took me to see him in prison. He had written her a letter asking for books and a new pair of tennis shoes—he was playing a lot of pick-up basketball in the yard to keep his head clear. On the ride out to the prison, I clutched a box of black Converse high-tops in my lap, my head bubbling with important things to tell him, thoughts which percolated up, burst, and disappeared—their one theme: Don't forget me.

I remember very little of our lives then, but that visit has the etched clarity and foggy blanks of a fever dream. We pulled into the broad prison parking lot and stepped out to face the gray facade punctured by a grid of tiny windows. Mother lifted her hand against

Lisa Michaels won the 1997 Jackson Special Award in Nonfiction for her memoir Split, *a portrait of the days of communes and antiwar protests and rallies held by the radicals of the sixties and seventies—from the point of view of a child raised by counterculture parents. Presently living in Seattle, she is working on a novel, based on the lives of a pair of newlyweds who took a homemade boat through the Grand Canyon in 1928 and disappeared. She is also a faculty member in the creative writing program at Antioch College.*

the glare, then pointed to a pair of arms scissoring in one of the barred openings. Was it my father? She hoisted me onto the roof of the car, and I held the shoebox over my head and shook it up and down. I thought I saw the man wave back.

In the waiting room, the guards called our names in flat tones, never looking us in the eye. They led us through a series of thick pneumatic doors and down long corridors to the visiting room. Once we were inside, I saw something soften in their faces. "Sit right here, missy," one of them said. Mother lifted me into a plastic chair and my feet jutted straight out, so I stared at the toes of my tennis shoes, printed with directives in block letters: left, right.

I sat still until a door on the far wall opened and a flood of men filed in. Out of the mass of bulky shapes, my father stepped forward, the details of his face reassuring in their particulars. He grinned and reached for me across the tabletop scribbled with names and dates, and despite the no touching rule, the guards said nothing. When he took my hand, every manic bit of news I had practiced in the car flew out of me. I was stunned by the dry warmth of his skin, his white teeth, the way he cleared his throat in two beats before speaking. Distance made me notice for the first time these familiar things, which proved him to be real beneath the clipped hair and the prison uniform.

Our conversation was simple. There was little we could say in the span of one public hour. He read me stories, which my mother had brought, cracking the pages wide and roving from bass to falsetto as he acted out the dialogue. I told him what I ate for lunch, and in the silence before he answered I remembered the tennis shoes, flushed with relief to have something to give him. "Look what we got you," I said, and then tore the box open myself. I beamed and bunched my skirt between my knees while he admired them. "All Stars!" he said. "These are the best. I'm gonna tear up the court."

At the end of the hour, the guard rested one hand on his gun, tipped back on his heels, and called the time. Panic closed my throat. I looked to my father for a sign—he would tell the man we weren't ready—but his eyes were wet and the corners of his mouth twitched down. I turned to the stranger by the wall and flashed a saccharine smile. "Daddy," I asked, leaning my cheek on the table and looking at the guard, "is that the nice man you told me about?"

The guard squinched his face at me, in what passed for kindness in that place, then made a slow turn and gave us a few extra minutes. Once they were granted, we had nothing to say. I sat there with all my feeling funneled down to the smallest aperture, until my chest hummed and my head felt light. Then the guard said, "Time's up," and we shuffled to our feet. In the clamor of chair legs and murmured good-byes, we could speak again. "Hey, what do you want for Christmas?" my father asked. I stopped in the doorway and stared at his dark bulk. I wanted him. But his voice was filled with a sudden expansiveness, and I knew I should ask for something he could give.

"Something purple," I told him. It was my favorite color then, and I let everyone know: I was staking out my turf in the visible spectrum. I still have a letter he wrote me that night from his cell: "It may take a long time, but I'll try to get you a purple thing. Here's a pretend one for now." Below it is a necklace with a carefully sketched purple star, ringed by faint marks where I once tried to work it free from the paper. This was the first of many letters he wrote me, each with a drawing in colored pencil. "Darling Lisa—Hello, Hello, Hello. I am very happy tonight. I got a guitar yesterday and am learning to play it. I am on a diet so I won't be fat at all—not even a little bit." Then half the page taken up by an abstract drawing: a grid filled with tangled clots of scribbling, a black anvil shape, a downward arrow, the symbol for infinity. "I call this picture, Being in Jail: JAIL. I love you darling, Your Father."

His notes were full of rhymes and playfulness: portraits of me with green hair, or of himself with the head of a man and the body of a conga drum. In places, his loneliness leaked through. "I will try to keep writing you," said one letter, "but it's hard when you don't write me back." I was pricked by guilt when I read these pleas, then quickly forgot them. At first his absence was a plangent note, always sounding in the background, but it became muffled as the months passed. In time, I had trouble recalling his face.

My mother made several visits to Billerica, but gradually she began to cut ties. My father had become increasingly focused on his political work in the months leading up to the demonstration, and his arrest meant she had no help in caring for me, no one to consult with, no air. She was furious at him, and fury made her feel free. We would move to Mexico and buy a piece of land. She would become a potter, maybe look for work teaching English. I would wear embroidered dresses and turn brown in the tropical sun. In the flush of her new-found independence, Mother went to a postal service auction and bought herself a used mail truck. She parked it outside of our apartment and gave me a tour. With a tune-up and a few interior improvements, she said, it would get us south of the border. The cab had one high leather seat, and a long lever that worked the emergency brake. To shift gears, you punched numbered keys on a small raised box. It looked like a tiny cash register, and Mother let me play with it while the engine was off. A sliding door led back into a cold metal vault, bare but for a few mail shelves. "This is going to be our cozy rolling home," Mother said, her voice echoing off the walls.

For the next few months, my mother worked as a waitress and took steps to make the mail truck road-worthy. The first rains of autumn had revealed a couple of leaks in the chassis, so she spent a weekend driving around Cambridge in search of patching material. On a narrow side street, she spotted a promising sign: Earth Guild— We Have Everything. She stopped in and asked the cashier if they had any sheet metal. The store was a kind of counterculture supermarket, stocked with incense, bolts of cotton, paraffin, books on homesteading, yarn and looms. But it seemed that "everything" didn't include sheet metal.

"What to do you want it for?" the woman asked. It was a slow day in the store. Had there had been a line of customers, impatient to buy beeswax and clay, our lives might have taken a different turn.

"I need to patch a hole in the side of my mail truck," my mother said. "Well," the woman offered, "we don't have sheet metal, but we have Jim, and he has a mail truck, too." She yelled toward the back room, and out loped my future stepfather, a handsome lanky man in square-toed Frye boots, smiling an easy smile.

Jim came out to the curb and looked over the rust spots. He and Mother talked about their vans, how much they'd paid at auction, where they were headed. Jim also had his eyes on Mexico. And at the very moment my mother dropped by, he had been building a kiln in the back of the store for the Earth Guild's pottery studio. It seems she had stumbled on a man who could help her turn her schemes into brick and wood. By the time they finished talking, the sun was low in the sky and they had a date to change their oil together.

Jim had embraced the counterculture, but not on political terms. He wore hand-painted ties, listened to the Stones, and collected

Op Art. When he met my mother, he was living in a commune in Harvard Square called The Grateful Union. "Those guys were uptown," my mother says. "Into spare living and Shaker furniture."

She and Jim soon made plans to head across the country under the same roof. We would take his truck, since it was considerably cozier than my mother's. A platform bed stretched across the width of the van, and a hinged half-moon table folded down from the wall and perched on one leg. We ate sitting cross-legged on the mattress. The walls were lined with bookcases, fitted with bungee cords to hold the volumes in place. On a shelf just behind the cab was our kitchen: a two-burner propane cooking stove, a tiny cutting board, and a ten-gallon water jug. Jim covered the metal floors with Persian rugs and hung a few ornaments on the wall: a plaque with the Chinese characters for peace, prosperity, and happiness; a yellow wicker sun.

Before we set out, Jim bought a small wood stove and bolted it to the floor near the back wall. The smokestack jutted out the side of the truck, the hole weather-sealed with the fringe from a tin pie plate. One of Jim's friends from the Grateful Union wired a stereo system into the van, and Mother sewed heavy denim curtains that attached to the window frames with velcro, so we could have privacy at night. The engine on these snub-nosed trucks bulged into the cab and was housed by a metal shell that served as a shelf for bags of mail. Jim cut a piece of thick foam just the shape of the engine cover, which would be my bed. A perfect fit. I was about the size, in those days, of a sack of mail.

In the spring of 1970, we packed up our essential belongings and set out on a year-long journey across the country, down the eastern seaboard and then across the low belly of the continent to California. The thrill of traveling sustained me for a while, but it was a difficult age to be rootless. I played with other kids for a day or two at a campground or a city park, and then we drove on. After a day on the road, Mother tucked me in on my foam pad, warmed from below by the engine's heat. In the footwell below me was a small pot we peed in during the night, and so I drifted off to the smell of urine and the tick of the cooling pistons. Now and then, when we were parked on some dark residential street, I would wake to the knock of a policeman, asking us to move along.

And move along we did, until our funds started to run thin, and Mother and Jim began to search for a piece of land, "our pie in the sky," as Jim called it. Mother was browsing through a copy of *Mother Earth News* when she saw a classified ad listing land for sale. She located the town, which had a population of two thousand and was marked with the tiniest speck the map allowed, and we drove up through San Francisco headed for that dot. We ended up buying a clapboard house in the heart of this coastal valley town, a half-acre plot that came with a stucco duplex. Later, Mother would say that you had to call the people who lived in those buildings homeless. Only two out of the four toilets worked. The ceiling plaster bloomed with stains. There were a handful of ramshackle sheds on the property and a line of rusted cars in the driveway. The yard was nothing but thistle and dry grass. They dickered with the landlord a little, and agreed to buy the place for $18,000.

Our new address was 10,000 Main Street. Apparently the town's founders had been anticipating an explosive growth period which never arrived. Just past our house, the only sidewalk in town ceased abruptly, the last slab jutting out toward the cow pastures and orchards down Powerhouse Road. We would hold down the end of the main drag, on about an acre of good river valley soil gone hard from neglect.

We moved into the front apartment, formerly inhabited by an old alcoholic woodcutter named Floyd, who died in his bed shortly after we arrived. It took us a week of scrubbing to make that place fit to live in. There was standing water in the sink that the neighbor told us hadn't been drained for six months. Mother made batik curtains for the windows, and lined the musty drawers with butcher paper. In the bedroom, the wallpaper hung in thick tatters, a yellowed flowery print laced with ribbons. We pulled that down and found a layer of cheese cloth tacked beneath it, and when that was stripped away, solid foot-wide redwood planks, rough planed from trees that must have been five hundred years old.

I was given Floyd's bedroom. Mother and Jim slept in the living room on a bed that doubled as a couch by day. I was not yet five, and it was summer, so I had to go to bed before the sun went down, which felt like exile from the world of light. I would press my face against the screen and watch the older neighborhood kids playing kickball in the street or straddling their bikes on the corner. One evening, not long after we had moved into the house, my mother and Jim came to tuck me in, and the two of them lingered for a moment. Mother sat on the edge of my bed and sang to me. Jim stood in the middle of the room with his hands in his pockets, looking out the western window at the torn-up yard, the bristle of cattails in the ditch, and the corrugated roof of Mel's welding garage across the street, where he went every afternoon to buy glass bottles of Coke from the vending machine. The novelty of the two of them tucking me in together in my very own bedroom set me humming with pleasure, and I wanted to say something in honor of this, but I didn't dare break their reverie. Even as I lay there, mute with happiness, I was conscious of the fragility of the scene—two parents, one child, pausing for a few moments together under one roof at the day's end.

Late in the summer of 1971, when I was nearly five, my father was released from prison. Friends of his were living on a commune in Oregon, and they had invited him to come and sort himself out. He came west, as soon as he was free, and gathered me from mother's place.

It must have been a shock to see him again, for I have no memory of our first hours together. I know we took a Greyhound bus up to Eugene, and a friend from the commune picked us up and drove us out to the property—acres of dry grass and scrub oak. There, my memories become clearer. The commune members were roughing it—no running water, no electricity, just a few ramshackle houses at the end of a long dirt road.

My father's attempt to unwind in the woods was a disaster. The sudden move from a cell to the wilderness seemed to leave him nervous and unsettled. The first day he tried to play the hip nudist and got a terrible sunburn. Then he drank some "fresh" spring water and spent three days heaving in the outhouse. I stayed indoors with him while he recovered, making him tell me stories. "Me and nature never got along," he said.

But as the days drifted on, we settled into the place. My father taught me to use a BB-gun in the field beside the commune's main house. Arms around me from behind, he cheered when we shot the faded beer cans off the stump. "Sock it to me," he would say, holding out his enormous, olive-colored palm. We ate homemade bread and black beans that the women in the main house prepared, swam naked in the creek flowing through the property. One wall of the room we shared was given to me as painting space. I spent the afternoons scribbling figures on the white paint as high as I could reach, faces with huge, lidded eyes and no mouths, rapt but mute.

One day we wandered into one of the many rough-framed buildings on the property to take shelter from the midday heat. Cinder block and knotty pine bookshelves lined the walls. Up near the ceiling, a long sagging board supported Lenin's collected works. A sink and countertop unit pulled out of a remodeled kitchen shored up one wall. There was no running water; spider webs stretched from the tap to the drain. A propane stove sat on the drainboard, and beneath it, on the floor, were jugs of cooking fuel and water.

My father moved to the open door, raised his arms up to the door frame and stretched like a cat. He was there in body—a body honed by hours in the weight room, on the courts playing ball with the other prisoners—but in another way he was fitfully absent. At five, I was having trouble pinpointing this. He circled the room slowly, traced a pattern in the countertop's dust, not pent up, but aimless, as if he had lost something and didn't know where to search. I squatted near the sink, playing with a set of plastic measuring cups, watched him closely. He moved through the doorway—for a moment framed by light, a dark cutout of a man—then passed out of view.

Thirsty, I decided to make a tea party. I went outside to see if my father wanted to play, and found him sprawled under a large oak tree near the door. He was staring up at the leaves, his hand spread open in the air above him, and didn't answer at first.

"Do you want some tea?"

He raised his head and his eyes slowly focused, placing me. "No thanks, honey." I went back into the shack and filled two of the cups from a jug on the floor. I pretended to have a partner for my tea, and chatted with him a while before drinking from my cup, thumb and forefinger on the short handle, my pinkie raised high.

From the first sip I could tell something was wrong. The water burned my tongue, and when I opened my mouth to scream all the air in the room was gone, there was only fierce vapor. I spat out what I could and yelled, feeling a white heat unfurl down my throat. My father dashed in, smelled my breath and the spilled gas and scooped me up from the floor. He ran with me toward the spring and over his shoulder I watched the shack jiggling smaller and smaller in the field.

It seemed lonely, canted off to one side on its foundation like a child's drawing of a house. The dry, summer hay swayed like the sea, and I heard his breathing, ragged as surf.

When we reached the spring, a bearded man was there filling a green wine bottle. Water spilled down a rock face into a pool bounded by ferns and moss. My father gasped out the story and together they hovered over me, making me drink from the bottle again and again. "That's good," they said, "You're doing really good." My father stroked my hair. And though I wanted to stop, I tipped my head back and drank for him.

That night we stayed in the main house. My lips and throat were chapped and burning. I began to have visions. A crowd of ghosts led by a goateed figure marched with torches through the room. I told this to the grownups and they seemed alarmed. Some of the other people staying at the house lit extra kerosene lanterns to soothe me, but I could still see the figures. The leader looked furious, driven, his whole body straining forward toward some unknown mission.

My father moved with me to a bedroom upstairs and held me in a worn corduroy arm chair, talking softly, telling me stories of what we would do together when it was light. The vagueness I felt in him during the day had disappeared. He was dense, focused, his legs pressed long against the sides of the chair, his arms around me heavy and still. I sat in his lap, leaning into the rise and fall of his chest. In my last rinse of delirium, I closed my eyes and saw his body supporting me like a chair, the long, still bones, and under him the real chair, fabric stretched over wood, and all of this twenty feet above the ground on the upper floor of the house, held up by the beams and foundation, and beyond that the quiet fields, silver under the moon, alive with animals, the punctured cans lying still by the stump. I saw us perched in the center of this, neither safe nor doomed, and in this unbounded space I fell asleep.

The Men in My Life

James D. Houston

I wish I was in the land of cotton.
Oldtimes there are not forgotten...
Dixie (1859), by Daniel Decatur Emmett

In 1809 my great-great-great-great-grandfather left Buncombe County, North Carolina, and crossed over the Appalachians into central Tennessee. I have thought a lot about that trip. Of the numerous trips it has taken to bring my family—that is, the handful of us scattered along this coastline—from the eastern edge of the continent to the western edge, that one looms largest in my imagination. I cannot say it looms large in memory. No one now living knows much at all about it, nor have I heard it talked about or seen anything written about it, apart from the dates and the names of counties, and the prices he paid for a couple of pieces of land, and the name of his wife, Temperance, the names of their four sons, Gideon, Louis, Reuben, Nathan, and their one daughter, Elinder.

His name was Noble Bouldin, a church-going farmer who came from a long line of farmers, as far back as lineage can be traced. The first Bouldin to cross the Atlantic, they say, was a fellow named

James D. Houston was born in San Francisco and has spent most of his life on the Pacific Coast, where he is recognized as an authority on Californiana. The winner of the 1967 Jackson Award, he has written six acclaimed novels, including Continental Drift *and* A Native Son of the Golden West, *as well as several works of nonfiction about the West. He lives in Santa Cruz, where he occasionally offers writing workshops at the University of California and sits in from time to time with local country-western bands.*

Thomas, a Warwickshire yeoman who landed at Jamestown in 1610 and quickly acquired some land along the James River. Perhaps he was the original immigrant ancestor. If not, there was another Bouldin, sooner or later, very much like him, who carried the seed, and Virginia was the homeland for almost two hundred years, until after the Revolutionary War, when the West began to beckon, the West, at the turn of that century, being Ohio, Kentucky, Tennessee.

In those days nothing happened suddenly. A family on the move might stop a while along the trail, set up a cabin and clear a piece of land, as Noble did, in 1803 or thereabouts. He paid a hundred dollars for fifty acres, between the Blue Ridge Mountains and The Great Smokies and worked it for a couple of years, no doubt picking up scraps of information here and there about what lay beyond the peaks in the distance.

Perhaps he made the next trip alone, the first time, scouting ahead before bringing his family farther than most white Americans had ever traveled and into territory few had ever seen. Perhaps it took a couple of weeks, or a month, with long days of solitary riding, during which he missed his wife and children, but also savored the solitude and the daily discovery of new terrain. On one such morning he may have got an early start and reached a ridge top just as the sun rose behind him, adding sudden clarity and sharp shadows to the rippling landscape, causing his heart to swell and his skin to prickle and his blood to run. He may have shouted something then, one long syllable of exultation.

Or perhaps not. Perhaps he was a born slob, unmoved by natural wonders, insensitive to color and light, and concerned only with grabbing the best piece of land he could find before someone else got hold of it. Maybe he was an ignorant, stubborn, hot-headed redneck, a rifle-toting hillbilly racist from North Carolina. But I prefer not to remember him that way. I prefer to dwell on his name—Noble—and to look in his farmer's heart for signs of noble character. I prefer to see him on the ridge top at dawn, like a wolf in the wilderness, celebrating with his voice, celebrating the miracle of his own life.

However it happened, he must have liked what he saw or had heard about. According to court house records, he sold his Buncombe County acreage for a two-hundred-dollar profit. Then he packed up his family and all their worldly goods and continued west. There were tools to carry, a plough, knives and rifles, a Bible or two, a fiddle. Noble was in his thirties then, halfway through the Appalachians and halfway through his life. I see him wearing a hat like the one Walt Whitman wore for the frontispiece to *Leaves of Grass,* a dark and wide-brimmed hat, tipped back. No one knows what he looked like. He passed away before cameras came along. I can only speculate, and hope, that he resembled Whitman, with that kind of questioning eye, the trimmed beard showing some gray, and the top button of his long johns showing underneath the open-neck shirt.

He would be walking in front of a horse, and Temperance would be riding, in order to hold and nurse the newborn daughter. There were other horses, perhaps a wagon or two, perhaps not. It was spring, and the ground was cool and damp, but no longer muddy, and by the summer of 1809 they had staked out a Tennessee homestead, in Warren County, near the banks of the Collins River.

After that, one thing led to another. Noble had already begat Gideon, who was thirteen when they made this journey. Gideon eventually built a house right on the county line, making it possible, so I have heard, to leave Warren County and cross over into Van Buren County just by stepping from the parlor into the kitchen.

In 1831 Gideon begat Montesque, the fifth of his ten children and my great-great-grandfather, naming him after the eighteenth century French philosopher. I will defend the mountainized spelling of this name the same way George Hearst once defended himself at the California Democratic Convention. The rambunctious, self-made millionaire father of William Randolph Hearst, George was hoping to be nominated for governor. One of his opponents had accused him of being so ignorant he had spelled the word bird, b-u-r-d. "If b-u-r-d does not spell bird," Hearst asked his fellow delegates, "just what in the hell *does* it spell?"

If M-o-n-t-e-s-q-u-e does not spell Montesquieu, what else in the world *could* it spell?

This fellow did two things that linger in the family memory. (1) Sometime before the Civil War he left the flat farm lands his grandfather and father had settled and worked, and he moved up onto the nearby Cumberland Plateau. In a region called Pleasant Hill he built a two-story house out of ax-hewn logs and began to raise his family. (2) When the war came along he did not fight for the South, as several of his brothers did. Montesque fought for the North. Or so goes the official version of that era—the official version being what I first heard from my grandmother, as she passed her memories on, during the years when I was growing up in San Francisco. Back in 1969, however, when I made my one and only pilgrimage into the Cumberlands to look up some of the surviving relatives, looking for the grandads and great-grandads I might have known, I heard another version, and one that appealed to me a lot more.

One of Montesque's grandsons was still alive, an aging cousin thrice removed, who had spent his whole life in those mountains, farming mostly. At eighty he was erect and spry and vigorous, wore a twill shirt, coveralls. He felt a special bond with Montesque, since he was the only one in the family, or in the entire world, for that matter, to inherit the name. I should say, he *almost* inherited the name. When it crossed the Atlantic, from Paris to Van Buren County, in the 1830s, two letters had fallen out, like teeth. And somewhere between the generations, a consonant had disappeared, so that this eighty-year-old cousin of mine had ended up with a name that is surely unique in the long history of French-speakers taking liberties with English and English-speakers getting even by taking liberties with French. His given name was *Montacue.*

We were in the front room of his old frame house in the little town of Spencer, Tennessee, sitting in two straight-backed chairs, when I asked him about this spelling. He shook his silvered head in true wonder.

"It's always mystified me," he said, "how a whole letter could get lost like that. When I was born, grandad was still alive and sure must a knowed how to say his own name. It aint like people up here got somethin so big caught between their teeth, they're afraid to let some air through. I guess that ol S just dropped out of sight about like the way grandad did during the war."

"Which war was that?" I said.

"The war," he said.

"I heard somewhere that he fought for the North."

"Nope. He never fought for the North. Not my grandad. Not Montesque Bouldin."

"That means he must have fought for the South."

"Nope."

Again he shook his head, not with wonder now, but with purpose and what looked like the beginning of a grin. "He didn't fight for the South neither."

"Well then, what did he do during the war?"

The craggy face opened. The eyes gleamed with pleasure. "Far as I know, he didn't fight for nobody. He just hid out til the whole thing was over."

"Hid out?"

"Hunted. Kept to himself. Stayed off the roads. Wasn't nobody goin to find a person up here who didn't want to be found. Wasn't nobody goin to come lookin for him anyhow. In these mountains. A hundred years ago. There's places I could show you right now, you could have all to yourself for six or seven months. You take where I grew up, over there toward Pleasant Hill, where grandad built his log house. You can't even git in there now. I don't know if I could show you how to *start* gittin in there, it's all so growed over."

As he talked, I was thinking, That guy sounds like my kind of ancestor. Not only was he named for an eminent man of letters, he seemed to have a mind of his own. There are some, I suppose—other cousins, on other branches of the family tree—who would call it sloth and cowardice, not to have fought for one side or the other, when his own brothers were out there somewhere slogging through the mud and gunsmoke of the 1860s. But Montesque's grandson obviously didn't see it that way. Nor did I, the great-great-grandson, dreaming of hide-outs.

As we sat there, grinning about this forerunner we had in common, and the memory of his independent spirit, I began to dwell on the episode, as I had long dwelled upon the trans-Appalachian passage. I began to see those mountains from high altitude, as if hovering in a hot-air balloon, and high enough to observe uncountable puffs of smoke rising from invisible rifle barrels far to the north and far to the south, a wide circle of silent puffs and cannon clouds. In the center, surrounded by forest, there is a softer puff, a misty cloud rising at the base of a mountain waterfall, and Montesque is standing there in his boots and his heavy trousers.

Next to him stands a little girl. She is six years old, already lean and tough-limbed, tough as hickory, the way she will be throughout her life. Her name is Arminda, though he calls her Mindy, his oldest and favorite daughter, who has just hiked two miles through the trees to bring him a pail of food. The pail is sitting on a rock, and she is looking at it because the hike has made her hungry, hungrier than usual. She is hungry all the time. She says, "You gonna eat pretty soon, pa?" And he says, "Fore long." And she says, "When you comin home?" And he says, "You miss me, darlin?"

"Mama says to tell you the soldiers come and gone and they didn't git near our place."

"Did you see em?"

"Mama says they look so sick and raggedy she doesn't believe they'll ever hike through these woods again. Or any other woods."

"Well, that's real good news, darlin. Now what we got to eat in that bucket?"

"It's only cornbread, pa. Mama says we just about run out of everything else."

"You tell your mama there is a bear likes to wander down to the far end of this here pool every evenin about sundown, and it won't be long fore he takes his last drink a water."

"You gonna shoot him, pa?"

"I might. Or I might just sneak up behind him and catch him by the neck and stick his head under the waterfall just like I'm gonna do you," grabbing her lightly then, lifting her under the skinny arms to swing her out over the pool, while she squeals with fearful delight.

Later, while they are hunkered down in the grass, breaking off chunks of cornbread, she says, "Pa?"

Through his mouthful he grunts, "Yunnh?"

"Can I stay here with you?"

He chews a while and looks at her and looks away and says, "No darlin. Mama needs you back home. And I'll be back home fore you know it. You tell her I said that too."

And much later, while she trots through the twilight forest, to make it home before dark, she is already remembering that lift over the water as if it happened long long ago, the ecstasy of it, as the man in her life, the one she loves more than any other, lifts her up and swings her around and out, toward misty plumes and the plummeting rush of white. It seems to last forever. And yet it ends too soon, too soon...

Or maybe this little meeting of the father and the daughter did not register deeply at all. Maybe it was just another day in the long months of days when he was laying low. I am only guessing here, a grandson-at-large searching for his past, making it up as I go along, searching for some way to account for the look in her eyes in the earliest photo of Arminda I have seen, taken right at the turn of the century. Forty years and nine children later, her stern and weathered face says, "Nothing lasts forever," and "Everything lasts too long."

Yes, Noble begat Gideon. And Gideon begat Montesque. And Montesque begat seven sons and daughters, among them Arminda, who was my great-grandmother, born in that two-story house at Pleasant Hill. Around the age of twenty-two she married into another mountain clan, Irish in origin, if you trace it back far enough, another line of farmers and small-time landholders who had arrived in Tennessee by way of North Carolina. Her husband's name was James Wiley Gulley. He too is in that turn-of-the-century photo, slouched next to her, and I am sure he contributed something to the look on Arminda's face, as husbands always do. She was well past forty by that time. She looks past sixty, sitting up straight, with her knees together underneath the full-length, neck-to-shoetops dress. Her lips are pressed tight, her hair is pulled tight against her temples. Her eyes are formidable, challenging, as if this camera is not to be trusted.

Her husband's eyes are slant-browed, seemingly at ease. He is leaning on the chair arm, with knees apart, wearing jacket and vest, but no tie. His hair is uncombed. Perhaps he has been drinking. It has always looked that way to me. This was their first and only family portrait. If he'd had a couple of quick ones while they were setting up the shot, I wouldn't have held it against him, being the father of nine children, in those times, which were hard times all across the land and particularly in the South. Behind him stands his oldest daughter, who has just turned twenty. On his knee he holds a son who looks to be about three, while Arminda holds their youngest, a girl not yet a year old.

It must have been a madhouse getting everyone dressed and in position for this picture, which represents about ten seconds in their combined years on earth. The camera clicks, and a moment later the faces unfreeze, a chair scoots back, the talk begins, as the son-in-law standing in the back row rips loose the chafing, high starched collar, and as great-grandma breaks out the corncob pipe she smoked. What I wish for here is a movie of the day they took this portrait, an hour before and an hour afterward, with all the grunts and belches and the curling smoke. And yet this frozen moment captures something essential, bearing out everything else I have heard about these two great-grandparents of mine. Unbending, severe, Arminda was the stronger, the family rudder, and J.W. was the lovable ne'er-do-well, a singer, a joker, a man "with a long streak of fun in him," as I heard one old nephew say.

Perhaps it was the inclination of Arminda, the oldest daughter, to take command of things, and the inclination of James Wiley, who had older brothers, to let her do just that. Or perhaps it was something about the characters of their two clans. The Bouldins tend to be built like trees, ramrod straight, both men and women, and among themselves they make remarks about the Gulleys, as people do—families, clans, tribes, nations—who have intermingled through the years. The remarks are made lightly, in intimate jest. The receding chins of certain Gulley men, I have heard it said, suggest uncertainty of purpose. In a friendly and kidding sort of way someone will point to a small, fenced and long-untended graveyard where Gulleys were buried, until it was abruptly closed back in 1912. The last grave dug there was filling up with water faster than the gravediggers could bail it out—a sign of the high water table at that particular spot, and also an example of the unfortunate choices Gulleys tend to make.

On the other hand, it may be that my grandmother was right when she said the Union Army left on her father a lasting mark, and that this is somehow the key to his character. She grew up listening to his tirades about Yankees. She often said he had re-fought the Civil War every day of his adult life. Too young to enlist, he was old enough to remember the day a detachment of Union soldiers appeared in their yard. He was ten at the time. His father and older brothers were off somewhere fighting on the Confederate side and had left young Jim behind to take care of his mama and be the man of the family. She was in labor, so the story goes, when these barbarian northerners arrived at the farm, like locusts, and left with every live animal and every scrap of food, including a stash of turnips and potatoes Jim had buried.

He never forgave them for what they did that day, stripping the farm while his mother lay there crying out with labor pains. The *them* he never forgave included that small band of soldiers, together with all officers and enlisted men in the entire Union Army, and every man, woman and child who happened to live north of the

Mason-Dixon line. In later years some of his grandchildren would deliberately take the northern side in the endless debate, just to get him started. They would prod him to tell that story again, hoping he would follow it with other tales of Yankee treachery and deceit and end up singing *Dixie,* his favorite song. (He did not know and so was never troubled by the strange irony that this Confederate call to battle had been written in New York City by a composer from Ohio):

> Then I wish I was in Dixie. Hooray! Hooray!
> In Dixieland I'll take my stand
> To live and die in Dixie...

That is how my grandmother liked to remember him, sitting on the front porch in Huntsville, Alabama, singing gospel songs or patriotic songs about the South.

Maybe this is why he chose to move his family out of the mountains and into a mill town in another state—to put a hundred and fifty more miles between himself and the hated North. Or maybe it was that decade's depression, and the near worthlessness of cash crops, that decided him to give up trying to scrape a living from his fifty acres outside Spencer. Or maybe it was some old restlessness in the blood that sent him in search of traveling money, when he agreed to team up with a brother-in-law and pick a large orchard somewhere down the hillside, on Bouldin land. These two men moved their families into a house near the orchard, for a month of picking and peeling and slicing and drying. They built two drying kilns right there and came up with sixteen hundred pounds of produce, which netted Jim Gulley about forty-eight dollars. With that and a covered wagon he and Arminda and their eight kids set out for Alabama. They kept fifty pounds of dried apples to eat along the way and carried fifty pounds of fresh apples to trade for other food. It took them a week to make the trip, which is not quite as fast as a person on foot could have walked it.

I see Jim in his coveralls, hunched above the reins. He does not hear the squabble breaking out amongst the kids crammed in behind him, nor does he notice the line of brown spittle staining his beard. He is chewing tobacco and thinking of their next stop, when he can step behind the widest tree and take a pull from the flask he has hidden somewhere on board, and he is dreaming the dream you always dream when you pull up stakes, of another start, or an easier life, or at the very least another way of doing things.

His family had been in Tennessee about sixty years. Arminda's had been there for ninety. In our patchwork legend, this wagonload of kids rolling south over rocky roads at the speed of three miles per hour is remembered as a kind of exodus from the homeland, the wagon pulled by donkeys and covered with bedsheets stretched over curving hickory staves.

Their destination, their Mecca, their Jerusalem, their Silicon Valley, was the Huntsville of the 1890s, a town which had recently become a new industrial center, fueled with Yankee money and drawing country people from all directions, to work in the textile mills. The shifts were long, and the pay was low (fifty cents a night, my grandmother told me). But the work was steady, and a man with a big family was considered a lucky man indeed, in those pre-child-labor-law days, when anyone ten years and older was employable.

Jim Gulley soon had five of his children drawing wages, though he himself never did go to work in the mills. He took odd jobs around town, when the spirit moved him, and delivered lunches to his bread-winning crew, then tended to hang around the mill, ostensibly to make sure they behaved themselves. More likely he was hanging out with his cronies, other fathers-on-the-loose with other lunches to deliver. He was in his mid-forties then, at a time when the average lifespan was about forty-two. Maybe he figured he had already outlived his generation and paid his dues and earned a rest, and what were children for anyhow, if not to comfort and sustain a man through his autumn years. Or maybe it was true, what his ancient nephews cackled about when I met them in Tennessee in 1969.

"Don't you know that's why he went on down to Huntsville in the first place?" one of them told me with a wink. "If I'd a had that many young-uns, I'd a done the same. Ol Jim, he was lazy, but wasn't dumb. And he never wore a long face neither. Wasn't nothin could get him down. I remember the time him and Bud Bouldin picked that orchard clean and dried all them apples. Jim was working over-time there for a spell, but he already knew he was on his way offa this mountain, ya see. He was whistlin all day long and singin so loud you could hear him clear to Memphis."

That formal family portrait was taken on the front porch in Huntsville, four or five years after they had settled in. It hangs now in my living room here in Santa Cruz, where I pass it several times a day, a portal, an opening into a long-gone world. I think of it as a door that swings two ways, into the past and into the future. The year was 1901, the threshold of the twentieth century. These great-grandparents, Jim and Arminda, could be any of the ancestors of the previous two hundred years. Their faces, their body angles, their clothes are of an older time. But that young girl at the far right, the one with the dark hair piled high, rolled and shining, with the thoughtful and sadly burdened eyes, she is my grandmother, Nora Alda Belle Gulley. Of the dozen people in this photo she will be the only one to continue the journey to the continent's farthest edge.

She is thirteen here, but like her mother, she looks much older. She is not a schoolgirl and never will be. She has already put in three years of ten-hour shifts at the cotton mill. She has her mother's long limbs and wears the same kind of dress, sleeves to the wrist, collar to the chin, hem to the floor, everything covered but the hands and the head.

She has her father's slant-browed eyes, and at thirteen she is showing at least one of his traits: she is not cooperating. In this photo she is the only one not gazing at the camera. She has glanced away. Perhaps a young man on horseback has just trotted around the corner, though I doubt it. The eyes don't seem aimed at anything specific. While her body sits on the porch, her mind is elsewhere. Knowing how her life turned out, I can read into her look the wistful foreknowledge of the man who will one day entice her, and father her children, and then disappear, the reluctant husband, the main man in her life, and a man in mine too, though I never met him, the grandfather who covered his tracks.

This is what I see in those young/old eyes. Already she is watching him walk away.

His name was Eddie Wilson, a young mill hand from Danville, Virginia, or so he claimed, who moved into their neighborhood in 1909 or 1910. So little is known about this fellow I call him Elusive Eddie. He had black hair and blue eyes, and like Jim Gulley he was a sometime singer who appreciated good singing when he heard it. Sixty years later I met a woman in Huntsville who said she once had a crush on Eddie. A few years younger than my grandmother, she evidently had watched their courtship with teenage jealousy.

"In the evenin, after work," she told me, "if it was warm, Nora would sit out there on the porch with her guitar and sing *Red River Valley,* and Eddie would yell across the street, 'You'd break the heart of any boy in Alabama!'"

Eddie too played guitar, and mentioned once that he had some Cherokee blood. He also liked to pick clover on the way to the mill and make up songs about it.

Or so I've been told.

Everything is vague, except the marriage date, 1910, and the fact that he was gone by the time my mother was born, and the huge silence that later surrounded his memory. Though family meant more to Nora than anything but heaven itself, she would never talk about this man who was the only man she married and the only man she dated after the age of twenty-two. Eventually he wrote and told her he had joined the army. A while later she sent him a photo of their baby girl. He then wrote from Griffin, Georgia, begging to come back. It was the only letter of his she kept, and she kept it hidden from the world until she was almost eighty.

"My dearest little wife..." it begins.

Three years after he had disappeared, he returned to Huntsville and in due time my uncle was born. But by then, Elusive Eddie was gone again, heading to Virginia, he said as he left, to borrow some money to put down on their house.

One of Nora's younger sisters witnessed this farewell and remembered her parting words to him. "Eddie," Nora said, "as sure as we're standin on the ground, I am never gonna see you again."

"I'm comin back as quick as I can," said Eddie. "I swear it."

She may have heard from him after that, but she burned all the letters. No photos have survived, and no information at all after 1923, which was the last time anyone remembers hearing he might have been spotted. It was near Danville. Many years later the brother of a friend of the family recalled seeing him in a cotton mill. "How you doin, Eddie?" he called out, "Long time, no see." But this fellow in his thirties who resembled Eddie and moved like Eddie and was back at Eddie's original line of work, told this brother of a friend of the family that he must be mistaken. The next day he had checked out of the mill, whoever he was, moving on. Where to? No one knows. Where from? We can only guess. Any relatives? None to speak of. A letter he had supposedly written to a sister, before he married Nora, came back to Huntsville unopened. Forty-five years later a phone-book poll of all the Wilsons in the Danville area turned up no leads. Once or twice Nora asked him to tell her the story of his life, but he never got around to it. In that one letter she saved, he wrote:

> You said tell you what I had bin doing these long yeares
> well darling you no that would fill a common size book
> and I will tell you all about it when I come...

She was seventy-nine when she finally dug out these pages and showed them to me, the grandson with a taste for history, pressing for evidence. Though she knew exactly where the letter was, she had not looked at it for decades. She put on her glasses and read it aloud, while color rose into her cheeks. She began to cry. My mother was there, and she too began to cry at the sound of this message from the long lost father. We all cried at the words rising out of his fifty-year silence. For me, it was the first real proof of his existence. Until then I'd had nothing to validate him, nothing as solid as a letter written by hand, on folded and fragile paper, in purple ink. Now his words, the voice of the missing grandfather, were coming from her throat, like the disembodied words a medium pulls out of thin air.

With money saved from her years of paychecks, Nora went ahead and bought a house in Huntsville, by that time knowing two things for sure: she wanted to make a home for her kids, but she did not want them growing up in the mills. When an older brother moved to Texas, in search of a drier climate for his wife's lungs, Nora soon followed, sold her house, put the equity into a quarter-section of the Texas panhandle, and went back to the farming life she had known as a young girl in Tennessee. Before long half her family had made this move, other brothers and sisters, and Jim and Arminda, who spent their final years out there.

On her deathbed, in 1926, Arminda summoned her grandchildren one at a time. My mother was fifteen then and remembers the last words she heard from this fierce-eyed woman born in a log house before the Civil War.

"Loretta," she said, "don't you never go ridin alone in a car with a man."

"I sure won't, grandma," my mother said, thinking 'Not if I can help it anyway.' And she may actually have tried, for a while, to follow this advice. But by that time, as we know, the world was filling up with cars. A few years later she was riding alone in one with my father, as they left Texas together, heading west and bound for California.

Nora eventually leased the farm and followed her daughter. She lived with us or near us, in San Francisco and later in Santa Clara Valley, for the rest of her life. She always considered herself a widow and tended to dress that way. In her view, Eddie was dead and gone. Yet she kept his name, and that in itself gave him a ghostly presence during the years of my growing up.

She had come west without a man, but I realize now how many she brought with her. She was a channel for all the southern names and places. She talked about life "up on the mountain," as if the mountain were rising right outside the window, between our house and Golden Gate Park. She sang songs her dad learned when he was young, and some of them were playful, like *The Crawdad Song:*

> Yonder come a man with a sack on his back, honey.
> Yonder come a man with a sack on his back, babe.
> Yonder come a man with a sack on his back,
> Got more crawdads than he can pack, honey, baby mine.

Others had a haunting and medieval sound, and years later I would learn, via the F. J. Child collection of *English and Scottish Popular Ballads,* that she was puttering around our kitchen humming versions of tunes that had crossed the Atlantic two hundred years earlier, to be carried into the Cumberlands along with the rifles and the plough:

> There were three crows up in a tree,
> and they were as black as black could be.
>   *With a humble bumble snigger-eye grinner*
>   *snooze-eye rinktum boozer.*

One of those crows said to his mate,
'What we gonna do for grub to eat?'
  With a humble bumble snigger-eye grinner
  snooze-eye rinktum boozer.

She was the channel for ballads, for voices, for all these ances-
tral details that otherwise might have been lost to me. She also
passed on a way of thinking about ancestry that is essentially
Biblical, and patriarchal. After the first few elementary grades, she
had no more formal education. But she studied the Bible every day.
It was her source and reference, her solace and inspiration. Wanting
to transmit the best of what she knew and believed, Nora would read
aloud at night from the Old Testament. The stories in *Genesis* had a
special appeal for her. With that soft, grandmotherly, mountain
voice she often read aloud from *Genesis:*

And Enoch lived sixty-five years
and begat Methusaleh...

And Methusaleh lived a hundred and
eighty-seven years and begat Lamech...

And Lamech lived a hundred and eighty-two
years and begat a son, and he called
his name Noah...

And Noah was five hundred years old, and
he begat Shem, Ham and Japheth...

Eight or ten years of this, when you are young and impression-
able can have a powerful effect. The elegant ring of the King James
Version itself can work a spell on you. It seeps into your blood and
into your way of measuring time and charting a family's path. Maybe
this is why the missing grandfather came to preoccupy me. There
was a place in the genealogy and in the nervous system crying out to
be filled. And maybe this is why I traveled back to the homelands in
1969, in search of patriarchs.

Or maybe it was simpler than that. I had lived with both my
grandmothers. They both came west to spend time with us. Having

known them and their unconditional love, I had no need to go looking for replacements. But the grandfathers were both out of reach.
Elusive Eddie had closed the door behind him, while the grandad on
my father's side had passed away in Texas before I was old enough to
make that kind of trip. I see now how consistently I have been drawn
to elderly men. I never went looking for a father figure, because my
dad was always there. He came home every night. But I have sought
out grandfatherly men, elders who seem to carry in their eyes and in
their faces some knowledge of ancient times.

Among the numerous old Bouldins and Gulleys I met during
that pilgrimage to Tennessee and Alabama, one drew me more than
all the others. He seemed to be the elder I had come searching for.
It was old Montacue, my great-grandmother's nephew, my grandmother's first cousin, a man of her age, who had never left Van Buren
County. He welcomed me as if we had known each other for a lifetime. Perhaps we had. I recognized him instantly and recognized
someone in myself, the subsistence farmer I might have been, or
could have been.

He led me to the shed outside his house where all the canned
goods were stored on shelves, sealed Mason jars filled with fruits and
vegetables. He handed me a quart of applesauce, just like Nora would
have done, if I had come visiting, pressing it on me, and then a quart
of string beans striped with sliced pimentos. As he was reaching
toward a pint of jelly, I protested. I was flying, I told him, and my
carry-on luggage was already crammed full. He refused to hear this
remark. Pushing the third jar into my arms, he nodded toward the
string beans and looked at me with a kind of relentless, stubborn
generosity. "Them Kentucky Wonders'll surprise ya, I guarantee it.
They're gonna taste mighty good when you git home."

We walked out into his small orchard, where the last yellow
leaves of autumn hung on the apple trees. I have a photo of the two
of us standing among the leaves, beyond his white frame house.
Gazing at it now I see that he looked exactly the way I always wanted a grandad to look, in his coveralls, his twill shirt, his ruddy cheeks,
his silvered hair. He was taller than I am, and that too felt good, to
have a grandad you can physically look up to, even at age eighty.

I idealize him, of course. I idealize them all. Having met him and some others of his generation only once, I can fill in most of the rest myself, create my own ancestry. We have to do a lot of that, in any event. We get some names and dates, if we are lucky, whatever trickles toward our own time. But most of it is lost. The number of teeth old Montacue had at sixty; what he thought at age twenty-five walking alone behind his mule; what he used to say when he made love, or what he failed to say—these are the details you have to fill in for yourself. It makes you wonder if there is any real difference between the making of your family's past and the making of fiction. In either case a process of very careful selection is at work.

In the paragraph above, for instance, I mention his coveralls and his ruddy cheeks. I left out his arthritic knuckles. Why? Maybe I forgot. Maybe I didn't want to go into it. Maybe I am superstitious, afraid that mentioning a cousin's arthritis will have an effect on my own knuckles later on.

That is just one example. The process of selection is a process of invention. Take Montesque Bouldin, and the two extant versions of his allegiance during the Civil War. Not only do I choose to believe what his grandson told me, I choose to see his non-combat record as honorable behavior, another form of heroism. Or take Noble, a fellow from Virginia, who passed through North Carolina on his way to Tennessee. Why start with him? Somewhere back there I had thirty-one other great-great-great-great-grandfathers of more or less his age. Anyone of them could serve as progenitor. But who were they? What were their names, their jobs, their passions? Some were Scots, some were German, some were Cherokee, some were Louisiana French, with maybe a little Cajun blending in. But who knows how much? What role models might they have offered, what identity supports? I'll never find out. They are invisible now, or receding fast, whereas Noble is remembered because the Bouldins happened to be ardent record keepers and bearers of the family flame and because Nora came west with her memories, and because she liked to talk.

My father's mother didn't talk as much, or know as much. On his side the family memory gets very dim around 1900. And I don't really mind. Thirty-two great-great-great-great-grandfathers is probably more than I could deal with. One is plenty, although in truth I could have let Noble join the others. I could have chosen to forget him. He just happens to appeal to me. He is a gift from my grand-mother, one I happily accept. So it is with all these ancestors. They create me. I create them. We give each other life.

Take Elusive Eddie, the man who passed through Huntsville on his way to who knows where. I will never be able to let him go. I still try to picture him, and when I do the picture is not black-and-white. The years before the First World War were lemon-tinted years, and grandmother's long dress touches the grass, with her hair piled high and her waist cinched tight, as her beau departs, moving off into thick sunlight. They are in a park in Alabama, beside a pavilion where a brass band plays. I see light glinting off the tuba, the trom-bone, playing background music for a distant voice, a young woman's plaintive voice, half humming, half singing.

Her arm lifts to shade her eyes, taffeta crinkling at the elbow. It is her one good dress, saved for rare occasions, for this Saturday stroll, only to find herself watching him leave, his slow-motion exit across the shimmering grass, his reckless boater tipped, his custard trousers lost in the glare off the lake, while she hums and sings:

> Man fell down and bust that sack, honey.
> Man fell down and bust that sack, babe.
> Man fell down and bust that sack,
> just watch them crawdads backin back...

She watches with eyes that were shaped at birth to expect this and every other burden, and yet in all these years he has not gone twenty paces, light so thick and luminous how can anyone escape.

Wealth

Sallie Tisdale

Access to space is wealth. Light is wealth. The way the country here rolls out and opens is wealth—a kind of luxury, almost decadent. So much work, but so much room. Two counties in Oregon—Harney and Malheur—are each bigger than eight different states; Harney County alone could hold Rhode Island eight and a half times. One of the first miners into the Klamath Mountains called them "the best poor man's country I was ever in." You could starve and freeze in magnificence here, not in a small room in a small house on a crowded street. And as much as anywhere, the land might provide. This place is an estate, a mansion. And we are alone in the wilderness, unperceived: the solitude and privacy are themselves immense, and we are in a place that has no human bounds but our own. The horizon, seen so vaguely and dreamily far away, a layer beyond a layer of hills and valleys we've never walked, is the reach of our private

Sallie Tisdale is the author of Sorcerer's Apprentice, Harvest Moon, Lot's Wife, *and most recently,* Talk Dirty to Me. *Her next book,* The Best Thing I Ever Tasted: The Secret of Food, *will be published in 2000. She is a regular columnist for* Salon.com, *and her work has appeared in* The New Yorker, Esquire, Harper's, *and other magazines. The winner of the 1986 Phelan Award, she now lives in Portland, Oregon. "The Phelan Award was the first 'big-time' recognition I received as a writer and it genuinely shocked me to win. It was a lot of money to me—money is time to a writer, and time is what a writer needs most. I began to learn then that I might really be a writer, be able to live this way....I was from a small logging town in the lovely Klamath mountains—far, far north of what most people consider Northern California—and bit by bit I'd found a way into a more urban world literature and writing and ideas, and the Phelan Award seemed like this good-luck omen honoring both."*

world. Our sense of ourselves in these big places gets bigger, because it doesn't bump up against anyone else's sense of space. There are no intrusions.

At every pass up and down the length of the Cascades, on every ridge where the pines stand up like the bristles of a toothbrush, is a border: the soil changes, the trees and rocks change, the sky and the temperature and the light change. The transition is both reliable and abrupt. Sagebrush and scattered ponderosa replace hemlock and vine maple; tules and cattails replace ferns. Most of Oregon and Washington lies east of the Cascade spine, where the fall color arrives first. In the space of a half-mile, you can go from summer green to autumn gold.

Leaving the Douglas fir below Mount Hood for the open land of the Warm Springs Reservation, the desert appears so suddenly it is as though a glass wall stopped the trees. Tall ponderosa pines with orange and black bark mingle with green grass like the colors of a kilt, like plaid. The canyons and talus buttes are filled with quail, rabbits, coyote, deer, desert grasses, and of course, rabbitbrush and sagebrush; the low shrubs are everywhere, covering the land like stubble on a pale man's face.

I first saw the high-desert country at the age of ten, dropping out of the mountains, into the horizon with a thrill. I was leaving the embrace of the hills, seeing for the first time the flat plate of the world. The particular occasion was a church trip to the Mount Lassen Lava Beds in northeastern California, and since then I've made many trips out there—into the marshlands of Tule Lake, where migrating birds winter by the thousands, and to the toothy trail called Captain Jack's Stronghold. In that spine of black lava and in nearby, equally desolate hideouts, the Modoc leader Keintpoos (called "Jack") and a shrinking band of men, women, and children, held out against hundreds of army regulars for six months. I could always imagine blood on the rocks out there, where little grows and the hard ground is sharp even through the thick soles of boots. When Keintpoos finally submitted because his people were starving—only to be hung for treachery—he submitted with these words: "I have said yes, and thrown away my country."

In the upper middle of the emptiness of eastern Oregon is a place known as the Painted Hills. The Painted Hills are weird mounds leaking the colors of mineral layers like paint—orange and yellow, black and dark green and rust. The soil here is a crumbly mix that looks from a distance like the texture of a sponge, and up close as though it had been milled to a uniform shape. In the spring, yellow bee plants grow in bundles along the indentations of the hills, outlining their shapes in crayon color. After a snowfall, the snow lies silver and as smooth as porcelain in clear air, unmarked, as though someone had draped a cloth of white silk over the land. All summer long, tourists by the twos and threes pant up the short trails to gaze down on the unbroken land, where fossils have been found, are still found, as though the ground grew them. There are signs posted telling people not to drive on the hills—on the hills as soft as the interior of an angel food cake.

East of the hills, the landscape becomes more varied. The Painted Hills are only part of an enormous fossil bed of the Cenozoic, an era when an inch of rain fell every three days in this now-arid plain. North are grey rock spires growing out of the flat ground like the towers of sand castles. The road through is shadowed and dark when the sun falls behind the cliffs; the fossiled land stretches for many, many miles. There are hills, and cliffs, and canyons, lonely ranches and small towns in the curving shadows of the cliffs, and far to the south, dark mountains rising above.

My great-grandmother, from whom I took the name Tisdale, lived her girlhood in Fort Rock, a town in southeastern Oregon near its geological namesake. Fort Rock is a very old, well-worn volcanic remnant, a tall near-circle of toothed rock, set down softly on the flat plain like a black crown. My great-grandmother used to go for picnics to a volcanic depression called Hole in the Ground. From here, the southern edge of the Blue Mountains is vaguely visible, and the land is penciled with narrow roads and hopefully fenced fields. North is Paulina Lake, a navy lake in the middle of Newberry Crater, a frozen lava flow around the tentacles of which trees have sprung and springs bubble.

Driving through the desert late at night, in midsummer, I passed one animal after another gambling with the road. I came around a curve and nearly flattened a peacock, a disappointed male dragging his long plume across the pavement behind him. One doe leaned back from my headlights, then forward, and suddenly darted across my path; I swerved right, then left, making a wild snake trail of rubber and missed her by inches, remembering the solid thunk of a deer on the fender of our car when I was a child: remembering her dazed, drugged freeze and then the leap, far too late, directly into steel. One feels a constant, fatalistic caution on these back roads at night, readiness for wild animals in the pool of light. A short while after I missed the doe, in a section of desert lit by a three-quarter moon, I passed two fawns, side by side in the other lane of the highway, standing still, waiting their fate.

Finally I reached Condon, leaving behind the desert for a little Oregon wheat town in open land. The whole place was strangely empty, wide, still in smoky yellow streetlights. I passed an intersection on the deserted main street and happened to glance to my left; the side street was filled with a dancing crowd, lit by the ochre light, still silent in my quick passing. Past the dance, all the streets were empty again, as though all of Condon danced. A few miles north of town, I passed a dark silo and was back in the flat, black land falling away from my white path on both sides of a sagging wire fence. All at once I could see a line of flame far away, radiant and orange under the black sky. It was nothing more than a straight line of flame, burning across the field like the signature of God in a dream.

Southeastern Washington and northeastern Oregon form a country called the Palouse, part of the immense Columbia River drainage. The Palouse is named after its natives, the Palouse Indians, who in turn named the Appaloosa horse, their favorite gift from the Spaniards. Vast numbers of people were expected in this country, which is outrageously lovely and fecund. The soil is a special kind, so fine and fertile you'd think it came through a sieve: loess soil, silt blown on the winds in the interglacial age, deposited hundreds of feet thick in places and full of growth. The Palouse is chiaroscuro, shaded draws and beams of light, stubbled fields of mezzotint and miles of wavering wheat. The county roads out here are sometimes no more than two dirt tracks cutting through a field of oats. The planted hills above the Touchet River ripple down the valley like a cloth rumpled into folds, as though someone had run his finger down the groove of the valley and gathered the grass into pleats. There is a native optimism here, and one hopeful year after the other it inspired grand plotting schemes, big schools, tall silos, even opera houses to spring from the fertile ground.

The land has texture, like corduroy. You can see it best when the fields are in cultivation, dark and light and dark and light in an undulant variation; from above it looks like a striped sweater tight across a bosom. The land is sexual and abandoned in the sunlight, frosted in the cold. A kind of wanton heat drifts off the soil here, all the slow curves above and beyond the winding road, all the mounds of barley and rye and wheat, like a feast of hip and breast.

The sides of the canyons through which the roads of eastern Washington are laid are stacked, and the top layer is usually talus here, a basalt formation of hexagonal columns lined up side by side. Talus forms military rows for miles, and then suddenly a colossal chunk is twisted as though a strongman had bent it in a show of strength. Talus has the texture of a heavily worked oil painting—paint layered on paint and scraped up to form ridges like frozen water, pulling the painting out and up from the flat dimension of the canvas. One's finger strays thoughtlessly to touch it. Tiny dots of green hide in the draws, tugging groundwater from soil tawny and ochre. The coulee country is a strange and pretty place, with alkaline lakes rising into dry, rusty cliffs topped by miles of unbroken pillars, and now and then a dewy field speckled with yellow bales of hay and round spoke-wheel sprinklers. Puffs of tall ivory cloud hang in the sky and drop black, cool shadows on the land. Distant flocks of birds stand still in the light sky, iron filings dropped on a tile floor.

The Wenatchee World, the daily newspaper of central Washington, is published in what it calls "the apple capital of the world and the buckle of the power belt of the great Northwest." Every part of its region is outsize, even its own image. What seem like rolling hills from the ground—unusually rolling, particularly curvaceous hills—are called the scablands. Scablands form from violent action of various kinds. They run like busy water across the land, and in fact came from water, the cataclysmic floods that so marked this basin. Some farms are marked with a smaller kind of scablands, separate mounds called biscuits, which look from the air to have the artificial pattern of a planned community; they may be the result, depending on the particular history of the area in which they occur, of glacial or water action, wind erosion, or even earthquakes. Ripple ridges rise fifty feet in the air and stand five hundred feet apart. These are the unbelievably large lines sculpted in the ground by the flowing water of floods, like the little wiggles of sand left by a retreating tide on a giant scale.

The canyons through which the roads wind are actually coulees, old water channels left dry by historical water, braided channels of a flood system so big it would have drowned Texas. The ancient highwater mark is a thousand feet above the road, its walls striped with rhythmites, piled layers of silt and mud from flood on flood. Boulders were washed from Montana and Idaho to western Oregon in these floods. These rocks are called erratics, for obvious reasons: they're the hoboes of geology. A ten-inch round stone of granite erratic is pocketed neatly in a wall of the Columbia Gorge, with a little room on every side to spare; it sits in its hole like a ball in a socket joint. The coulees and channels can't be seen for themselves except from above, because the meandering trails they make run not for miles but for hundreds of miles. The lost, dry waterfalls are miles wide.

Washington state has nearly eight thousand lakes and reservoirs; more than eighty percent of its energy comes from hydroelectricity. There are so many reservoirs here and they are so incongruous at times as to be embarrassing; they seem dropped in the lap of tall timber or dry brush like moist dreams. Sometimes I come around a curve and see a bowl of water hanging in midair over a dry chasm, its dam jammed against the canyon walls like a shim. We destroy the land in order to inhabit it, destroy those parts that held the most light and hope: the streams, bright moisture in the midst of dryness, the surprise of a river bubbling up from the ground and shaded by riparian trees, drowned under the still water of an irrigation dam.

Just north of Yakima, in southeastern Washington, the big hills go dead into sagebrush and the opportunistic rabbitbrush that colonizes overgrazed lands. The view is all sere brown and grey with crumbling basalt ridges breaking through the powdery soil. This is the Yakima Firing Center and Military Reservation and not much else, rumpled coulees and silky hills and the tatting of sage. East of here, not even sagebrush grows, and the fields produce rocks instead.

But at the top of the ridge, you can see the distant, smoky smudge of the North Cascades, and below a valley of green and yellow fields. The fields themselves are filled with precise rows, fresh, prosperous, abundant. This is irrigation land, silos and barns and roving sprinkler heads for corn, fruit, wheat. Orchards lie in a cleft, an oasis of apples and peaches like a wet heart held in a dry hand. The unfettered sagebrush, with its tender perfume, holds down the soil with its tangled roots. It crawls right up to the edge of orchards marked off as though with rulers. Here the wild land, the natural shape and colors of the land come to a halt, and an inch away, grass grows amid the order of hybrid apple trees and the mist from spray hanging in the air. The radio stations play Mexican songs.

In Miocene times, cypress, gingko, and hickory grew and outsize mammals prowled, lakes moistened the humid basin. In the Miocene, lava poured out of fissures in the eastern Washington ground, making one of the largest, deepest sets of basalt flows on the planet. Faults lifted and shifted and buckled the land, leaving the enormous lava plateau leaning slightly to the north, off balance. A million years ago, a brief blink, the Ice Age: the glaciers moved down into Washington, Idaho, and Montana five to ten thousand feet thick, digging out channels and damming enormous lakes with the waters of the Columbia. Lake Missoula covered western Montana before it broke through and flooded the plateau again and again.

The Grand Coulee (the granddaddy of coulees) is a huge trench marked here and there by lakes. It is fifty miles long, ranging from one to six miles wide, with steep walls of columnar and vesicular basalt almost a thousand feet deep. The Grand Coulee begins north of where the Grand Coulee Dam now stands and descends far south of it, with Dry Falls near its center.

Dry Falls is not a falls, but a series of sheer, dry, slowly eroding walls—three and a half miles of walls curved and layered one upon the other and standing more than four hundred feet high. The land comes flying from the invisible horizon through the haze of summer air, splitting and twisting on its arid course, opening here and there with fissures and cracks large enough to swallow whole towns. It flies up to the edge of the cliffs in shades of brown and tan, and drops into space, drops hundreds of feet down to distant ground wet with small lakes. Then the ground climbs in a vertical wall and races on again.

The main road passes Dry Falls on the other side of its burst into air, slightly higher than the height of the walls, so that one looks slightly down and across the wide, empty space. It is too much to see in one sweep of the eye; frame by frame, you must turn your head from one side to the other, straining to find the farthest reach of cliff in the hazy distance, to encompass the width of the falls.

The small lakes at the base of the cliffs are called "pothole" lakes, or "kolk" lakes. They are round hollows dug during the Ice Age floods of the Pleistocene epoch by the force of falling water, by the grinding of boulders in the spinning stream. (All the lakes of the Grand Coulee are really kolk lakes, puddles left behind of what used to run fresh by the cubic mile.) The floods that carved out the coulees and the gorge were so enormous that what we call Dry Falls—this series of overlapping cliffs—was under water when they ran, like rocks and troughs on the bottom of a stream. The sheer drop of Dry Falls—more than twice the height of Niagara Falls, higher than Victoria Falls—was nothing more than a bump in the river bottom.

A five-hundred-foot wall of glacial water poured through Wallula Gap when the earthen dam broke, draining "in a few hours," says the geologist John Eliot Allen, with a force ten times the combined flow of all the rivers in the world. Such a flood didn't happen once, or twice, but at least forty times, and smaller floods ran through by the hundreds. I can see it coursing over the four-mile width of Dry Falls Butte and down, down, too much water to get through the gap, climbing the walls to twelve hundred feet loaded with debris, chunks of ice and boulders, dead bodies, backed up and eddying in its rush. The river was a constantly widening and narrowing channel, powdered with the ash from various volcanoes. The huge quantity of flood water, sometimes a mile or two wide and steady and forceful, would be funneled through a gap only a few hundred yards wide, suddenly extreme in its power and mad rush to get through.

The Columbia River is older than the Cascade Mountains. What we consider the Columbia Gorge—seventy-five miles of great, ridged walls of stone beside its lower banks—are the piles of stacked basalt flows through which the ancient Columbia ran. The floods cleaned soil off the slopes of the gorge, tore off the ends of streambeds, leaving behind the abrupt hanging valleys and rivers turning to the veils of waterfalls.

Inside the pump house of the Grand Coulee Dam, every inch of floor and wall and air is vibrating at a high frequency; the air wiggles inside my ears. This is the old-fashioned space age—the space age of the new American technocracy, circa 1940. It's that white man's optimism again. The pump house is a long, long hall several stories high, with twelve giant green pumps spinning electricity out to Washington's power belt. There are catwalks and dials and arcane emergency equipment, rotary phones and not a soul in sight. I'm reminded of the cheerful movies we saw in elementary school, narrated by a middle-aged man with horn-rimmed glasses and a knee-length lab coat, carrying a clipboard. He points at esoteric machinery and chalked equations and discusses the magic of electricity, the momentous victories of the West. Even the toilets in the bathroom down the hall are like the short, round toilets I sat on in third grade, trying to get away from the movie.

Rows of huge, white-ringed tubes pumping water from the reservoir are plopped on raw ground and rise over the steep cliff behind the dam. The cliff, the scrub, the dry grass beside the road, the camel-colored land rising away into the distance on every side is arid and dusty. But the visitors' center is surrounded by a neat square of lush green grass. The dam, which rises from frothy water, is so wide and tall it seems to be a stage set. (The dam is almost a mile wide.) Cars glide by across its top like little toy cars on an elevated track, stopping now and then so little toy people can stand by the edge and look down to the swirling pool and little Coulee City below. The school, the motels, grocery stores, houses, the little Colville Reservation Museum are all below, in the path of the towering, artificial lake above and behind the dam. A constantly changing digital display by the edge of the water gives an up-to-the-second record of how much wattage has been produced here. The Grand Coulee generates more electricity than any other plant in the world. There will be none bigger around here: so many large hydroelectric plants exist in Washington now that there are no large-scale sites left. I have vertigo from the height above, from the drop below, and the vision of bursting dikes; I have vertigo from the millions of horsepower and kilowatts, millions of cubic yards of excavation, truckloads of cement to make a feet/second pumping capacity. The dam is a statistical menace; it leaks numbers.

Two guides in the visitors' center glance around quickly before quietly answering my question about suicides off the dam. Only one, they say: an Air Force major named Joseph Benner who leaped from the new section of dam in the winter of 1987. He didn't jump from the length of the dam spanning the water, the enormous, seductive tilt of concrete disappearing below the distant water of the river. Instead, for reasons that might have been more masochistic than strategic, Benner jumped off the railing of the section built over cliff, a sculpted angle of concrete dropping into boulders. "He hit and skinned himself all the way to the bottom," the young man says, and they shake their heads at his idiocy.

There are bleachers beside the circular visitors' center, by the hotel near the lower pool, and in the sandy parking lots over the water, in front of the dam. By nine-thirty on a summer night, when the light is finally gone beneath the towering edge of the cliff, the bleachers are full of cheerful people. Cars line up along the crescent edge of the parking lot, facing the dam with a sort of reverent attention. A bright half-moon drops behind the spooky pump pipelines crawling into darkness over the hills. The woman beside me leans over to say she and her husband had driven over from Spokane for the night, just to see the show.

A laser light show is projected onto the flat, grey expanse of dam on summer nights. Just before it begins, the spillway gates at the top are opened one by one, and lines of foamy white water pour down the dry front. A pulsing music begins (repeated on a local radio station) and precise neon lines dance across the screen of water. Gargantuan horsemen gallop and fish leap, waves roll and fields of wheat grow, in garish purples and daffodil yellows. Over the electronic mood music, the booming voice of Mr. Columbia River narrates his story.

It is the prettiest piece of propaganda I have ever seen. Mr. Columbia River exults in the achievement of the dam, explaining with a patient wisdom the necessity: the need to destroy the salmon runs, drown the towns, inundate the ancient Indian lands, to flatten his own wild roar. It was necessary, says the deep, comforting voice, so that man—White Man—could raise crops and live where no agricultural people had even considered living before. He admitted the sin of the deed and invited with his admission compassion and clear-eyed hindsight. We are watching history written not for the re-education of history's victims but for the new generation of conquerors; it is history for the children of the winners: an apologia, a vague rationale, an expectation of more. It is like selling hamburger with Mr. Cow.

A few days after I watched the Columbia River dance across its own crypt in neon light, I crossed into the North Cascades. I had turned west again, and slightly north, leaving the flat coulee land. On the way through Colville, Washington, I passed a large sign with an arrow pointing to the left:

DEPT NAT RES
MENTAL HEALTH
ALCOHOLISM
GOLF

I was walking up a switchback trail beside Cutthroat Creek, and came into a chaos of fallen trees. One swatch of mature trees had been knocked aside, by some freak of weather or avalanche, the season before; the trail passed under and over the trunks of noble firs and hemlock lying tangled together. I happened to glance down and saw the ground moving right at my feet—moving as though the soil itself had somehow come to nightmarish life.

When I looked more closely, I could see the ants. They were engaged in a phenomenon of antdom called slave-making. Large red ants with big pincers battled much smaller black ants for possession of the black ant larvae. They swarmed across the trail. I followed the action back to a decaying log ten feet long next to the trail, and then down the trail and across the path to another dead log. Each of the red ants was carrying a white oblong egg as big as itself in its mouth, and racing from one log to the other. In slave-making raids, masses of invaders surround a nest, and the besieged ants attempt first to seal off their nest and then to defend or escape with individual larvae. Thousands of red ants overwhelmed relatively few pitiful, panicked black ants, only a few of them with eggs. A few black ants scurried wildly around as though in panic. I saw two red ants fighting a black ant for possession of an egg, and as I watched, the egg was torn apart and shredded, a defeat that seemed so pathetic to me that all at once my eyes blurred with tears. All the pearly larvae would be carried back to the red victors' nest, hatched, and imprinted with the scents of that nest, to work for life in nurturing their conquerors. The red ants formed a determined, implacable battle line over my shoe. I picked up a red ant with an egg on the end of a stick, and it raced to the middle, stopped, turned around and raced back to the end, stopped, and returned, back and forth until I gave up and laid the stick back down.

The North Cascades spread east and west of the long north-south line, a far more haphazard and convoluted set of pinnacles, ridges, and peaks. (Washington's topography is so rough that even now, large parts of the state are unsurveyed.) There are no single white mountain cones in the North Cascades, no wide plains paying homage to a mountain queen. In the North Cascades, the average visitor confronts a convolution of trails, sheer walls, and ragged rocks separated by thick evergreen and a multitude of waterways. On the east side are many little jewels of cold lakes, bordered with tules or covered in lilies. The winding, narrow road passes through birches and larch, spruce, hemlock, and pines. Little one-lane roads beckon to each side, to a campground here, a Bible camp or fishing resort there. The Forest Service proposed something called "star-fish conservation" in the North Cascades, a clumsy attempt to weld development with preservation. "Star-fish" refers to the appearance of such a plan: it would preserve the rock ridges and snowy draws that range out from a central spine like the arms of a star, while developing the valleys.

In the foothills of the piny Cascades are great groves of birch, each a foot in diameter, and cottonwoods. A small storm of cottonwood blossoms floats across the sky, like torn pieces of cloud. And then these give way to moist, green meadows with grass and wildflowers, and someone's dream house on a distant hill.

I stop for ice cream in Tonasket, where a thermometer in the shade reads one hundred degrees. The woman in the little store is playing old 45-rpm records and humming to herself. My daughter and I contemplate the array of candied flavors, and my husband orders vanilla.

The proprietor, who has been almost silent, suddenly begins to speak.

"I have a philosophy about ice cream," she says. "It takes a really strong person to order vanilla. Everyone always tries to talk them out of it. You know, 'Why order plain old vanilla when there's all these other flavors?' So you have to be strong to resist that. Young or old."

She hands my daughter a giant cone of something called Goo-Goo Cluster—chocolate, peanut butter, caramel, and marshmallow—and gives her a bright smile.

I think there are really two idylls here, two dreams of Eden. One is the lush idyll lived west of the mountains, in the wet valleys where everything grows easily, without effort. The second idyll is this one: growth and comfort born from luck and hard work. It is vanilla, plain and pure, a luxury doubly sweet.

The North Cascades Highway winds through scooped valleys and hanging cliffs. This road is a marvel, carved over decades through a granite tumble and still closed part of the year, drowned under drifts of snow. We had climbed up from Early Winters Valley and stopped a while at Kangaroo Ridge, turning to look back at the ribbon we'd traveled. I crawled down a boulder and perched behind a low log fence on a flat dish of rock hung high over the valley. It is a long, soft, green tongue tucked in between painfully sharp, bare peaks. Trees slid off the slopes in waves. I felt a sudden vertigo, the slap of height, and mass.

We stopped again at Diablo Lake, a glacier-fed lake opaque with the mountains' detritus. We came around a curve and saw a rest stop, and then a REST STOP CLOSED sign, and a crescent lot filled with trucks, vans, cars, lines of backpacks, milling people, and a small helicopter. All that day, helicopters had passed us every which way, disappearing over the cliffs. It was fire time, and not a whiff of smoke seen and the trees green beside us.

We followed the highway down, skirting a ledge on the cliff above the lake, finally dropping almost to its surface. There we found a parking lot, a dark pine grove, and a rocky spit jutting out. Diablo is filled with suspended particles of rock, which makes rivers grey and lakes jade. This powder is called rock flour; it is sanded off boulders and crushed to clay by the icy foot of a glacier, and then dribbled down from the peaks in melting snow. Diablo Lake is a milky aqua lacking any of the glassy quality of water, filling the valley like a puddle of spilled paint. Hill on hill of firs leaned up and back from the lake, turning to run into a narrow valley at lake's end, and out of sight. The highway came down, crossed, and turned away past our place. Cars slowed at the bridge, the people pointing at the strange water, and then drove on. We settled on the pebbly bank and darted at the waves. Nearby, a man leaned over a flock of floating Canada geese, tossing bits of bread at them. I tried to imagine swimming in water so impossible to see through, so spooky and seductive at once.

Then the air split with a boom, a pounding noise that quickly broke into a steady, panting *whapeta-whapeta,* the sound of long, flat blades slicing sky. From the far end of the lake, where the water trickled away, a huge helicopter came down, dropping in an arc from the end of the valley. The double rotors splattered the water into foam and the copter came down to hover right in front of us.

"Small fire," the parking lot volunteer had told me when I asked about the people at the rest stop. He was a retired mobile-home owner monitoring parking and picnic sites for the busy rangers. He was glad to talk. "A hundred acres or so, six miles south," he added, pointing into the tip of the valley. "It's nasty. Problem is, it's on a cliff. The jumpers are hanging on ropes and the fire's falling down on top of them. So they're dropping water."

We weren't alone on the narrow tongue of land; a half-dozen people shared the corner: children, a young couple, several older people I associated with the RVs along one side of the parking lot. We watched the helicopter coming in and saw the enormous red pail hanging from its underside. The pail hit the water with a bang and then slowly sank while the engine hummed. It lifted with a sudden, hungry whine and turned on an axis, without haste, and lumbered back away, mist flying off the top of the bucket like steam. Six minutes later, by my watch, it was back, swinging the empty red cup, sliding in close so we felt spray in our face. The noise bounced off the trees and back.

"Wow, this is a lucky chance," one man said to his wife, and I knew what he meant—this random combination of drama with beauty almost narcotic in its depth. Another man had a video camera and an Albertan accent, and he carefully filmed the sequence, lowering his lens to catch the disappearance of the bucket, raising it to follow the pilot's perfect spin. The Pacific Northwest is a gallery of land, a maze in which one room holds one view—another room, another view. Event and place blend with a twist like the twist of a Möbius strip, turning so it has only one side. Adolescent flocks of flowers run right over the random drapery of snow in springtime, bordered by larch and dark dashes of pine dripping like dye down the mountainsides; we live right in and through such things. The meadows are wet with light; the summer sun is as sharp as a knock to the head.

Every six minutes the copter returned, and we waited, timing the pilot, glad for another view. The conversation drifted into speculation—fuel capacity, flying speeds, death by burning. The bucket took three thousand gallons of Lake Diablo every trip, a great vat swinging back on its cable as though reluctant to follow. We stayed, cheered by the friendly, holiday feeling among the strangers on the spit. We stayed until the helicopter veered off the valley and up, instead of back to the lake. The crowd broke apart. And finally we left, too, down and out of the mountains, through hidden flame.

Dormitory Initiations

James Broughton

How did I happen to be acting Ariel in a military academy when I was ten years old? This was due entirely to my mother's desperate widowhood. After my father's death she launched a relentless campaign to find a rich second husband.

She said, "I'll never again let a man pull the wool over my eyes. Your father left me nothing but debts. Money would disappear and I never knew what he did with it. I was so green, I was taken in by his good looks. He could charm the pants off a snake."

Dressing us in expensive clothes, she took us to expensive resorts winter and summer—Tahoe, Del Monte, Coronado—where she flirted as fashionably as her desperation allowed. To make me more presentable she gummed my head with a glue called Bandoline. This was supposed to make my hair lie flat in a pompadour like the Kaiser's, whereas it preferred to fall forward in bangs.

I resented being made to smile at prospective stepfathers. I had forever lost the chance to laugh enough with my real father. Not surprisingly I moped more than I smiled. Sometimes I couldn't restrain

---

James Broughton, who has made films, written poetry, and produced plays, was "born a gleeful poet in a solemn family"—a survivor of military school, Stanford University, the merchant marines, and a career in journalism before finding his place in the arts at just about the time he won the 1946 Phelan Award, a prize that arguably launched his life. His memoir, Coming Unbuttoned, *from which this excerpt comes, tells the story of his life among luminaries like Alan Watts, Anais Nin, W. H. Auden, Robinson Jeffers, and the Beat poets. Born in Modesto, California, he currently makes his home in Washington.*

my tears. This annoyed my mother: "What a namby-pamby sissy. One look at you and you start boohooing. You're just too sensitive for this world. If you don't quit this sulking I'll give you something to really cry about."

Any self-respecting poet would have felt too sensitive for my mother's world. Convinced that I was a liability in the eyes of any he-man suitor, Olga would introduce me as some pitiable mistake of nature. She never understood that sissies like poets are tougher than they look, that they learn early to sidestep and outwit and endure, that they giggle rather than growl because, being pariahs, they are free to laugh at the delusions of the world and to kiss the joys as they fly.

Despite the handicap of two small sons Olga had marriageable assets. She was a lithe dancer, a lucky gambler, a stylish dresser. She also possessed a hearty laugh though she didn't find much that was funny. Like the rest of her German clan she could switch in a twinkling from sentimental sobs to toilet jokes. One of her habitual sighings was, "I've been so busy all day I haven't had time to fart." Her days comprised a heavy schedule of gossiping, shopping, and mah-jonging.

Very few of her husband candidates did I like. Scott Hendricks had huge black eyebrows and two huge dogs but was stingy. Wendell MacPherson smelled of horses, had a big nose, and owned a yacht. I liked the way he wrestled me but Olga thought him frivolous. The handsomest was Elliott Flugelhoff but she couldn't countenance being a Mrs. Flugelhoff. She scoffed when I asked her why she didn't marry Borge Nilsen. He was the husky blond ranger in Yosemite who at Christmastime had taken us cross-country skiing from the Sentinel Hotel. I worshipped his rugged warmth. I can never forget the toboggan ride he took me on one icy morning. He lay completely and snugly on top of me till I felt I was part of him, and off we sped down the steep slope at such exciting speed that when we reached the bottom I wet my pants. Maybe it was my first orgasm.

In the end Olga picked a man neither handsome, sophisticated, nor fun-loving. A self-made lumber baron from Hoquiam, Washington, Will Wood was not only rich, he was determined to get richer. Of my mother he often said, "I adore the ground she walks on." For years he would spoil my appetite at the dinner table by repeating, "Your mother is the most wonderful woman God ever made." As if that were not enough he would sometimes serenade her right in the middle of the roast beef with a loud outburst from *The Desert Song:* "One alone, to be my own, the one my worshipping soul possesses..." She would grin appropriately and not even look embarrassed.

Will had disliked me on first sight and the more he witnessed of my talents the more disgusted his dislike became. He especially disapproved of my theatricals and my theatrical behavior. In the attic playroom I had set up a rickety stage with some discarded drapes for curtains. There I often forced my baseball-loving brother to portray villains or servants. Sometimes for my leading lady I had to make do with cross-eyed Jane Newhall from across the street. I much preferred sultry black-haired Gloria Zander whose mother told fortunes in a storefront on Fillmore Street wearing gypsy costume. Gloria was my favorite playmate: she shared with me the movie magazines that she stole from the drugstore.

One day when Olga came home from a bridge party earlier than expected Gloria and I were in her bedroom playing dress-up. I had donned a beaded chiffon evening dress and a lamé cloche. In silver high heels I was sashaying about with a fan of pink ostrich feathers. To Gloria I had given a smaller purple fan that matched a velvet opera cloak. I had already decorated her with Olga's pearls. Hearing the front door slam and Olga's voice calling out I panicked. Hastily stashing the fans in their drawer I stumbled on the high heels and fell to my knees, tearing the dress, as my mother entered the room.

"What's going on here?" Her familiar fury became cyclonic. Seeing Gloria, whom she loathed, she cried, "My God—my pearls!" Removing them quickly and flinging off the cape, Gloria fled from the house. Then Olga said, "Now you, Jimmy Broughton—take off my dress!" The fact that I was naked underneath it only outraged her the more. She reached for her riding crop and beat me unmercifully.

That evening when Will Wood came to call she told him the whole story. He denounced me as the worst sissy he had ever heard of in his entire life and announced that he could not tolerate the prospect of living in the same house with a creature like me. Therefore I must go or he would. He said, "The next thing you know that boy will be sitting down to pee."

She and Will held a solemn conference. They agreed that making a man of me required stern measures. It was Will who proposed the military as a cure for my perversity. It was he who located the academy in San Rafael. It was his chauffeur who drove me over to the school with my suitcase of uniforms and name-labeled underwear. It was he, I suppose, who paid the tuition. Feeling well rid of me, he married my mother before the year was out, while I vowed that no one anywhere would make me into a man anything like him.

The dormitory for the youngest boys was a two-story barn with all the doors opening onto a central hall. I could not believe the bleakness of the narrow cell I was expected to occupy: bare wooden walls, bare floor, bare bulb from the ceiling, bare cot, uncurtained window looking out on the railroad track of the Northwestern Pacific. I felt I had been condemned to prison, under sentence of death.

When I heard someone in the hall approaching my door I ducked into the narrow closet, pulled its door shut, and crouched there until it grew dark and a bugle blew and footsteps came and went and the door to my room opened and I squeezed farther into the corner of the dark closet and then the door closed and everyone went away and I realized they must have gone to dinner and this way I would get nothing to eat, I would starve and be found dead here in the morning and no one would care, and it would serve my mother right. And I threw up in the closet.

How did I survive that barracky place that smelled of varnish and disinfectant and the urine of boys? I had never had to sweep my room or make my bed or polish a brass doorknob or load a rifle or carry it on my shoulder. I had never had to stand at rigid attention, pull in my butt, suck in my gut, and wear a heavy khaki uniform and puttees. Nor had I ever gone for cross-country runs at daybreak, been regulated by buglers, or eaten tasteless, overcooked food. The most energetic game we had played on Pacific Avenue was Kick the Can.

At home I had been surrounded by women, scolded by women, taught by women, and been the playmate of girls. At the military school I was surrounded by male bodies, male smells, tough talk, rough games, sharp commands, tests of strength, dirty jokes, and dirty tricks. Inevitably I was made fun of. But so was everybody else.

We were all misfits whose parents didn't know what to do with us. As fellow exiles we found congeniality. We even found affection.

My miserable cell had a magic peephole in the wall above my cot. It looked into the adjoining room where the house officer was billeted. I could hear Sergeant Naylor coming in after my lights were out, could hear him breathing after he got into bed. One night when I put my eye to that peephole my curiosity gasped. Where he stood naked leaning against his bed, Naylor's bare strong thighs and his amply developed genitals directly faced me. Apparently he was looking at a magazine by his overhead light bulb. I had never had an opportunity to observe any man's privates that closely. As the fingers of his right hand began to stroke his penis I saw it rouse and rise as he caressed it. Awed by the vision of a man enjoying his sexuality I went about for days in wonder. Could I do that with mine? Did all men inside their underpants sport shape-changing and explosive pendants? Even Jesus, under his diapers?

The anguish of my first weeks of school devastated my digestive system. Whatever I could not stomach, I threw up. So I was throwing up all over that military academy. No more than two months after school began I was hospitalized in San Francisco with acute appendicitis. The operation took place two days before my tenth birthday. The surgeon told me he had difficulty removing my appendix because, he said, "it had enlarged to bulging." He said it was the largest from anyone my age in the history of the hospital. He gave it to me in a bottle to take home.

All too soon I had to return to San Rafael. To impress the other boys I brought my appendix with me. One morning before reveille a pug-faced redhead named Clark Pettit slipped into my bed and begged me to show him my scar. In appreciation he showed me the scar on his thigh from the time he dropped an ax. We also compared appendages.

I liked the close touch of other fellows. To slide into bed alongside a warm body alleviated my loneliness. The most warmth that first year came from a brawny pal named Cole Brand. Despite his smelly feet he was roughhousingly affectionate. He was the first boy I slept all night with. He taught me to play pool, to swim the Australian crawl, and to spit intricate patterns onto a stone wall.

For my theatrical performing I gathered other admirers. Aside from acting Ariel for the official school play, I portrayed leading ladies in Archie Bianchi's impromptu melodramas. Archie improvised these lurid entertainments in the study hall on Saturday nights to amuse the boys confined to campus on weekends. Since he was addicted to opera, his plots thickened with heroines who died of unrequited passion or who stabbed villains and themselves. Sets and props were imaginary and when two female characters had to encounter, we had a problem: there was only one wig. To say nothing of a shortage of flowered bedspreads to wear. Most of the boys applauded my bravura speeches and my transvestite charms. I even received some Hershey's Kisses and Wrigley's Spearmint. So it didn't matter whether the same fellows jeered my ineptitudes at rifle drill and football. I didn't mind being called a pansy, a fruit, a fairy: they were pleasanter things to be called than a creep, a scumbag, or a shitface.

Whether or not I was being made into a man I was at least finding that I liked living among men. One morning I discovered that Hermy also lived at the school. Or nearby anyway. Because just after dawn he was standing by my bed, smiling and radiant, still three years older than I. He asked me if I was glad he had arranged my "escape" from home. He said I had to be free to experience fellowship and resourcefulness, and added, "Keep alert, be receptive. Wonders await you. Remember, adventure is not a predicament."

How lucky I was to have Hermy in my life. By the end of the first year I realized that, far from being a prison, this school in San Rafael offered me less alienation and more affection than Will Wood's dark brick house in San Francisco.

And then a year later in 1924 the military academy suddenly became a place where literature was more important than riflery. Instead of a disciplinary haven for the unwanted it became a civilian prep school, the Tamalpais School for Boys, modeled on New England institutions, tailored to the bright sons of the western well-to-do. It acquired a new tennis court and a new dormitory, grace before meals, horsemanship, no uniforms, a whole new teaching staff, and longer reading lists. There I remained until I was ignominiously removed after four years.

In that school three persons nourished my appetite for poetry. One was the new headmaster, a jovial, oratorical Yale man with a frumpy wife and three tall daughters, Dr. Williamson by name. At chapel many a morning he recited poems like "The Highwayman," "I Must Down to the Sea Again," and "General William Booth Enters Into Heaven." He introduced me to the Louis Untermeyer anthologies and the *Oxford Book of English Verse* as well as dictionaries, thesauruses, and crossword puzzles. Thanks to him I fell more deeply in love with the sounds and subtleties of the English language. I also loved Dr. Williamson because he chose me to play the piano for the chapel hymns and endured my wrong notes.

Secondly there was my classmate, James Walker Benét. In Untermeyer there were two Benéts, Stephen Vincent and William Rose. Jim was the only son of William Rose Benét, then poetry editor of what was called in those days the *Saturday Review of Literature.* Bright-freckled, snub-nosed Jim Benét became my adored inseparable friend and my first fellow poet. We went everywhere with locked arms. One of our favorite games was to attempt every traditional verse form and compare the results. Jim had more facility than I, just as he had more literary connections. His aunt and uncle were novelists Kathleen and Charles G. Norris who lived in a hacienda in Palo Alto and entertained visitors like Alexander Woollcott and Sinclair Lewis.

Jim received long letters on blue notepaper from his father in New York, at that time in great distress over the irrational behavior of his second wife, the poet Elinor Wylie, who believed she was the reincarnation of Percy Bysshe Shelley. Ten years later, when I went to New York to become a great American writer, William Rose Benét generously gave me my first magazine publication in the *Saturday Review:* a rather flaccid lyric entitled "There is No Death."

The third inspiring person in the school provoked a sonnet a day, sometimes as many as a dozen. The cause of my literary outpouring was a stocky blond named Littlejohn, captain of the baseball team and two years older than I. I don't think I ever showed him any of my poems, but I owe to him the erotic exhilaration that writing poetry has given me ever since. Even now when I think of him I get an erection, remembering the beauty of his.

Though his legs were too short for his long torso and his chin too recessed to be ideal, Littlejohn was a golden wonder of a young man. All of his hair, including his eyelashes, armpits, and pubis, shone like white gold. Furthermore he possessed radiant skin and intoxicating body odor. More than once I wondered if he was Hermy in human guise, or some other form of angelic avatar.

In the evening he would play records for me on his windup Victrola. He especially liked Ruth Etting singing "Come To Me, My Melancholy Baby." In the morning he came to my bed before the other boys awoke and taught me the erogenous language of love. For as long as an hour he would cradle me in his arms to initiate my body to the wonders of touch and the surprises of rapture. He showed me how tender, tactile, and passionate a true comrade can be and how the body can be a temple of holy ecstasies. I wasn't sure if this was what Hermy meant by the Big Joy. But I am sure that Littlejohn inspired my lifelong faith in the redemptions of love.

This rhapsodic first romance did, alas, cause my peremptory removal from the school. By the time I was fifteen and he seventeen Littlejohn and I were dreaming of a future life together traveling around the world or living in New York where he said he had a sympathetic uncle. In fact Littlejohn spent the Christmas break in December of 1928 visiting in New York. To him there I made the mistake of writing a passionate letter declaring how much I longed to kiss his body again. A mistake, because my mother intercepted it. Ever the suspicious snooper searching for evidence to prove me a disgrace, she would rifle my drawers, cut open my locked diaries, eavesdrop on my phone calls. In this case she grabbed the letter off my desk saying she would mail it, and tore it open as soon she left the house. She made no excuse for this betrayal. Returning home in glowering triumph she called me on the carpet in my stepfather's presence, saying:

"I had no idea what a despicable squirt you are. God knows I've been a good mother to you. And this is how you reward me. Doing everything possible to make me ashamed of you. Acting like the worst kind of pervert. Carrying on with this filthy boy. You are never to see him again, do you hear?"

I had crumpled in tears. "You opened my letter! You promised to mail it!"

She went right on. "I'm at my wit's end. What am I going to do with you? You're an absolute disgrace. Obviously you can no longer be trusted. We'll have to take you out of that school at once. You will stay here at home where we can keep an eye on you at all times."

I cried out: "But he was my friend, my closest friend—"

"I don't want to hear any more about it. You've upset me enough for one day. It's all decided. You'll get over this despicable behavior or I'll settle your hash for good."

Will Wood said to me, "You should be ashamed—upsetting your mother this way. If you were my son I'd give you one helluva tanning. I'd give you the licking of your life." It was also Will Wood who said to me a month later:

"Whenever you think you're ready for it, I can fix you up with a good, safe prostitute who'll teach you the ropes."

In January I had to enroll in huge Galileo High School in the Marina. I was ordered to come directly home from school. After dinner my stepfather locked me in my room. Then he went around the entire gloomy house locking the doors and windows. He even kept a loaded pistol in a drawer beside his bed. He cautioned me always to shut the large window in my room. This was a double French window that gave onto a light well and paralleled an outside stairway of the apartment house next door. With sufficient effort any stranger could jump across into my room.

I deliberately left that window open night after night hoping for that stranger. I didn't care what he might steal as long as he stole me. I imagined him a swashbuckling hero as embraceable as Littlejohn who would free me from my imprisonment. We would sail around the world like triumphant pirates luxuriating in voluptuous capers.

By day the big public high school seemed a corral of roughnecks and squealing girls. I made few friends. One was Freddie Devereux who took me to his house to sample his mother's bathtub gin and to dance to his recording of the ballet music from *Aïda*.

Sometimes I had encounters on the street, such as the perfume sales-man outside the drugstore who offered me $20 to go to a hotel room with him. I was too scared to accept, but he bought me a maplenut ice-cream cone anyway.

In order to gain additional time before my evening incarcera-tion I persuaded my mother to let me take piano lessons. Although the teacher she found for me, tweedy and bony Miss Hamm, was a devotee of Chaminade, I insisted that she let me explore Bach and the "Rhapsody in Blue" which Littlejohn had introduced me to with Paul Whiteman's original recording. A further solace I found in churches. There I could feel freer and less miserable, thinking of the Jesus whom my grandmother had adored. Jennie had died after her gallstone operation and my grandfather had surprised the town by eloping with a stern Battle Creek dietician who gave massages and high colonics.

In Grace Cathedral while swallowing his flesh and blood I asked Jesus how to best dispose of my mother and her insensitive husband. Receiving no useful answer I hoped Hermy would turn up and have some suggestions. Locked in my room at night, I wrote O'Neillian dramas violent with matricide, patricide, and suicide.

Will and Olga disliked my presence in the house as much as I disliked being there. I had to endure glum dinners with them in the dining room where the walls had been painted Granny Smith green. Any dining place of that color ever since has given me an urge to puke. Olga scolded me: "Some days you drive me crazy, you're so sullen. Can't you make some effort to be pleasant? You ought to be nicer to Will. If you just flatter him enough, you can get anything out of him."

I remembered this advice when in the fall of 1929 she went to New York to stay with Aunt Marion Ohlandt who was now a Mrs. Alwin Wild. She had been a wealthy widow when a suave Welshman married her, put her in a Park Avenue penthouse, and gave her a stainless-steel limousine in exchange for her entire inheritance.

Left at home with Will, I wondered how to try loving my enemy. Maybe if I went to work on him I could persuade him to let me go to another boarding school. I began by admiring his neckties, his golf scores, and his baritone. I buttered him up until he began to smile at me and take me to the movies. Soon I asked him if he would like to have me sleep in my mother's bed alongside his. After all, weren't we buddies now? Once ensconced beside him at night I tried more intimate blarney.

Since he wore only his open pajama coat and made a point of letting me see his manhood, I questioned him about his sexual prowess. He was shamelessly proud of his substantial member and how many women it had pleased and how much my mother loved it. I praised his equipment till he glowed and preened. When I asked him if I could measure his erect cock he said, "That's enough now, son. Go to sleep."

When the stock market crashed Aunt Marion's husband jumped out of her penthouse window and Olga returned abruptly from New York. Will made me promise not to say anything to her about our intimacies and offered me a set of golf clubs. I opted for higher stakes: would he send me to the boarding school where my brother was, the Menlo School for Boys in Menlo Park? Will made one proviso: that I should take boxing lessons.

Menlo School was supposed to prepare boys for Stanford. The ancient white oaks were the only attractive thing about the place. Otherwise its primary function was to keep boys too exhausted from violent exercise to have much interest in sex or serious learning. This satisfied my sports-minded brother. But there was no chapel in the place, no theatricals, no art classes or music, only debating societies and competitive games. I worked on the school paper and tucked poems among the sports copy. I lasted only halfway through the first boxing lesson, falling to the floor in a faint. The coach didn't seem to mind. He laughed, patted me on my behind, and told me to switch to tennis.

My first roommate was named Bob Baird. He called me Roomie and gave me his white rat to sleep with. His favorite amusement was lighting my farts with Ohio Brand matches. My second roommate, a hefty bodybuilder named Eldridge, wanted me to feel his biceps and smell his armpits. I found more refreshment in long talks about movies with the smartest boy in the school, wry and pudgy Waldo Salt. In our grown-up years he and I pursued different approaches to cinema. In those teenage times we tried to outshudder one another with our juiciest fantasies.

I remained at Menlo for a year and a half. As a graduation present in that summer of 1931 my Aunt Esto took me on a trip across the USA in her Model A coupe. We looked at national parks and local monuments all the way to the brand-new Empire State Building. On Broadway I was enthralled at matinees of *The Green Pastures* and *Street Scene*. Then we went to Washington to visit an elderly cousin, Helen Nicolay, only daughter of Lincoln's secretary John George Nicolay. Helen wrote historical novels for boys and lived with a Miss Spofford who wrote indelicate verse. They took us to the Freer to see the Whistlers.

In Pittsburgh we stayed with a former sorority friend of my aunt's whose younger married sister had juicy lips, bloodshot eyes, and no qualms. She seduced me under the orchids in the greenhouse. This excursion compensated for my frustration of the summer before when at Cohasset Beach on the coast of Washington State a smoldering nymph named Barbara Owens kept showing me her breasts till she wearied of my timid advances and scooted off behind the driftwood with a fullback from Seattle.

Fiction

from Catherine Carmier

Ernest J. Gaines

Brother set the pan of water on the washstand and turned on the light. Jackson raised his head and looked at him.

"Just getting ready to wake you up," Brother said.

Jackson looked toward the door that Brother had left partially opened. He could hear the people talking and moving around in the other room. The house was so full of cracks that the voices came through the wall as clearly as if the people were on this side.

"What's going on?" he asked.

"The party," Brother said, going to the door to shut it.

Jackson sat up on the bed and passed his hands over his face. He had gone to sleep in his shorts and undershirt. The rest of his clothes were thrown over the back of a chair beside the bed.

"I was tired," he said. "How's it going?"

"All right."

Ernest J. Gaines was born on a Louisiana plantation in 1933. At age fifteen he moved to Vallejo, California, where he attended school until 1953, when he was drafted into the Army. In 1955 he resumed his studies at San Francisco State University, and went on to receive a Wallace Stegner Fellowship at Stanford University. His first novel, Catherine Carmier, *won him the 1959 Jackson Award, and concerns, among other things, a young man named Jackson who has received a prized education in California and returns to his Louisiana home to find himself estranged from the people and the community in which he was raised. Since* Catherine Carmier, *Gaines has become one of the nation's most prominent writers, and has written* The Autobiography of Miss Jane Pittman, Bloodline *(a collection of stories),* A Gathering of Old Men, In My Father's House, *and* A Lesson Before Dying.

He looked at Brother and smiled. He and Brother had been best of friends before he left here—they had been inseparable. He did not feel that way about Brother now, and he wondered if he ever could again.

"What time is it getting to be?"

"'Bout eight thirty."

"How long has it been going on?"

"'Round sundown."

"Is that water on the washstand?"

"Yeah. Miss Charlotte sunt it for you to wash your face."

Jackson passed his hands over his face again. He was still very tired. Instead of helping him, the three or four hours of sleep seemed to have made him feel worse. He felt groggy. He wished there was no party at all. What would they say when he told them he was going back? Would there be a party for him then?

He got up from the bed and went to the washstand. The warm water felt good on his face and made him feel much better. After throwing the water out through the window, he came back to the chair to get his clothes.

"Sounds like a big crowd," he said.

"Pretty good size."

He sat on the bed to put on his shoes, then went to the chif-forobe mirror to comb his hair. In the mirror, he could see Brother watching him.

"Well, I guess this is it," he said, turning away from the mirror. "Listen, I might not recognize some of the people in there," he said to Brother. "How about standing close by, huh?"

Brother nodded his head. Jackson continued to look at him. He started to put his hand on Brother's shoulder, but he changed his mind. He could not make himself feel about Brother as he did before.

When they came into the other room, a woman standing by the door threw her arms around Jackson and kissed him fully on the mouth.

"Been waiting right here just for that one thing," Olive Jarreau said. "'Clared to the rest of 'em, I was go'n be the first one. But, my God, Jackson, you done growed up there some. Just look at you there. Just look at you. Lean here, let me kiss you again. Let me kiss you again." She kissed him on the mouth. "You see this boy trying to be bashful 'round here," she said to the rest of the people. "You see that—much bread he done ate in my kitchen. But, my God, Charlotte got herself a man here. Ain't that little old skinny boy that left. Well, how you been, Jackson? How you been?"

"All right, Mrs. Olive."

"Yes, sir, he done growed," she said, not hearing what he had said. "And you already to start your teaching, hanh?"

He shrugged his shoulders and did not answer. Aunt Charlotte had really spread the news, hadn't she?

"I guess you have to look 'round some first," she said. "I guess that's the best. But I hope it's somewhere close so you can teach some of my great-grandchildren. You didn't know I had great-grandchildren, did you?"

"No, I didn't."

"Yes—Lord—Toni done married and got children going to school. And when you left here she wasn't nothing but a child herself. Yes, indeed. But, Jackson, you look some nice. Ain't married yet?"

"No."

"Come back to get one of your home girls, huh? Well, that's nice. Never forget the home people. No, sir, don't ever forget them. Ain't no place like home. No, sir."

"Jackson," another woman said, "your aunt busy in the kitchen, and she told me to car' you 'round to meet the people. I'm Mrs. Viney. You 'member me, don't you?

"Yes."

"I 'member when you got baptized. You sure was a great little Christian. I hope you still keeping up the good work."

Jackson did not answer her. He could not remember the last time he went into a church. But whether or not Viney expected an answer, Jackson could not tell, because as soon as she had asked him about the church, she was introducing him to people standing close by.

Some of the people—the older ones in particular—were like Olive Jarreau; but the majority of them were not. They did not know what to do around him. He had to make the first move. If he held out his hand, they took his hand. If he spoke to them, they spoke in return. If he smiled, they did also. But when he had shaken their hands, spoken to them, smiled with them, he could not think of another thing to say or to do, and neither could they.

After Viney had introduced him to everyone in the living room, including the small children who were in school or might be starting school the next semester, and assuring them that they had better be nice because Mr. Jackson might be their teacher, she led Jackson out on the porch. The boys and girls sitting in the swing and along the railing of the porch were too interested in each other to pay Viney and Jackson any attention, and Viney led Jackson out into the yard where she hoped, as she said, the men folks would show a little more respect for someone with his learning. The men were arguing about something before they came into the yard, but as soon as Viney and Jackson came up to where they were, the conversation came to an abrupt end. The men shook Jackson's hand and spoke to him, but they did this just as the others had done. They waited for him to make the first move. He had been educated, not they. They did not know how to meet and talk to educated people. They did not know what to talk about. So let him start the conversation, and if possible they would follow. But once Jackson had spoken to them and had shaken their hands, he was as lost for words as they were. Viney noticed how uncomfortable everyone was, and she tried to start a conversation by saying that Jackson had come back here to teach. The men looked at Jackson and said, "Yes?" "Un-hun." "That's good." And that was as far as the conversation went. A long period of silence again. Everyone was waiting for someone else to do what should be done. Viney said, "Well, I guess that's all you ain't met, yet; let's go back in."

The men watched them go back up the steps, and their conversation was resumed only moments later.

"Well, he done met just about everybody," Viney said to Charlotte, when she came back into the kitchen. "And I reckon'd I'm go'n be heading on home."

"So soon?" Charlotte said.

"Yes. Put this old self to bed," Viney said. "If I don't see you 'fore Sunday, I'll be seeing you at church."

"Yes, I'll be there," Charlotte said.

"Good night," Viney said, and went back into the living room.

"Ain't you hungry, Jackson?" Charlotte asked him.

"Not right now," he said. "Right now I'm trying to cool off."

"No wonder you hot," Charlotte said. "That coat and tie on—
but I reckon'd that's what they teach y'all, though."

Jackson moved toward the screen door but did not go outside.
An old woman sitting at the table raised a spoonful of gumbo to her
mouth and looked at him. She drank a swallow of beer, but did not
take her eyes off Jackson.

"Well, Jackson?" she said.

He looked over his shoulder for the person who had spoken to
him. He recognized her immediately and came to the table where
she was.

"Madame Bayonne," he said, smiling.

"Sit down," she told him.

He pulled out a chair and sat across from her. She was a tall,
slim, black woman, with the sharp features of the Caucasian race.
She might have been seventy years old, she might have been older.
She wore a small black hat on a pile of gray hair. And she had been
Jackson's teacher before he left for California.

"You are grown," she said.

"I've grown some."

"You are a man now."

"I'm twenty-two."

She looked at him closely and admiringly. He had always been
her favorite student.

"You look very well yourself," he said.

"I manage to get along."

"Do you want to eat now, Jackson?" Charlotte asked him.

"Yes."

She turned away, and he heard her dishing the food; then she
was back again.

"You want something to drink with it?" she asked, setting the
plate before him. "Got all kinds o' soft drinks there."

"I'll take a beer," he said, looking at Madame Bayonne. But
Madame Bayonne wanted no part of it, and she looked away.

"A beer?" Charlotte said.

"I drink," Jackson said, looking up at her.

"Is that nice?" Charlotte said. "And in front of the children, too?"

Jackson looked around, but saw no children watching him. He
looked at Charlotte again. He could tell by her face that she was still
against his drinking the beer.

"A Coke'll do," he said.

She opened a bottle of Coke for him and set the bottle and a glass on the table. She went back to the stove, and he could hear her saying something to Mary Louise about him. Both of them looked at him and Madame Bayonne sitting at the table.

"When are you going back?" Madame Bayonne asked, looking at him. Not exactly at him, he felt, but through him. She could always tell what you were feeling or thinking before you knew yourself.

How do you know I'm going back, he said with his eyes, when all the others seem to think I've come here to stay?

She did not say any more, she did not have to. She made a sound in her throat as if to assure him that he had no other choice. She raised the bottle up to her mouth, still looking through him.

"About a month," he said.

"When are you going to tell her?"

"I don't know," he said, eating. "I didn't know she expected me to come here to stay."

"You were supposed to come back," she said. She said it as though it was a vow he had broken—as though he had promised a girl he would marry her, and after she had waited ten years, he decided to back out of it.

"That was a long time ago."

"People like that never change. She remembered you said a long time ago that you would come back. She doesn't pay any attention to what is happening around her. These things mean nothing. The only important thing in her life was that you were coming back here one day."

"It's been so long since I said it."

"But you did say it. And she has been living in that dream ever since. Now you must tell her the truth."

"How?" he said.

"It's going to be hard, but you must. Do you want me to do it for you?"

"No. I'll do it myself."

"She wouldn't believe me, anyhow."

"Will she believe me?"

Madame Bayonne nodded her head. She continued looking at him—not only at him, but through him. Those eyes know everything, he thought.

"Yes, she will believe you," she said. "And it will be the worst moment of her life."

"Am I to blame for that?"

"Yes," she said.

When they were through eating, they sat at the table talking a while. The people continued to come into the kitchen, but no one went to the table where Jackson and Madame Bayonne were sitting. They wanted to meet Jackson—for Charlotte's sake at least; but even for Charlotte's sake, none of them would go near Madame Bayonne. Madame Bayonne had very little to do with the people in the quarters now that she had retired from teaching, and the people, though they respected her very much, looked upon her as an eccentric old woman from whom they kept their distance. Even Brother, who got along with everybody, stood by the window with his bowl of gumbo. He had looked forward to eating at the table with Jackson, but when he saw Madame Bayonne sitting there, he had told Mary Louise that she could put his food on the shelf in the window. Mary Louise had understood, smiled, dished up the food—a bowl of rice and gumbo that could have fed three people Brother's size—and set it on the shelf before him. When the food had cooled enough so that Brother could hold the bowl in his hand, he turned away from the window with the bowl and looked at Madame Bayonne and Jackson.

"Well, I think I'll be going," Madame Bayonne said.

"Why so early?" Jackson said.

"I've seen you," Madame Bayonne said. "That's what I came for."

She leaned over to get her walking cane that lay on the floor under the table. She could not reach it, and Jackson had to get it for her.

"I'll walk with you," he said.

"No. You ought to stay. This is your party."

"I need the fresh air," he said, standing up with her. "I'll be back in a few minutes, Aunt Charlotte," he said to his aunt.

Charlotte nodded her head, but everyone in the kitchen could see that she did not like the idea of his leaving the house. She had given the party for him, to celebrate his homecoming, and he should have showed consideration by staying there. He and Madame Bayonne went through the front room toward the porch.

"You have a nice crowd," Madame Bayonne said, when they were in the road.

"I'm sure they didn't all come to see me," Jackson said.

"They did," Madame Bayonne said, "if only to talk about it tomorrow. That's human nature."

"What's happening around here, Madame Bayonne?" he asked.

"In what way do you mean?"

"I don't know. In every way. The people, what are they doing?"

"Nothing. Now that the Cajuns have just about taken over. Nothing."

"What is this about the Cajuns taking over?"

"Just as I said. They have taken over the plantation. They have wrangled and wrangled until they have gotten everybody else to quit farming. Now those five cousins have it in their hands."

"Didn't Bud Grover—he's still alive, isn't he?"

"He's alive."

"Didn't he have anything to do with it?"

"Bud Grover is so lazy and drinks so much, I doubt if he knows where he is half of the times."

"But how did they make the people quit?"

"They kept asking for more land. Each year they showed Bud Grover where they needed more land. Bud Grover took the land from the Negroes and gave it to them."

"But why, when the Negroes were sharecropping just like the Cajuns, why?"

"White is still white, Jackson," Madame Bayonne said. "And white still sticks with white. But there are other reasons, too. This uprising by these young Negroes now is one of them. He's proving to them that they need him much more than he needs them. The other reason, of course, is that the Cajuns have always made more crop for Bud Grover than the Negroes have. They've always had the best land—being white they got that from the start; and they have organization. That Villon bunch has always worked together. Having the best land and being able to work it all together, they grew twice as much. When you make twice as much, you can afford to buy more equipment, better equipment. Once they got the equipment, they wanted more land to work. So Bud Grover gave them the land—acre by acre until the Negro's farm was too small to support him. He quits, and the Cajuns get it all. The next year another one quits; the next year another one. Now, they've all quit. All but one."

"Raoul?"

"Yes. They're letting him run for a while—the way you play with a fish before jerking him out of the water."

"Why?"

"Because he's killing himself working, trying to keep up with them. Besides he's neither white nor black; he's not standing on a soapbox preaching against the treatment he's getting."

"If he did?"

"He and his kind never will; you ought to know that."

Jackson looked at the big, old house that they were now passing. A light burned in one of the rooms, but the rest of the house was in darkness. He looked at the trees in the yard and he remembered how he and Catherine and Mark used to play behind the trees. He remembered how he would have to leave before Raoul came home because Raoul did not like dark people. Then, when he got home, Charlotte would whip him if she knew he had been down there, because she knew how Raoul felt, and she was afraid that Raoul would hurt him if he ever caught him there.

"I saw Catherine today," he said.

He could feel Madame Bayonne looking at him. "Did you?"

"Yes."

She was still looking at him. "You all had anything to talk about?"

"Not much."

"I'm afraid she has her hands full there," Madame Bayonne said.

"How's that?"

"You seem interested?"

"No, it's nothing," he said.

Madame Bayonne looked at him a long moment before going on. "She has two of them on her hands, three when that other one is there," she said.

"I don't understand."

"It's a long story."

"How's Mrs. Della?" he asked, after they had gone a little farther.

"She's there, but that's about all that you can say for her," Madame Bayonne said. "Catherine just about runs things now."

"Mrs. Della shouldn't be that old?"

"By years, no. But life has been hard on her. She's defeated. Finished. You remember the boy."

"Yes. He was killed just before I left."

"His memory is as fresh in that house today as it was the day it happened. Neither Raoul nor his people will ever let her forget it. I doubt if she really wants to forget him. She loved him just as much as Raoul loves Catherine. I'm sure you remember him."

"Yes."

"You fought for him enough."

"I liked his sister."

"You liked her a lot, didn't you? Or I should say you two liked each other a lot."

"I suppose so," he said, looking down at the ground—remembering.

"And now?"

"You can like a person so long," he said, but still keeping his eyes down on the ground.

"Some people like forever," she said, looking at him.

"I'm afraid I have other things to think about," he said. But Madame Bayonne thought she detected something false in the way he said it.

They were between two walls of corn now, a patch on either side of the road. It was very dark here, because the moon was behind the patch of corn on the right. Jackson could smell the sweet dry odor of the corn, and it reminded him of a field he had passed earlier that day when the bus had stopped to pick up passengers along the road, and he had opened his window for only a second.

"There was a house there once," he said, nodding to the left side of the road. "The Washingtons, didn't they live there?"

"Yes; they moved to Baton Rouge," Madame Bayonne said. "The house was torn down and everything was plowed up. That also belongs to the Cajuns.

"But it gets worse as you go farther down the quarters," she said. "Houses don't sit between houses any more; now they sit between fields. It's all right at night. It's quiet at night. But in the day you might have a tractor running up to your fence any time."

"And the people are leaving more and more?"

"Yes. Going to Baton Rouge, New Orleans. Some who have money go up North. But most of them hang around Baton Rouge and New Orleans."

"What are they doing there?"

"Whatever they can."

"There was a house there, too," he said, nodding to the field on the left again.

"Yes. Robinson. When old Robinson died, the children all moved away. I suppose they were glad he died. They hated the country, anyhow."

"Why haven't you left, Madame Bayonne?"

"Why? Moving around is for the young—the restless. I'm old now. My daughter has been trying to get me up North—Seattle. But why should I go? Let them pay me for the service I've done for this state."

"How do you make out? All right?"

"As well as can be expected. I don't have to pay rent, and I have the privilege of keeping a garden."

"Does anyone pay rent?"

"No. You can stay here for free. As long as you keep your nose clean. You don't have your farm any more—no; the Cajuns have taken that. But you can stay here if you want to."

"As long as you keep your nose clean?"

"Yes—as long as you keep your nose clean. I'm at the age now that these things don't bother me any more. I have only a few more years left, and I would love to live them in peace."

"Don't we all?"

"Why did you come back, Jackson?" Madame Bayonne asked.

"Pardon me?" he said.

They were in the heart of the quarters now, and he saw what she meant about the houses and the field. Most of the houses on the left had been torn down and had been replaced by patches of corn and sugar cane. The houses that still remained looked so worn and dilapidated that Jackson knew it would be only a matter of time before they would be torn down also.

The right side of the road was different. Not only were there more houses, but they were in better condition. The yards were clean and many of them had flowers. The scent from one of the flowers—jasmine, he thought it was—permeated the air. He had heard voices from the porch as he and Madame Bayonne came up to the yard; but as they came closer, the voices ceased. Then after they had gone, the people began talking again.

"To tell her you could not come back?"

"No, it wasn't exactly that. And maybe that was part of it."

"You have finished now?"

"Yes."

"What are your plans?"

"I haven't any."

"You must have something in mind."

"Nothing concrete, Madame Bayonne."

"What will you do when you go back?"

"I don't know."

They had stopped in front of her house now—a small three-room cottage that looked no better or worse than any of the others on that side of the road. There were several little trees in the yard—flowers, too, that almost hid the house from a passerby. Madame Bayonne leaned on her walking cane and tilted her head back to look up at Jackson.

"Something is bothering you, isn't there?"

He was not looking at her; he was looking far away. He frowned and made a sound in his throat as though to say, "Do you have to even ask that?"

"There is, isn't there?" she said.

"I'm like a leaf, Madame Bayonne, that's broken away from the tree. Drifting."

"You are searching for something?"

He nodded; he was still looking away. "Yes. Searching."

She nodded now. "You were always searching. Always wanted to find something strong—something you call concrete. Always."

"Always?"

"Always," she said. "It was the same here when you were small. And even then I was afraid for you. Terribly afraid."

"Why?"

"Because you're searching for something, Jackson, that is not there. It isn't in California, and it isn't here."

"Then maybe it's some place else."

"No. It isn't there either. Men, not only black men, but all men, have looked for it, but none have found it. They have found a little of it, but not all. I'm sure some of it is in California, and some of it is here also. But all of it is not in any one place."

"I must search."

"It isn't to be found."

"I cannot bow, Madame Bayonne."

"I suppose by bowing, you mean you can't put up with the things you would have to put up with here."

He nodded. "Yes."

"Then your only alternative is to go back."

"There's no place to go back to."

"What?"

"They promised us, Madame Bayonne, they promised us. They beckoned and beckoned and beckoned. But when we went up there, we found it all a pile of lies. There was no truth in any of it. No truth at all."

"There must be some truth."

"There's no truth. They don't come dressed in white sheets with ropes. But there's no truth."

"That's why you're here?"

"I came for a while, and then to leave again. I don't know where I'm going. But it would be impossible here."

"Then it has to be there."

"Has to?"

"If you can't stay here."

He looked at her thoughtfully a moment, as though he had been thinking of some other alternative. She did not like what she saw in his face. He looked away.

"Maybe it's me."

"In a way, it is."

"In a way?" he said. "Not all the way?"

"No. Because there are many just like you. Aren't there?"

"There are."

She nodded. "I saw it in the beginning. I saw it in you then."

"I'm not looking for a paradise, Madame Bayonne."

"I know what you're looking for. Dignity, truth—you want to make something out of a senseless world."

"Is there anything wrong with that?"

She looked at him, but did not answer.

An owl suddenly left an old pecan tree about a hundred yards from where Jackson and Madame Bayonne were standing, and went flying over the field and across the road. The owl flew so low over their heads that Jackson could almost hear the beating of its wings. He watched it fly over the house and into the night. He wondered what had caused it to leave and where it would eventually stop.

"Even he must leave sometime." Madame Bayonne had taken one quick glance at the owl, and had looked at Jackson again. "I wonder what he ever did to anyone, what was promised him, what was not fulfilled?"

Jackson turned to her. "Do you understand?"

Her eyes said it. Her mouth did not. She understood.

"Good night, Madame Bayonne," he said.

"Good night," she said.

She went into the yard, and the tall flower bushes and the trees in the yard seemed to envelope her, hiding her from him in the road. Or did these things hide the road, the outside from her? He walked away.

The party was over. All but three people had left the house. Mary Louise and Charlotte were in the kitchen washing dishes; Jackson and Brother sat in the swing on the porch. Jackson had taken off his coat and tie and had rolled up his shirt sleeves. Brother sat beside him drinking a beer. In a rocking chair, at the other end of the porch, sat an old man sound asleep. His snoring could be heard all over the place.

It was after midnight. A heavy dew had fallen, and there was a slight breeze from the direction of the swamps. The breeze stirred the leaves in the mulberry tree at the corner of the porch.

"Finish this beer and take him in," Brother said.

"Can you handle him by yourself?"

"Oh, yeah."

"I'll give you a hand if you want me to."

"I can handle him—I do it all the time," Brother said. He raised the bottle up to his mouth, threw his head back, and drank about half of the beer. He looked at Jackson again. "Anyhow, you got something up here to take care of," he said.

"Yes, a good night's sleep," Jackson said. "And I need it."

"I mean Mary Louise," Brother said. "What you think she hanging 'round here for?"

"She's helping Aunt Charlotte with the dishes, I suppose."

"Don't take you ten years to wash no dishes," Brother said, and grinned.

He got up from the swing before Jackson could say anything, and took the empty bottle inside. When he came back on the porch, Charlotte and Mary Louise were with him.

"Done cool off," Charlotte said. "That's a blessing. Saint Ambrose still here?"

"Just getting ready to take him in," Brother said, going over to the chair where the old man sat snoring. "Okay, Saint Ambrose, let's get to getting," he said.

He pulled Saint Ambrose out of the chair, but Saint Ambrose went back down again. He pulled him back up, but again he could not keep Saint Ambrose on his feet. Jackson went over to help Brother take him out to the car.

"He must 'a' had one too many," Brother said.

"You ever knowed when he didn't?" Charlotte said.

They had a hard time getting Saint Ambrose down the steps and through the gate because he was heavy and no help to them at all. After they had gotten him into the car, Jackson shut the door. Brother went around and got in on the other side. He looked at Jackson again.

"What time you getting up tomorrow?"

"I don't know. Eight; nine."

"Probably come by and we can go riding somewhere if you want."

"Yes, that sounds all right."

Brother looked toward the porch where Charlotte and Mary Louise were, and leaned closer toward Jackson.

"Don't mean to be prying," he said; "but y'all can have that whole house to y'all self over there tonight. Herb's working in Baton Rouge."

Jackson smiled and looked away. But Brother could tell by his smile that Jackson was not interested in what he had proposed.

Brother shrugged his shoulders and sat up. "Just thought I mention it," he said, starting up the motor. "See you tomorrow."

"Take it easy," Jackson said, standing away from the car. Brother drove off, and Jackson came back into the yard.

"How did you like the supper?" Charlotte asked him.

Charlotte had dragged the rocking chair to the center of the porch, and now sat rocking and fanning with a piece of white cloth. There weren't any mosquitoes tonight, but bringing the piece of cloth along whenever she sat outside had become a ritual with her.

"All right," Jackson said.

Charlotte looked over her shoulder at Mary Louise. "Ain't you go'n sit down and cool off?"

"No'm, I ought to be going," Mary Louise said.

"I spec' you want Jackson to walk you home?" Charlotte said.

Mary Louise looked at Jackson, but did not say anything. She did not move from where she was standing either.

"Talking about shame-face," Charlotte said to Jackson. "You better take her on over there. She'll never ask you."

"About ready?" Jackson asked Mary Louise.

Mary Louise nodded and started toward the steps.

"I'll be back tomorrow when I get through at the Yard," she said to Charlotte.

"Good night," Charlotte said, and watched them go out of the yard.

She knew she did not have anything to worry about from Mary Louise. She had watched them together tonight and she had watched them this afternoon, and she knew there was nothing between them.

When they came into the road, neither one said anything. Mary Louise wanted to talk; she had so much on her mind to talk about, but where should she begin? Where do you begin after ten years?

Actually she had not been waiting for him. She had said it many times and meant it sincerely. "No," she had said, "not him. But the first one that love me and can respect me and who I can love and respect, that's the one I'm go'n marry." But none of the boys who courted her, who took her out, seemed to be the right one.

When she took Charlotte's place at the Yard two years ago, she ceased courting altogether. All of her time was devoted to the Yard, her house, Charlotte's house, and the church. When boys attempted to escort her from church, she told them very politely that she was with someone already. If the boy insisted, Charlotte came to the rescue. Then when they were alone again, she would tell Mary Louise, "You know, you getting 'round that marrying age now. You got to spec' that kind o' 'tention."

Mary Louise would nod her head, but would not answer.

When all of her friends were getting married and asked her what was she waiting for, she told them very simply, "The right one." When they heard that Jackson was coming back—Charlotte had told everyone in the quarters that he was—and asked her if he was the one, she told them no. But he was, and he was not. One day she could not believe for a moment that he could possibly look at her. The next day she saw them together as husband and wife. One day she saw him getting off the bus with a girl walking behind him. The next day she saw him rushing toward her with opened arms. She was ready to expect almost anything.

"Thanks for what you've been doing for Aunt Charlotte," he said.

"It wasn't nothing," she said. "I was glad…"

She could not say any more. But why, when all the time she was bursting over with things to talk about? It was not love she wanted to talk about. No, not love at all. But him. She wanted to know about him. What had he been doing? How had he been? What were his plans now? She did not want to tell him anything about herself. Nothing interesting had happened to her. Nothing interesting had happened to the place—but that it was going down faster and faster. No; she only wanted to talk about him.

He opened the gate for her and she went into the yard. He followed her up the walk. She was going to detain him some way or another, but it was he who suggested it first.

"Can we talk a moment?"

"Yes. Want come inside?"

"No. Out here will be good."

"Let me get a chair."

"No. The steps are all right."

She used her handkerchief to wipe off a clean place for him. It was a small white handkerchief with her initials embroidered in it. A boy had given her a dozen of them for her birthday a year ago.

After sitting down, they remained silent a while. What was it he wanted to say to her? After all, he did not come back there with a wife…

"How've you been?" he said.

"All right."

"You look nice."

"Been getting along all right."

"I thought you'd be married by now with a house full of kids."

"No. Still single," she said.

He leaned forward, rubbing his hands together. She looked at him, thinking: I don't care what it is. Anything—I'm ready to hear it. Say it so I can be free. Say it so I can know what to do tomorrow, so I can know how to feel tomorrow. 'Cause as long as you don't, I'll never know which way to go...

"I have something to say to Aunt Charlotte," he said. "I don't know how to say it."

Mary Louise hesitated a moment before asking him what it was that he had to say.

"She thinks I'm coming back here to stay," he said.

Mary Louise's heart leaped into her throat. She stared at Jackson as if he had just confessed to murdering someone. Tears rushed into her eyes, and she raised her hand to her mouth to keep from crying out.

"How can I say it to her?" he said. "From what I hear, that's all she's been telling everyone. It's impossible. But how do I explain it?"

She had wanted to say these same words to Miss Charlotte. When he first left, everyone thought he would come back one day to teach there. Three or four years after he had gone, she still thought he would. Then suddenly all of the young people started leaving. Those who weren't being drafted or volunteering for military service were all going to the cities or up North. And she had asked herself then, why should Jackson be an exception? Why should he come back, when all of the others were going the other way? No, she had thought, he won't ever come back. I might's well get interested in somebody else 'cause I'll never see him again. So she had started dating. Different boys called on her two and three times a week. But the right one never did come along.

Charlotte might have been partially responsible for this. Not that she did not want her to get married. She definitely did want her to get married. But whenever they were together, she was continually bringing up Jackson's name and his returning. She, Mary Louise, had wanted to caution her. Several times she had wanted to say, "Miss Charlotte, you know, many o' the young people leaving and going—" but each time she thought about saying this, Charlotte would seem more confident than ever of his returning. If she showed any doubt at all, Charlotte would show her a letter from him. No, Charlotte would not let her read the letter, and whether or not Charlotte was showing her the same letter over and over, she did not know, because Charlotte would keep the letter at safe enough distance so she could not identify the date. But, nevertheless, she began to feel that maybe Charlotte was right and maybe he was an exception after all. And about two weeks ago, Charlotte did get a letter from him, for it was she, Mary Louise, who brought the letter from the store. The letter had said that he would be here next week. It did not say whether or not he was coming to stay.

"How would you do it?" he asked.

She was still crying, and did not answer him. Jackson sat up and turned to her.

"What's the matter?"

"Nothing," she said. "I don't know how to do it. Not that."

"She really thinks so?"

Mary Louise nodded her head. "Yes."

They were silent a long time. He sat forward on the steps, looking at the little beads of dew sparkling in the grass along the fence. Something pleasant stirred in him. He felt like going out there and rubbing his hand over the grass. He wanted to feel the wetness of it, he wanted to feel the soft prickling touches against the palm of his hand.

"Well, I think I ought to be going," he said.

But he did not move, and he turned to Mary Louise sitting beside him.

"Why were you crying?" he asked her.

She shrugged one shoulder. "I don't know."

"Did you expect me to come back?"

"I don't know. I reckon'd I did."

He started to tell her why he could not come back, but he was tired, and, too, could she possibly understand what he was saying? Could she understand all, not part of, but all of what he was saying about North and South? She probably would not—how could she?—when the North had been pictured for her as it had been pictured for him before he went there. But he had found out that it had its faults as well as the South. Only the faults there did not strike you as directly and as quickly, so by the time you discovered them, you were so much against the other place that it was impossible ever to return to it.

But it had taken him a long time to discover these faults, because he was too involved with his books to stand back and look for them. Hearing his mother complain about the shabby neighborhood they had to live in only because they were Negroes, or hearing his stepfather complain about his job, did not make him aware of these things either. They lived in a slum neighborhood because they did not have enough money to live in a better place, and his stepfather had to work as a laborer because he did not have the education to hold a better position. But he would not have to live under these conditions; his instructors had already told him so.

When did he begin to notice the faults? When? It was hard for him to see them when he sat in a classroom, surrounded by white students, while in the South the problem of integrating the school was causing so much trouble. It was hard to notice them when he went out for the school track team, running side by side with anyone, and then leaving most of them behind. It was hard to notice them also when he went swimming in the same pool with all the others. So when did he begin to notice them? When?

It had happened suddenly. It had sneaked up on him. No, no, it had not. It had only come less directly than it had in the South. He was not told that he could not come into the restaurant to eat. But when he did come inside, he was not served as promptly and with the same courtesy as were the others. When he went into a store to buy a pair of pants or a pair of socks, he was treated in the same manner as he had been in the restaurant. And when he and his parents were looking in the papers for another place to rent, he remembered how his mother's finger made an imprint under each place that said "colored," when all the time there were other places which she would have preferred living in and which were much cheaper. The imprint under that one word, because it was made in San Francisco, would be imprinted on his mind the rest of his life.

These incidents were not big. They were extremely small when you thought of them individually. But there were so many of them that they soon began to mount into something big, something black, something awful.

When he first went to California, it was understood by his mother and his aunt that he would go there to be educated, and then return to the South to work. But before he had finished the high school, he had become so discouraged by what he had seen and by what had happened to him that, if home were any place other than the South, he would have returned then. But there was no returning home. The North with all of her faults made it clear to you whether you were a Negro from the South, an Indian from New Mexico, or a Chinese from Hong Kong, that in spite of her shortcomings, conditions here were better than the ones you had left, or you would not have left in the beginning.

So the struggle for survival—or better yet, the struggle to keep his sanity—had begun for him. He found no help at home from parents who were continually complaining about the conditions in which they lived, and neither did he find solace in the church as he had done when he lived in the South. He was in college now, and he soon realized that he was not alone in this struggle. Not only was the red boy from New Mexico and the yellow boy from Hong Kong in it, but the white boy, born and raised in Dayton, Ohio, was in it, too.

"What is your problem?" he asked the white boy from Dayton. "You have everything."

The boy grinned and looked at him as though he were a fool.

"Look around you," the white boy said. "Look up, look down; look to your left, look to your right. Do I have anything? Do I have anything, really?"

"Then, why don't you tell them to stop? Not only what they're doing to me, but what they're doing to you, to themselves."

"Don't you think I have?" the boy from Dayton said. "Don't you think I have? I tell them with every breath I take. Your struggle is no worse than mine. I'm sure your cross is even lighter to carry."

So the struggle went on. The little incidents, the little indirect incidents, like slivers from a stick. But they continued to mount until they had formed a wall. Not a wall of slivers that could be blown down with the least wind. But a wall of bricks, of stones. A wall that had gotten so high by now that he had to stand on tiptoe to look over it.

It was then that he decided to leave before it would be impossible to look over this wall at all. He was not coming home. No, the South was not home, it had not been home for a long time now. But he had chosen the South because he knew people there, and because he had to go somewhere to think for a while. He had finished college now, and he had to leave San Francisco to think about what he was going to do from then on.

But could Mary Louise understand any of this if he tried to explain it to her? He looked at her sitting forward on the steps. He remembered how they had sat like this the night before he left for California. She was his girlfriend then, and they had exchanged many kisses, whispers, and many hugs and touches, which would have been frowned on by Charlotte if she had seen them. But sitting there beside her now, he felt none of this. He only felt a deep respect for her that he might have felt for someone in his family.

"It's getting late," he said.

"Oh, I'm not sleepy."

She looked at him and smiled. But it was hard to smile, because only a moment ago she had been crying.

"Don't you have to go to work tomorrow?"

"Yes, but couple hours' sleep all I need. Don't take me much."

"Well, I better let you get them," he said, standing up, and looking across the yard at Charlotte sitting on the porch. "Aunt Charlotte is still up."

"She'll be up till you come back."

Jackson looked at Charlotte, wondering when he would tell her he was going back. Maybe he would do so tomorrow. He did not feel like talking to anyone any more tonight. He turned to Mary Louise again.

"Well, I'll see you tomorrow," he said.

Mary Louise nodded, and Jackson went out of the yard. When he turned to shut the gate, he saw Mary Louise still sitting there watching him. He waved at her, and she waved back. Jackson walked away.

Moving

Mark Coovelis

We had to move because of the stairs. Our old house was one of those tall brown-shingled places you see all over Berkeley, and it had stairs everywhere: up from the walk to the front porch, and then upstairs to my parents' bedroom and the study, and again up to my sister's and my bedrooms. I remember the stairs well—the polished banisters, the worn carpets. The banister's curve on the first landing was as smooth and cool as the inside of a conch shell.

My father hired two boys from the college to help with the heavy things. I suppose he made an announcement after class one day asking for help. I try to imagine it. I have a snapshot of him that was taken at about that time, over thirty years ago. He's sitting on the front porch of the old house in a chair that he's brought outside from the kitchen. There's an open book on his lap, face down to mark his place. He's turning toward the camera, smiling from behind his close-cropped beard. His blond hair is white in the sun. He's a young man, younger than I am now.

I imagine he looked like that in front of his class. I see my father surrounded by silence before he clears his throat, changes gears so to

"The Phelan prize gave me credibility," says Mark Coovelis, who won the 1987 Phelan Award for a collection of short stories. "It was a letter of introduction to a handful of writers' colonies like Yaddo and McDowell, where I was able to write Gloria." Gloria is his highly acclaimed mystery novel for thinking people, which has been published in six languages. For several years, he was a journalist on the crime beat for the El Dorado County Mountain Democrat. Today, he teaches high school and lives in Auburn, California.

speak, to ask his favor. It must have been hard for him to ask. But what he said was probably very simple: I'm moving Saturday, and I need a couple of able-bodied men to help out. There'll be plenty to eat and plenty of beer. If you're interested, see me during office hours. Thanks.

Long before we finally moved, the stairs had been a problem for my mother. When the pain first came she leaned on my father's arm to mount them and used a cane that had belonged to her father. My father cut it down it down to size and presented it to her with a ribbon tied to it. He brought it out with a great deal of fanfare, announcing that even though it wasn't her birthday or their anniversary or Christmas, he had a present for her. He often gave us presents out of the blue, but he liked to pretend that each time he did so he was being unusually generous. My mother accepted the cane as though it were a piece of jewelry. I can still see her untying the ribbon with a flick of her wrist, the way she held it in both hands for a minute before standing up to test it out. My father took great pride in his work. He told us how careful he was to cut it just right, how he polished the brass end piece before replacing it. After my mother's trial run with the cane, my father took it and examined his work once more, then he leaned it against the dining room wall, where it remained for the rest of the evening, until it was time to go upstairs.

It's because Mother's Chinese, my sister told me; she had bound feet in a past life.

Ondine was twelve, and full of such ideas. My theory was not so mystical. I blamed it on the horse. My mother lived in a walled enclave in Shanghai before the Japanese invasion and revolution. Her father was a prominent musician, the pianist Kai Hua-Chiang. He had studied in Paris, Brussels, and New York, where he acquired a lot of modern ideas. Before the Japanese invaded, he sent my mother to school in London, where she studied English and horsemanship. Riding astride the huge beast did not come naturally to her, and she fell. Years before there was a hint of pain, my mother's fall was one of those things that grew in the family memory like a significant incident in history, our private Nanking so to speak. During her years in London, she believed she would return to Shanghai, but the wars changed everything. Mother was in the hospital, recovering from her fall, when she got news that her family had fled China and was living in a three-room apartment in San Francisco's Chinatown.

And fifteen years later, when her pain returned and kept growing worse, the family remembered the fall again, differently. Now, it was as though time traveled in a straight line from the moment she hit the ground to the present, the way pain travels the nerves.

Ondine showed me a clenched fist. Mother's feet were like this, she said. For me that was not explanation enough for why our mother stayed upstairs all day. When I felt her absence from the kitchen in the afternoons after school or at dinner when she felt especially weak, I feared she was not really upstairs at all, but gone. When I felt like that, I would go upstairs and look for her, and I'd find her in my father's study, sitting in his reading chair. We would talk. She spoke with the soft vowels of the British between the clipped consonants of a Chinese accent. She told me about her life in the walled garden in Shanghai, how she and her sister played catch with the lichee fruit. But I was not very interested. I tried to explain the rules of baseball to her. I told her about the infield and the outfield, the pitcher, catcher, and umpire. I explained the difference between a good pitch and a bad one, about three strikes and four balls, three outs. She listened as though interested, her high, fine eyebrows raised in expectation, as I demonstrated the batter's stance, swung my phantom bat, and hit the invisible pitch right out the upstairs window.

Everything changed after the operations. In the wheelchair she was the same height I was, and when my father wheeled her around I could walk next to her and talk to her. Everything seemed much better, but that was after we got the new house, the one without stairs.

Later, my father told me he looked for the right house for a long time. My mother liked nice houses and most one-story houses were, he said, either too small or too ranch-like. Our furniture was mostly Chinese and it wouldn't be right for a ranch-style house. He found the house while Mother was still in the hospital. During that time he was not around very much. Often he spent the whole night at the hospital, coming home as I was leaving for school, his suit wrinkled, his tie spilling out of his jacket pocket.

A woman came to stay with us while my father was out. Her name was Sylvia, and she read from the Bible all the time. She spoke to us in Spanish and cooked spicy meals full of tomato sauce and ground beef. Ondine was outraged. She cooked her own rice and sat in the family room watching television, eating with chopsticks. So, often, I ate dinner alone with Sylvia. I did not speak a word of Spanish, but I pretended to understand. I let the singing accent lull me into a daze. It was good to hear a woman's voice talking away, and I wanted it to go on forever in my head, like a song I had memorized. She broke into English to tell me that my mother would have her legs in heaven, and it made me very angry. I cried out that my mother was never going to die, and if she did, she wouldn't need her legs anyway, because angels have wings. She said *sí*, but God would make her whole again.

When I asked my father if mother would have her legs again in heaven, he just looked at me. Those days he seemed enveloped in silence. Then he asked me who said that, and I told him Sylvia. He turned his head away from me. He didn't know what to say to a nine-year-old boy about heaven, I guess. Now I have a sense of his God, but then I had nothing but Sylvia's vision. When he finally turned to me and spoke, his voice was as steady and deep and serious as ever. He said not to listen to Sylvia when she talked like that.

The day my father took us to see the new house, I played Little League. I pitched and won. Afterwards, I rode my bike up our street with my mitt hanging on the handlebars and my uniform shirt unbuttoned. The air smelled like grass and dust, sweet and harsh and hot. The shadows were blue, and when the sun hit the chrome bumpers of the cars parked on the street, I was dazzled. My world was, for an instant, electric.

When I got home everyone was waiting, ready to go. My mother was downstairs already with her hair brushed, and she was wearing a dress. The only time I had seen her so dressed up since she returned from the hospital was when her friends came with presents to celebrate her recovery. That was the first day I had missed her legs. Nothing came out from beneath her dress. She was sitting there like that when I rushed in saying that I had won the game. She hugged me. I had learned to lean in over the big wheel of her chair naturally by then. I can remember how she smelled. It was very different from the grass and dust outside. Sometimes I get a hint of that smell on a woman in the summer and I remember the day my father took us to see the new house.

His voice had a bell deep inside it when he told us that we were going for a ride, and also as we drove from Berkeley along the tree-lined streets with the windows down and he told us all about Piedmont, that it was a fine place with fine houses and nice people. My mother said she always wanted to live in Piedmont. My father said her dream had come true. But as we drove on the quiet streets I looked for something special about this new place and I couldn't see anything. It was a lot like Berkeley, with old houses and trees that reached out over the road. What I noticed most was that there was almost no one out on the street.

The house was in a cul-de-sac called Sea View Court and it was off Sea View Drive. My father explained that the new house didn't have a view at all, only the houses on the drive had the view. He said we could walk to the end of the block to see the Bay if we wanted to. That, he said, was good enough for him. My mother liked the idea of a cul-de-sac because, she said, it would be quiet.

The white stucco house had only one level, but it sprawled out in all directions as though they had built all the rooms onto it one at a time. Inside, we found it vacant, and when my father spoke his voice echoed down the halls. He wheeled my mother over the hardwood floors and showed her where all the furniture could go and asked her if she noticed how nice the light was inside and if she liked the fireplaces. He opened all the closets and wheeled her right into them to show her how big they were. Ondine told us where she wanted her piano to go and stood there as though her hands were poised over the keys. She sang dum-Dum-de-dum-Dum and we all laughed. There were five bedrooms and we looked into all of them, my father telling Ondine and me to choose the ones we liked best, and telling my mother that she could have a hobby room, and that he'd have a study. When the tour was over, my mother said that it was strange, but she felt as though she were going around in circles. It's just this chair, she said, it turns me all around. My father said no, no, the house has a secret. He rolled my mother across the empty living room and opened the drapes for her. Outside the windows, green, alive with light, was a garden surrounded by the new house. He opened the glass door and wheeled her out onto the patio. He stopped in a patch of sunlight and told her to look up, she could see the sky. When she raised her chin to look, he leaned down and kissed her on the forehead. Ondine and I stood back and watched from the door. My father turned her around to face us, and they both were smiling the way people smile in pictures of a wedding.

The morning we moved the college boys drove up in an old car and sat parked at the curb for a while. I was up the street on my bicycle saying goodbye to Matt, my best friend. Matt asked who was in the funny car, and I said I didn't know. When they got out of the car, the boys looked as big as my father, who was coming down the steps to greet them. My father introduced me while I was still straddling my bike. They looked at Matt, a blond, freckled kid. When my father put his hand on my shoulder they looked embarrassed and smiled. One of them said, your Dad tells me you're a great pitcher, and I said yeah, pretty good.

I wished I were older that day, and bigger. I wanted to help carry the chairs and tables, all my father's boxes of books, the couches, paintings and mirrors. All afternoon I rode my bike in circles in the street, watching them.

By the time the last load was finished, it was late, almost nine, near sunset on a summer night. My father threw my bicycle in the truck last thing, and then went inside again. The boys stood by the truck with me and waited. In a while, Ondine came out with the folded-up wheelchair. One of the boys took it from her and put it in the truck next to my bike. The other boy gave me a sip of his beer. It tasted salty, the way your lips taste after swimming in the ocean. I handed the can back to him and said thanks, and then I saw my father carrying my mother in his arms. He carried her down the stairs looking toward the car, but my mother was looking at me. She was light in my father's arms, like a child. Father put her in the car and Ondine got in with her. He came over to the truck and asked the boys to follow him over to Piedmont. I asked if I could ride with the boys, and he asked me if I was sure I didn't want to ride with the family. I said I was sure.

I rode with the boys high up in the cab of the truck. The sun was going down and it was the beginning of summer and I was nine years old and we were going to a new house. The truck strained out of the driveway as the boy moved through the low gears. Like cat claws, the lower branches of the trees scraped the roof of the cab. I looked down at my father's car, a two-tone, blue and white Ford with fins. I could see the two heads in the back seat, my mother's and sister's, the same height, my father's head in front, and the glint of his eye-glass frames as he looked left for traffic. We followed, the truck whining in low gear up the empty Piedmont streets.

Leaving the old house was like shoving off from a dock into the current of a river. For a year, I drifted as though in an eddy, watching my mother enjoy the garden my father found for her. After she died, the current took me up, and soon I was as old as those boys, and then sooner I was as old as my father was then. From my mother, I inherited small hands and the long earlobes that she said promise long life; from my father, a good beard and a propensity for silence. Now that I'm in the rapids of middle age, I know what his silence was all about.

Late in the summer, my mother and I sat together in the garden. Ondine was practicing the piano inside. The music sounded bright— clear notes rising upward. Mother sat with her back to me, one wheel half-hidden in the lemon bush. She was picking lemons. When she pulled one loose, the tree quivered, making a rustling sound. She said, Ondine is good. When she plays, I hear your grandfather. Then she swung around, her lap full of the yellow fruit. Here, she said, as she tossed a lemon. She watched it arc toward me like a baseball. Her high, fine eyebrows were raised in expectation.

Winners on the Pass Line

Dagoberto Gilb

In an office swivel chair, Ray Muñoz faced his jobsite and a pane of fixed glass. He'd missed a few days of work without explanation and the field superintendent was due anytime. He would be expected to say something. Only one of the foremen had even brought up his absence this morning, asking with an uncomfortable laugh whether Ray had tied one on or what.

The majority of the men were huddled in pairs and small groups near the coffee truck next to the gate, holding styrofoam cups and sandwiches and burritos, the steam from which quickly became indistinguishable from the overcast sky. Ray could hear a couple of them near his window talking about the leftovers they still had from

Dagoberto Gilb has won many awards in addition to the 1984 Phelan Award, including a National Endowment for the Arts creative writing fellowship and a Whiting Writers' Award. The Magic of Blood, *his collection of stories—part of which earned him the Phelan prize—won the Hemingway Award and the Texas Institute of Letters' Jesse Jones Award. He is also the author of a novel,* The Last Known Residence of Mickey Acuña, *and he lives and teaches in Austin, Texas. He has been described as a working-class Chekhov, able to describe the world of trucks and prejudice and layoffs and blue-collar work. So many of his characters, like those in "Winners on the Pass Line," are from a world rarely described in literature—an unsentimental view of working-class Californians, Latino and otherwise.*

Thanksgiving, about Christmas, about the sex in the movie last night and about what they were probably going to do today at the job. They were sitting on a stack of large but not full sheets of plywood waiting for the foreman to start them to work. When the time came, Ray rocked in his swivel chair and watched the wobbly manlift roll up the cable line to the eighteenth and the nineteenth floors where most of the men unloaded, and then to the roof where the lift clicked off to let two laborers load several empty oxygen and acetylene bottles. He saw the operator pull the cage door together when they were finished and the counterweight rise as the manlift coasted down where stragglers were waiting for the next trip up.

Ray thought about how only a few years ago he believed he'd be wearing leather bags into retirement. Never did he imagine a chair and a secretary. He worked construction with callused hands that made the tools feel like they had grips, hands that held so many nails and hammers for so many hours they stayed clenched like fists in his off hours. But they earned him a living, not a rich one, but enough not to be ashamed. He remembered how his wife changed his thinking about that. She told him he should stop thinking like he'd just crossed the border and couldn't do better and to remember the where of his birth, to think about the miracle of possibilities on this side. He knew she was right about miracles because he could touch her with his palms and fingers, always cut and smashed and lumpy with splinters, always dry because of cement and rust, and they could still record the sensation of such a contrary texture. That she fell in love with him should have sent him back faithfully to Mass every Sunday. There was no other explanation: she'd been to college and still married him and lived his life of wages and alcohol, rented apartments and, when children came, rented houses which would never have been homes otherwise. Houston was her idea. He never would have left El Paso. But she was convinced there were opportunities and she was the smart one. And soon there was a new truck, then a new house, and finally, when he got this job, a savings account he planned to surprise her with someday.

His secretary peeked through a crack in the door. "You're here," she said as though he never was. "Sorry I'm late. I'm making some coffee right now." He didn't say anything to her. He'd fired his last secretary six months ago for not typing well enough and being on the phone too much, but the real reason was that she'd been coming on to him and that was too disruptive to his life. He'd already had his youth, was what he'd decided, and this new world, Houston, had offered him winning dice: while his childhood friends were still struggling near the border, he'd become a superintendent in a major construction company. He was on a roll and he didn't want to complicate the betting.

He should have known better. Looking back, it was easy to see. Just as his wife had started teasing him about that secretary, she'd been telling him about all the women she worked with at her job in the federal building, about all the fantasies and even affairs that began at their more than an hour lunch breaks with lawyers and government administrators and sometimes diplomats. She even told him about the one she met who spoke—besides Spanish—French, German, and even some Russian. He just never suspected, probably because he was so preoccupied with his new status. He just never suspected that she'd moved with the times too.

Before the phone call, Sylvia Molina had been methodically packing their luggage, neatly folding all the clothes that she and her husband and their youngest son might need. She'd been thinking about the things she had learned growing up, because this certainly was not one of them. Vacations were a time when her father got to sleep in and nap in the afternoon and talk about it happily if it was a gift from the job, or worriedly if it was because he was unemployed. She could only remember taking a trip once, to Durango, when her grandmother on her mother's side died. Her father's parents were from this side and lived with them.

"Are you just about done?" her husband asked.

"Uh-huh."

"And Jimmy..."

"Is already over at Peter's." She said that strongly and it even surprised her.

"Is everything okay?"

She could hear the department store's Christmas music in the background. A voiceless Noel. "I'm a little nervous. I don't know why."

"We'll have a good time. Look, I'll be home in an hour, maybe two. I gotta go."

Sylvia hung up the phone guiltily. Everything mental told her that the trip was going to go well. A weekend in Las Vegas before her husband got bogged down with the holidays and then inventory. They'd catch a show, gamble, have a few drinks, eat out. Neither of them had been there before. And it was she who'd wanted to do something exciting.

Excitement, she believed, must be a word belonging to her generation. Her mother had never mentioned the concept to her. What might pass for it in their home came through living next door to Mr. Rodriguez, who would often come home drunk in the middle of the night and would sometimes try to get in his locked front door instead of sleeping in his car. Mrs. Rodriguez would scream at him and the neighborhood about whores and the devil, diseases and lice. Then there was Rudy Rodriguez, their oldest son, who had brought police cars to the street more than once, and Mike, their next oldest, who was a football star at UT-Austin and even tried out for a pro team. She didn't remember her sisters seeming too concerned about the feeling of excitement either. The older one married when she was twenty, and the big thing in her life was a wedding ceremony and reception and her first baby. She never wanted to leave El Paso for even a drive. Her other sister went to college to get married but ended up a schoolteacher and, as far as she knew, was still a virgin.

Sylvia herself had chosen security when there'd been a choice. Her husband now hadn't been her boyfriend then. But he wanted to marry her and had a degree from college and good job with a future, which was the life she was leading today. He was already a floor manager at a major department store in Huntington Beach, they were paying off a mortgage on a four-bedroom house in an almost new development only a mile from the ocean, and they lived on a stainless street where there was no concept of race or creed and where the gloom of unemployment and bad times she heard about over the color television seemed as distant as Mexico. Though they were by no means rich, they could make all their payments on time, and for her birthday her husband had even bought her a microwave oven she never asked for or wanted.

She didn't often think about the boy she didn't marry. She was in high school, which he'd only been to for two years before he dropped out. He lived wherever anybody would let him if he didn't have money, and sometimes that was in the county jail. He told her he loved her but she probably would have let him even if he hadn't said it. That was a winter night when a windhard hail broke out the windowpane in his rented room off Montana Street. He got up naked, his eyes the only part of him that seemed to have to adjust to the black wind, water cresting his cheekbones and rolling down his back, and he took nails and a hammer from his workbags and made a shutter out of an empty dresser drawer he disassembled with his fist. It was still cold but they were laughing under his blankets because he said there was nothing to worry about, they still had two more drawers with nothing in them.

Ray withdrew all the money from his account. It was, by accident, a thousand for each of their ten years. Not much by Houston standards, but enough to make him feel gold-plated, when he visited back home, and it might have been only the beginning. It had crossed his mind more than once to put it down on some land—he imagined building a house near the river, planting some trees, raising thoroughbreds, starting up a ranch not unlike the one his father spent his life working on—but he never kidded himself about how far away he was from that. He didn't know what he'd do with it now. He'd been considering a swimming pool, but he always recalled the lean, unemployed times when he wished he'd had enough of a cushion to wait for the better jobs. Good and bad construction workers, including superintendents, came and went for lots of reasons, and he'd taught himself not to be surprised when he was handed an extra check on pay day with "layoff" stamped on it. This time maybe he could have kept the job, but he didn't offer the company's field boss an excuse for his time off because he didn't want to talk about his wife and children. He didn't know how to explain such things because he'd never learned how and it never occurred to him that he might have to. Layoff checks were to be expected. They always made some sense.

He took the money from the account and cashed his checks. The ten thousand he wanted in hundred-dollar bills. He agreed that he was acting a little crazy but it was a decision as certain as the cash would be in his pocket and the bank manager spent several hours making sure he got it once Ray assured him that he knew exactly what he was doing.

He drank only one beer on the airplane. He sat next to a window in the non-smoking section and no one sat next to him. Sometimes he shut his eyes, but he didn't sleep. When he opened them he'd see the wing of the airplane shudder. There weren't enough clouds to look at, and the earth seemed only slightly more alive than one of his hundred-dollar bills. Thinking like this shamed him somehow, and he prayed he'd be forgiven such a huge ingratitude.

Sylvia relaxed considerably when she saw the green road sign that told them Las Vegas was 175 miles away. She'd examined her map too many times and her husband had noticed. He'd wanted her to go to the auto club and get a new map and make reservations through it because that was what they paid for. But she insisted that she could do it all herself. Everything about this, even calling for hotel prices and making reservations over tollfree telephone lines, even marking out the simple route on a map, had become like a statement of independence for her, a muscling-up in challenge to what in any mind was a contented, idyllic life. And she took it very seriously. She was determined to have things go her way, to direct the flow of events without suggestions or advice or cautions. She was doing this with "her" money, allotting a certain amount for the hotel, food, entertainment, gas, a certain amount for her husband to gamble with, a certain amount for her gambling. She'd figured all this as a debit in her bookkeeping, but she also figured that her winning would verify something, would mean something, though she had no idea what. Winning was her hope, and though she pretended otherwise, she clung to it religiously.

"Do you see that sign?" her husband said to their son. "'Eat Gas!' Those oil companies think of everything."

The boy was fidgety and Sylvia told him to go to sleep and when he woke up they'd be there, even though she knew that if he did she'd pay by having to stay up late with him. She could have easily left him at home with the older boy, but she wanted him along for an excuse. With him, they'd have to do their gambling separately, in shifts. She gave her husband another reason for taking the four-year-old along.

"It's great to get on the road, isn't it?" her husband asked her. "And in a big, comfortable car. Who would have thought? Think we'll see Frank Sinatra?"

She smiled. She never doubted that she made a good choice marrying him. He was ordinary in the best ways, watching football games on Monday nights, taking the children to amusement parks every month and her to a restaurant every week or so. His pride would show when they went back to visit their parents, and when someone asked him where they lived, he would say down the street from Carlos Palomino, though in fact they had no idea where the fighter lived, only that it was supposed to be within the same city limits. His small exaggerations like that made up for his unstartling existence, kept him in touch with his neighborhood friends still linked to the less affluent, working class suburb he grew up in. He was a good man, and, most importantly, he loved her.

"It's pretty here," she told him.

He chuckled at her. "I guess."

"In a different way. It's still open. The sky looks like El Paso's."

"I guess I see what you mean. I guess."

Ray came to gamble, but instead he wandered through casinos and lost money, betting randomly at dice tables the house favorites like the hard ten and hard four and any craps, and, while at the roulette table, the single numbers and always the double zero. Each time he played a twenty-dollar bill from his paychecks and each time a dealer or a croupier would turn his green paper into red chips which would be eased away and clicked into perfect stacks. He was aimless enough even to play the dollar slots, and when he won sixty dollars, his first winning since he got there, he tinkled and spun away the time until every silver dollar was gone on a triple and double and single line play. When he decided he wanted to sit and drink he settled on seven-card stud with a ten dollar buy-in and alternated between whiskey, his Houston drink, and rum and coke, his Juárez drink. He tried to fill flushes when he had three of the same suit and the high hand showed the same face cards, and he would raise with a low pair under and a low pair up and invariably lose to a full house or a flush. During one hand, he stayed in on three raises each on the last two cards when he had a chance of a high straight, and lost to three nines. After this he simply played drunk, seven rounds worth, waiting for more cards that never came to drop in front of him, losing three hundred dollars more. When he finally stumbled through the tall heavy doors of the casino and stood underneath the heaven of hundred-watt bulbs above the main entrance, watching old men with young women exit limousines with two-hundred-watt shines, with the bells and tingles and shuffles, the melody of all this ringing between his ears like a phrase from a song he heard on the car radio when he walked into work, it occurred to him that he didn't have to do it this way, that he could win.

He lay down on the bed of his hotel room, listening to the television he'd left on while he'd been out. The movie was *Lawrence of Arabia* and the voice he heard was Anthony Quinn's. He didn't feel drunk anymore, but very alone, and sad. Those days he'd spent in his empty house were angry, and he'd paced, opening drawers and cabinets like he would find something, waiting like he knew what he was waiting for. He'd cried like his youngest son and he only slept an hour or two at intervals throughout the day and night. He wanted to feel alone, but in the morning newspapers scuffed sidewalks and cars would drive off, children would walk to school. In the afternoon he could hear a neighbor's soap operas if he went to the right window in his house, and a meter man passed through his back yard. In the evening the cars would return and there'd be football, basketball, rock'n'roll. From midnight to dawn a digital clock whirred. He was in this new world and he could be hidden, but not alone. Here he was. He turned off the television, letting the darkened room loom with images of the wooden steps outside his office, with a picture of his wife changing her clothes near him, of his children boarding an airplane for a stay in El Paso while he and his wife sorted things out, of his own childhood there, the dirt baseball diamonds, the dirt driveway where he pulled the engine from his first car, the girls he loved so purely, the candles he lit on holidays, the stupid fights he won and lost, his marriage and the move from El Paso and his mother's tears, his father's bony handshake—all as distant and dry as that blue sky, as a story he could tell his children who could speak only English.

He heard voices in the hallway. Young men persuading young women to go in. When their door closed, their existence muffled away, and that was good to him. He had even been about to fall into sleep when he heard something that squeezed his heart until he stood up, frightened, and held still for several seconds. He nudged his shoulder into a wall and heard the hymn music coming from the room next door, from a television or radio. Jesus, the lover of my soul, sung by a choir, accompanied by an organ. He went back to bed relieved. He couldn't take any more surprises and for a moment he thought he'd gone over the ledge. He felt very weary now, even thought he would get some sleep, and he stayed on his back, in the center of the king-size bed, getting up many times throughout the night and morning to drink and to piss, expecting sleep any time, resting in the dark.

"What's all this stuff about El Paso?" her husband asked.

"I don't know," Sylvia said like a thief.

"Are you homesick? Is it Christmas? You could go there this Christmas if you want. It's only me that has to be around home this year."

"No."

"Because you don't have to stay home. You could take the boys back with you."

"I don't want to go. I didn't realize I was talking about it that much."

"You could stay those two weeks school's out. I could get an airplane and spend the day."

"I don't want to. Honest. There's just something about Las Vegas that reminds me of it, that's all."

Her husband sighed and fell onto the bed. "You were talking about it before we got here," he reminded her.

Sylvia didn't argue because he was right. She felt embarrassed and wanted the subject changed. "We can all see the Captain and Tennille," she proposed.

"I don't know why you're acting so weird about it. Wanting to be with your family is as Mexican as having babies."

"Let's eat dinner and everything."

"All right," he yawned, stretching on one of the two hard beds in the bright hotel room.

"We'll go make a reservation at that booth we saw in the lobby and you take a nap."

"Good thinking," he said, yawning again.

She took her son's hand and the room key and went out the door and said hello to the two maids, a Black and an Asian, who stopped talking as she and the boy passed almost running.

Once Ray made the decision to win, he knew the first thing to do was to have control, so he began by observing the play at dice tables and cards without drinking or gambling. He passed many innocuous hours and finally took a seat at a seven-card stud game and tested his will. He set a two-hour limit on himself. He didn't play when he got bad hole cards, and when one of the players was on a winning streak he didn't stay in if he had a weak though solid hand. When he held a good hand he bet moderately and raised only the last two deals. When he left the table it was with forty dollars more than he had when he sat down.

Later that evening he removed his envelope with the ten thousand dollars from his safe-deposit box at the hotel and walked it to a Texas Hold 'Em table which required a two hundred dollar buy-in. A simple game, each player getting two cards down which he combines with five cards the dealer turns up on the middle of the table, it is also a game of big winners and big losers, and this one was for particularly high stakes, even by Vegas standards. Already a second row of spectators strained to see over those in the first row, who snuggled against the metal railing that partitioned them off from the players, all of whom showed a minimum of a thousand dollars in green twenty-five-dollar chips and red five-dollar ones.

Ray took the seat at the top of the oval and counted out five thousand dollars, which were quickly transformed into chips for the dealer by a young woman, and his swell of stacks beat all but two of the players, an obese New Yorker with a slobbish cigar and a bag of green chips, and a slit-eyed, deep Southerner who hid under a cap and peered above several highrise-like piles.

Ray played conservatively in the beginning, in order to follow the betting. He quickly discovered that there were really only three serious gamblers—the Southerner, who bought a few hands with large raises and was challenged only one time by the New Yorker, whose two pair beat one, and a Hollywood movie type who lost with average hands, but whose pocket was so full of hundred-dollar bills he didn't seem to worry about it, and an Arab who would never show his cards.

After two hours Ray was about eight hundred dollars down. He had won a hand, dropped out of three, and paid to see two. He'd drank one shot of whiskey early to settle his nerves and it must have worked because, even though he was behind, he felt a confidence he hadn't remembered since he married his wife, since he accepted the job as superintendent. It was something that only happened to a person a few times but which was as palpable as silver dollars in the pocket: he belonged there, an equal to the best, his hidden status hovering over him like a fawning lover. He knew, and he was certain they knew, he was going to walk away a winner.

His chance came about an hour later when he got two tens underneath, spades and diamonds, and the first card the dealer showed was a seven of hearts. The guy from Hollywood bet unusually high, five hundred, and only the Arab and the Southerner, besides himself, stayed. The next card was a two of spades, and he stayed in for the next five-hundred-dollar bet, and for the five hundred more the Southerner used to scare away the other two.

The dealer turned a ten of clubs and Ray met the Southerner's next five hundred with a thousand-dollar raise. When the Southerner notched it up another, he matched it and shoved in all the chips in front of him.

"Let's play 'em up," the Southerner smiled when he called the bet. The table was excited, but no one moved. Ray didn't really understand what he was supposed to do.

"Let's see what ya got there, friend."

"Turn 'em up," suggested the New Yorker. "He wants to negotiate."

He showed his tens. The Southerner had two hearts. It was three tens against a possible flush.

"I'll give ya two to one on the pot," offered the Southerner.

Ray didn't even think it over. He shook his head confidently.

Jack of hearts.

"Fifty-fifty," said the Southerner, who'd stood up to see.

Ray shook his head again.

Two of hearts.

The Southerner was immodestly happy and the spectators breathed loudly as he pushed his chair away and reached in for the pot and, nearly hopping, stacked his mound of winnings to new heights. He talked volubly to the players sitting beside him and gave an unsporting stare of triumph at the loser.

Ray counted out four thousand dollars more. He felt more dazed than defeated, weak-kneed but standing. He was more disappointed than angry, not at the Southerner or himself, but at the deeper injustice of things. It did not make sense. It was not fair.

He thought that maybe he should pull out right then as the cards were being dealt around again. If he backed out, he could spare himself more loss. That would be the sensible thing to do considering the realities of unemployment, even in Houston. And chances were that he would be wearing those work bags again. He felt blurred by his insecurity, but in this fuzz he made out a queen on the table to match the queen-four in his hand.

He stayed in, as did the Arab and the moviemaker, as did the Southerner, who seemed to be playing this one for fun while he continued to reorganize his chips. After the dealer turned up a four and an ace, Ray upped the pot by five hundred on his two pair, and all stayed.

The dealer turned over another four and Ray made it another five hundred. The Arab dropped out, the moviemaker saw the bet, and the Southerner raised it another five hundred.

The last card was a king. Ray bet another five hundred on his full house, figuring the Southerner to play for that. The moviemaker considered the stakes and his chances, then threw in his cards.

"That plus five," said the Southerner carelessly.

Ray saw that and bet the rest without hesitating.

"I gotta see this one, amigo," the Southerner said. "Let's see what you can do."

Ray matched his queen-four to the table's queen-two fours.

The Southerner could barely contain himself. He flipped over a king-four and hugged the chips to his corner, crying for some racks to put all his money in. The New Yorker laughed. The other players felt no happiness for him, though they showed no signs of pity for the loser either.

Ray walked evenly to his hotel, contented only by knowing that in this defeat he had not been a fool because they were such strong hands that he couldn't have played them any other way. He couldn't say that about many losses. He'd done this gambling to win, and someone else had the better luck, and only luck. It was not always so simple. His wife, for instance, had left him for a richer man who she'd fallen in love with.

He was not sure what to expect next because he was taken by an unusual mood. Late by work standards, it was still early in Las Vegas. He turned off the lights and opened a window to a windless, cold desert, a range of mountains, and below, a tall, arching sky. He listened for something but all he got was some hotel machine and puffs of traffic. It was maybe okay that he lost, even justice of a kind. It was fresh like the cold air, like the winter air in El Paso.

Ray Muñoz closed his eyes on the bed. He waited to shiver with some strong emotion. Instead fell asleep in the chilled silence of the sanitized hotel room.

"I don't see how people can do it," her husband said after his night out alone. "It goes too fast and hurts too much."

"Did you win?"

"In a sense. I stopped contributing to the cause."

Sylvia looked away from him.

"You know, I think they've got it rigged, because when I played the dollar slot machines I won right away, on my first pulls. Something like thirty or forty dollars. I thought I had it made, but I never won again after that."

"Is that all you played?" she asked, angry.

"No, I played some blackjack too. It's something, this place. There's so much happening. This man that sat by me was playing twenty dollars a hand and was winning for a long time, but when he started losing he started betting more money. That's how it is here, easy come, easy go. I think the guy was drunk. Did you know that all the drinks are free? Anyway, I couldn't take it. I don't think I can take winning or losing, though it is fun to watch. I wandered all around the casino and counted all the money that other people lost. That felt better than losing all mine."

"Mine," she said seriously.

"Ours," he said automatically. "And I can't waste it. Maybe if it was money someone gave me and told me I *had* to gamble with."

"I did," Sylvia said.

"And then again I doubt if I could do that," he laughed without hearing her. "Hey, we're gonna have to take the baby to the circus shows they have at night. There were these stunt motorcyclists driving inside this ball and it scared the pants off me." He yawned. "I tried to win him a stuffed animal while I was up there. How long's he been asleep?"

"A few hours."

"Too bad they don't have babysitters. It'd be fun to have a drink together." He pulled her down on the bed and even touched her breasts.

"He'll wake up," she said.

He rolled off. "I guess I'm a little drunk already." He looked at the television screen. "What're you watching?"

"I just found it an hour ago. It's a program on how to play the casino games."

"They think of everything, don't they?"

"It's exciting."

"It's not worth the risk though."

"Do you really think that?"

"Yes. I really don't think you can win. Las Vegas exists because people lose. The only money I'd like giving them would be to own a piece of it."

She turned off the television. "I've already seen it twice."

"Leave it on. Maybe there's a Frank Sinatra movie."

Ray slept twelve uninterrupted hours, got up and drank water at the bathroom sink, and slept three more. When the sleep was over, and he shook the blood loose in his veins, he felt what he least expected, like he'd won.

He counted the ten crisp hundred-dollar bills he still had. He counted seven twenties he had in his wallet.

His plan had become very simple. He would go back to El Paso and see his children, he would talk to his brothers and sisters, listen to his mother, visit his father's grave, and, no matter what happened tonight, he would go home a winner.

Sylvia stood under a wide archway that divided the hotel lobby from the casino. For two days she'd seen and heard this, but now she was by herself, awed by how quiet it really was and how alone it could make her feel.

She wanted very much to age past this stage in her life. She didn't think it was right of her and she felt guilty and spoiled. Had she not been so fortunate, had she made different choices along the way, she knew she would probably want nothing more than what she had, and she would have undoubtedly settled for less.

She had no idea what her purpose was in this. She didn't know what kind of answer this would present her with, what she would do with it. She only knew that winning would be an answer, and that losing would be an answer. She didn't know which would be preferable, and still she was determined to win.

That evening Ray turned the thousand dollars into chips and leaned into a craps table. He played intelligently, and when he didn't feel right, he didn't place any bets. He waited for the dice and a hot hand. He was up, but not making a killing.

Sylvia had not been doing well. She took cards for blackjack and lost, she laid chips on red and black numbers for roulette and lost, though both by the inconclusive nibble of small wagers. She was more short of time than patience or money. And though she had been afraid of craps because the betting was so complicated, and though she was aware that she could just as easily spend her fortune waiting on the click of a ball at a spinning wheel or the snap of a laminated card on a baize table, she knew it had to be the padded tumble of dice.

At first Ray didn't find anything too special about the attractive woman who came to stand across from him, and it was only because he didn't want to bet on a few rolls that he noticed her choosing the poorer odds on the table, like the field and the hardway numbers. So he watched her, and then he stared at her, and he did this until he felt he had to, until the casino had become nothing more than a faded backdrop of noise and light and color to her. Like the sight of a pretty girlfriend long forgotten, she flushed him with such a strong emotion that it didn't seem a memory but an awakening as conclusive as the one he'd left his hotel with. He stared, certain he didn't know her and never had.

Sylvia had very early become used to men's eyes, and had learned that even though she couldn't ignore them, she could walk away from them. But rather than being distracted by this large man who gawked at her so childlike, she became more focused and sharp. His unwilled admiration was the warmest luck she'd played with all night.

When she was offered the dice by the stickman, Sylvia was down to her last three nickel chips, while Ray was three hundred above his original thousand. When she accepted the dice and bet one five-dollar chip on a pass, Ray put four hundred on the same and then the full extent of the double odds on her point of four, which she threw on the next toss. He put up a thousand on another pass while she let her ten dollars ride and threw a ten. He backed his thousand with two more on the odds, which, like the four, paid two to one. She rolled two times before a four-six combination appeared.

"Winners on the pass line!" the stickman barked. "The table's got a shooter!"

Ray counted out five hundred dollars worth of the chips the dealer gave him in winnings and slid them over to Sylvia. "Please," he said. "Give it back only if we win."

She might have refused, but she was gagged by confusion. She picked up the dice and threw.

"Seven! *Big* winners on the *pass* line!"

Ray wouldn't take back the money he'd left her in the pass line area, and Sylvia considered setting the loan aside in the rack in front of her, but gave into it, to him, and played the line. She had become the one watching now, watching him, and never had she felt so in control and out of control at the same time.

Ray bet on her pass with certainty and when she had a point he took as many come and odds bets as he could get, and she shot lots of numbers. Sylvia let Ray's pass line money ride and made her point three more times in a row, which multiplied into winnings of four thousand dollars. Ray quit when he counted close to forty thousand, and it took racks to carry the chips to the cashier's window.

"Thank you so much," Sylvia said uncomfortably, as though she were standing under her front door porch light. She held out the money she owed him.

"I want you to keep it," he told her in Spanish.

She believed that he was not making some haughty or suave or even the slightest of an insincere gesture. But she did expect him to say something about a drink or food. She'd already thought of how probably she'd have to say no, say something about her husband and son who were waiting, but he did not ask, and it did not seem because he was so overwhelmed by his winnings.

Sylvia checked to see that her husband was asleep beside her and listened for her son's breathing in the bed near them. She touched herself slowly. At first it was her hand and then it was not. At first she made her stiff fingers tingle across her skin, and then her palms flattened and her fingers softened and bent. Sometimes the hand would even reach her face, her lips, her eyes. She was warm and unlonely. She felt young and she liked the familiar cold air settling above the blanket. She knew that she could not leave the window open long, but she let herself enjoy every moment it was.

In bed much later that night, Ray was thinking again of Sylvia. He had not cheated on his wife in those ten years of marriage, and though as a young man he had a better than average share of dates, he had not had that many lovers, and those he did have he looked back on as much in defeat as in conquest. Maybe he'd be different this time out. He thought of Sylvia and he felt her as though she were next to him on the vacant side of the bed. He felt her without moving, sexually, and he liked it very much.

Sylvia and Ray stared at one another as he came into the restaurant for breakfast. He'd chosen the place randomly and seeing her again, by chance, inspired some strange confidence in him.

Sylvia didn't want to draw him into a conversation so she looked away. Sitting there, patiently waiting for her husband to eat his meal, tested her until she realized that Ray wasn't going to say anything. Then she felt very alive.

When her husband finished, Sylvia stood, glancing at Ray self-consciously. Her son scooted the wooden chair away from the table noisily and ran out to the other side of the glass door and smashed his face on it to see back inside. He made faces at Ray who smiled at him from his table.

"Big tip or little?" her husband asked her. "Maybe we should save some to make up for all the losses. We still gotta get home." He left twenty percent.

She couldn't let herself look at Ray on her way out, but she walked down the restaurant's aisle worried about her appearance. When her husband caught up with her, she still couldn't think of what to say.

"Are you feeling okay?" her husband asked.

"Just sleepy is all."

"Too much action without the old man last night, huh? You can nap on the way home."

She took his hand.

"You sure you don't want to go and visit the family for Christmas?"

"No, really, I only wanted to do this. And I had a good time. I always wanted to know about Las Vegas, and now I do." She squeezed his hand.

Outside the restaurant, on the famous Strip, Ray couldn't help but notice the flat plain of black asphalt that belted the underlying desert, couldn't help but realize that the miracle of these steel and concrete casinos and hotels and restaurants were doomed by the wind and the sun and the sand, couldn't help but feel good that he was moving around in this impermanent place like a winner.

Cross-Country

Anne Finger

This is Roger's idea of fun. Not mine. The whole you-and-me-and-the-open-road-babe, just-the-two-of-us-with-the-wind-in-our-hair-and-a-song-on-our-lips, the mountains and the desert and then the cornfields rushing past us on either side: all his idea.

"Enterprise, 23 miles." Roger reads the sign aloud. "En-ter-prise," he repeats (for my benefit), savoring the word on his tongue. Yes, we are driving away from Berkeley, away from pretense and in-tel-lec-tual-i-za-tion, driving towards the heart of America, where people aren't ashamed to name a town Enterprise. No, sir.

Roger pulls out his journal. Four hours on the road and he's already filled up seven pages. I have a feeling this trip is going to turn into a Significant Experience for him.

"Elizabeth—" Roger points his finger. "An eagle!"

I'm not going to be the one to tell him it's a hawk.

Anne Finger won the Jackson Award in 1984 for a collection of stories that included "Cross-Country." She is the author of the novel Bone Truth, the story of a lame artist who must deal with an unplanned pregnancy while recalling a childhood with commu-nist parents in the McCarthy era. With Gary Eberle, she also cowrote a novel, Angel Strings, that pokes fun at the New Age industries that thrive in California soil. She cur-rently teaches at Wayne State University in Detroit, Michigan.

"God-damn! An ea-gle!" Roger hits the heel of his hand on the dashboard.

A pretty puny hawk at that.

Roger picks his pen back up, looks at his watch. I check the highway, then glance down at his journal. Roger has written: "Eagle, 11:57, 22 1/2 miles outside of Enterprise, California."

"Are we there yet?"

Two o'clock in the afternoon. On the road since eight this morning. Wrinkled clothes, the seat beginning to get sticky with sweat, that peculiar grubby feeling that only driving can give you.

"Huh, Roger? Are we there yet?"

"Elizabeth—" says Roger.

There is no there to get to; this is a trip without destination. Just the two of us and the car and the North American continent, going wherever our (his) fancy pleases.

"An object at rest," Roger once said to me, folding his coffee filter in half, then in quarters, running his fingernail down the crease, "an object at rest tends to remain at rest; an object in motion tends to remain in motion."

That was Roger's explanation for why we couldn't go on a vacation for the four years that he was working on his Ph.D. in clinical psych. Roger believes that one's life should be guided by scientific principles.

"Hot air rises," I said, watching Roger pour a level measure of coffee into the filter. "The universe is expanding. Couldn't we just take off for the weekend? Go to L.A. I'll drive. You can study in the car—"

Roger was silent.

"Everyone has certain patterns they tend to fall back on," Cindy, my therapist at Student Psychological Services, said.

"Roger has two. Rational explanation and silence."

A concerned look came over her face. "How does that make you feel?"

Roger is silent now.

"Huh, Roger? Are we there yet? Are we? I have to go to the bathroom. Can we stop and get a burger?"

Eyes front, hands clenching the steering wheel.

"Ignore behavior you wish to extinguish." I lean over and tickle his ribs; he breaks down and smiles. "Roger, look." I point to the side of the highway. "Stickney's. Fourteen miles. Shakes. Burgers. Genuine Indian Jewelry. Roger, I want a shake and a burger. Roger, will you buy me some genuine Indian jewelry? I have to go to the bathroom. I feel carsick..."

I curl up in my seat; close my eyes.

After a few minutes, Roger asks: "Have you ever been here before?"

"Huh," I moan in my best 'I-was-almost-asleep, what-is-it-you-want-now?' voice. "Roger, I've been everywhere. Yeah, I've been here before."

Oregon? Definitely. This highway, this stretch of road? Most likely.

In third grade, I stood up in class: "Ma'am, I've been in thirty-eight states."

"That's very interesting, Elizabeth," the teacher said. She had purple fingernails. "What does your father do?"

"I've been to Wyoming," I said. "And Texas."

I pick up my purse from the floor of the car, rummage in it, setting three plastic pill bottles in my lap.

(The first psychiatrist I ever saw refused to prescribe medications for me. "Pills can't cure a philosophical outlook," she said.)

I take three pills: one Elavil, one Valium, one Librium. The "l" sounds are very important, suggesting calmness and serenity, while the letter itself is steadfast, upright. Zs, Xs, Ks—those crazy shapes, sharp angles, veerying off in different directions—those sorts of letters would never do. Calmness, serenity: what they actually deliver is a slight fuzziness that insulates me a bit from the world. And they make me sleepy.

Lulled by my Librium, elevated by my Elavil to the higher plane of sleep—

"Elizabeth—"

"Jesus, Roger." Speech thick and slurred, and this time it's no act.

"Elizabeth, there's no point in going on a trip and then not seeing anything."

"I've seen it all before. My father was big on seeing everything too." One night—I couldn't have been very old, seven, maybe only six—my mother leaned over into the back seat of the car: Rachel, Elizabeth, Karen, Jeannie. Wake up. Your father wants you to look at something.

Back asleep, until my father screeched the car over to the shoulder of the highway: then we all sat bolt upright. The car had stopped. What had gone wrong? Dark night. We had been asleep for hours and hours. What was it my father wanted us to see: snow? an interesting rock formation? the stars, the moon?

"My father thought sleeping was a waste of time. It could be so much more profitably spent. You could be hounding your congressman with letters about social workers who were trying to destroy the American family. Or bugging the welfare department for more money. You could be—"

"Elizabeth."

"You could be figuring out some way to get the Salvation Army to give you a free refrigerator or beating your children. You—"

"Elizabeth. Shut up."

You would never know it from what goes on inside this car, but Roger is actually very much in love with me.

As a matter of fact, three days ago he asked me to marry him. It was in our apartment on Durant Ave. in Berkeley. Perhaps "asked" is not the right word. What he actually said was, "Elizabeth, we ought to get married."

I did not even switch off the vacuum cleaner.

"Elizabeth—"

I bent my shoulders and went after a clump of dust under the sofa.

Roger unplugged the vacuum.

"Elizabeth," he shouted, even though, with the vacuum off, it was no longer necessary.

Roger followed me into the kitchen, stood over me as I washed the silverware.

Roger has a very logical argument for marriage:

1. I am highly neurotic and do not know what is best for me.	1. Axiomatic statement
2. Roger not only knows what is best for me, he can make me do it.	2. Inductive logic: when he met me, I fantasized daily about suicide; was so insecure that I found it difficult to leave the house to go grocery shopping; worked as a maid at the Holiday Inn, despite the fact that my IQ had once been measured as 148 on the Stanford-Binet scale. I was unable to do the following things: drive a car, figure out a tip in a coffee shop, ask for a box of Tampax in a drugstore. After five years of living with him, I am the proud possessor of a B.A., a driver's license, and a credit card.
3. Roger wants to marry me.	
4. Quod Erat Demonstrandum. Marriage.	
	3. It has already been proven that Roger knows what is best for me.

It was not the first time Roger had proposed to me. We have a pattern. Our proposals/fights go in two stages: in Stage One, Roger repeats the above logical proof. In Stage Two, Roger says, "Elizabeth, if you don't marry me, I'm going to leave you."

Three days ago, in Berkeley, I had just finished rinsing out the coffee pot when Roger said: "Elizabeth, if you don't marry me, I'm going to leave you."

I began to scrub the frying pan.

"You can't have your cake and eat it, too."

"Roger," I sighed, "you have such a way with words. How do you think of yourself? As German chocolate? Maybe a Boston cream pie?"

"Either you're committed to this relationship or you're not."

I squirted some more Co-op Economy Pack Liquid Detergent onto the scrubber, worked on a particularly stubborn piece of fried egg stuck to the bottom of the skillet. (I do all of the cooking—except for frying the eggs. Roger believes that women are biologically incapable of frying eggs.)

"Kampgrounds of America, five miles," Roger reads.

"Roger, we are not staying anywhere where they substitute a K for a C. Absolutely not. I refuse." I have certain standards. I pride myself on the fact that although I did have a crazy upbringing, our family never had plastic roses on the table or pictures of children with huge eyes staring at us from the wall.

Parked at our assigned space at Kampgrounds of America, Roger takes the tent out of the back of the car, shakes it onto the ground. I watch him staring at the collection of poles and stakes, doubtless trying to remember his Boy Scout days.

I sprint to the car and grab my air mattress, then sit at the picnic table, huffing and puffing it full of air.

"Elizabeth," Roger calls, "come give me a hand."

"It's your job to pitch the tent. You're a man."

"Jesus, Elizabeth. Cut the crap." Roger is a feminist in the following situations: (a) when the garbage needs to be taken out; (b) when the rent is due; (c) when a fuse is blown.

"You know," Roger says, "you'd be perfectly comfortable sleeping on the ground."

All those years in Berkeley when I said: "Let's get away," I had in mind getting away, not only from the city of Berkeley, but also from lugging groceries, dishes three times a day, and trips to the laundromat: the old ceaseless round. In my dream, Roger would put down his books and I would put down my sponges and, wrapped in a silver cocoon, we would wing over cities, flying away, away. We would lie in the sun and call room service at three in the morning, demanding mango yogurt and steak and kidney pie. But Roger wants to "really travel," as he puts it. Not what he knew when he was a kid: taxis to the airport, planes to Florida, and air-conditioned hotel rooms.

Sleeping in a tent and ten hours a day on the road: that was not what I had in mind.

When I wake up in the morning, Roger has rolled over onto my air mattress, pushed me onto the ground. He lies with his knees drawn up to his chest in his mummy sleeping bag.

"Oh, you dear sweet little fetus," I whisper.

Roger doesn't know it, but I am thinking about leaving him.

We have been living together for five years. For four years and eleven months, I have been trying to decide whether to stay with him or not.

I make lists:

Reasons for Staying:

I really love Roger.

I would be lonely without him.

He would get the car.

I might end up with someone worse.

Reasons for Leaving:

I'm not all that sure I even like Roger.

It would be so nice to wake up in the morning next to someone new.

Sometimes I think if I see him going through his morning ritual (folding the coffee filter exactly in half, exactly in quarters, frying the two eggs in the frying pan reserved for that purpose) that I will scream.

They balance each other out.

We are on I-5, headed towards Seattle, when Roger says, "Elizabeth, I love you."

"Violins, please," I say, gesturing to an imaginary orchestra in the back seat.

"Shut up."

"Roger, you once said, and I quote: 'Your sense of humor delights me. Delights me.'"

"I love you," Roger repeats.

I stare out the window.

"Either you're committed to this relationship or you're not."

"Or else I'm ambivalent."

"We're either going to get married or we're going to break up," he says.

I say nothing.

"Your move," he says.

"Pass."

I reach into my purse, pile make-up into my lap. I examine my complexion in the mirror. Last year I stopped smearing my face with Bio-Klear, Pimplefree, Acnex. I am twenty-three years old; in two years I will have to start worrying about wrinkles, will have to ask myself the question, Should A Woman Over Twenty-Five Use Soap On Her Skin? The raging hormones of adolescence have settled down; I have not yet begun to shrivel. These are my Golden Years.

"Roger," I say, as I remove an errant bit of mascara from beneath my eye, "what would you do if I left you?"

"You'd never leave me. You're too deficient in ego strength."

Roger knows these things: periodically, he administers Rorschach tests, MMPI's, thematic apperception tests. ("An ink blot, Roger. It looks like an ink blot." "True, Roger. It's true. I believe that I am a special agent from God." "Tell you a story. A story? Once upon a time there were three bears...")

In Seattle, visiting Roger's friends: Mary Anne serves us zucchini and brown rice casserole. Her macramé is hung on the walls. The young professional couple—Mary Anne is an editor; Clive is still in podiatry school. After dinner, we listen to Keith Jarrett. Boring, boring, boring.

Clive and Roger sit in the corner, a map spread between them. Roger is saying something about "getting off the beaten path." Clive shakes his head slowly, "super highways."

Mary Anne and I sit in our own corner. "Have you gotten any difficult stains out of your clothing lately?"

"What?" Mary Anne asks.

"Forget it. Sorry I asked."

"Oh, Roger," I say as we undress for bed that night, "when I look at Mary Anne and Clive and see what the future holds for us..." I clasp my hands and swoon onto the hide-a-bed.

Roger says nothing.

"We will get married. Everything will be very *neat*. You will be a renowned clinical psychologist. I will take classes at night in jewel-ry-making. Or maybe cake-decorating. We could perpetuate the race. Just imagine, cuddly little versions of you and me."

"End of this discussion," Roger says.

"It's not a discussion. It's a monologue."

At two in the morning, while Roger, Mary Anne, and Clive sleep, I creep to the telephone.

Katie's sleepy voice says, "Hello."

"'Look not too long in the face of the fire, O man! Never—'"

"Elizabeth!"

"'Never,'" I repeat, "'dream with thy hand on the helm!' How you doing, cupcake?"

Katie and I met in Miss Hoffman's English class our junior year in high school. Miss Hoffman believed, not in analysis or interpreta-tion, but in memorization. Hence, the lines from *Moby Dick*.

"I'm *fine*," Kate says. "Is something wrong?"

"I...I think so. Yes, I think something is wrong." Then: "I'm in Seattle. Tomorrow we're going to go see the Space Needle."

"That's very nice," Kate says. "It's five in the morning."

"I woke you up," I say.

"You're with Roger?"

"Who else? He's going through his second adolescence. We have this damn tent in the back of the Toyota. We're picking up hitch-hikers and having relevant conversations with them. We're looking for the heart of America. It's his final fling. After this he's going to settle down, become Roger Grossman, Ph.D.; clinical psychologist. Grown-up. Married."

"To you?" Kate asks.

"No, to Catherine de Medici. Sorry. To me."

"Elizabeth, don't do it."

"Kate. I know—" I start crying. "I know—that I shouldn't. But I don't know what I'll do. I don't know what I'll do."

"You'll get an apartment, a job..."

I should listen to Kate. A self-described radical feminist, she is also extremely pragmatic. When I first told her about Roger (the wealthy family, the brilliant future in clinical psych.), her precise words were: "It might not be such a bad idea. I mean, for a while."

"Kate. I keep telling jokes. I'm so funny and witty and amusing and charming. I can't stop. Is that a symptom of a nervous breakdown?"

"Maybe," Kate says. She's an expert on the subject, having had two.

"How do you know when you're having one? I mean, as opposed to constant, nagging neuroticism?"

"It's like an orgasm," Kate says. "You just know. Are you O.K.?"

"No," I cry. "No. I'm not O.K. I'm not," and hang up the phone.

"Roger, I used to live here. No, no. I'm not kidding. This town. This town. I did."

"I believe you," Roger says.

"For three months. I was in second grade. Roger, come on, please stop—"

No one place; no mama standing always aproned in the same doorway, welcoming children home from school; no street that was *my* street, walked up and down again and again. No. Childhood: a succession of images: first, an old black car (actually, there were many, always old and always black). A wrinkled tree I loved in California. The dance of the telephone poles as we rushed past them, on the road to somewhere better.

"Food," I say.

"All right," Roger says.

We pull off the highway, drive past a McDonald's.

"Roger, I'm hungry," I wail.

"We'll find someplace better."

"This is Montana. It may be miles and miles—"

Roger does not answer.

I open the glove compartment, pull out a Triple A guide book. "Montana has a population density of two persons per square mile," I read.

"We can go to McDonald's in Berkeley. I want to go someplace real," Roger says.

Twenty-two miles later, we finally pull into a town.

There are as many pickup trucks as cars parked along the street, and Roger is beaming.

"Elizabeth, roll down your window." He pulls the car over to the side of the road. "Hey—Excuse me. Hey—"

The guy stops.

"How you doing?" Roger asks.

"Oh, Jesus, Roger, we're not in Berkeley," I mutter through clenched teeth.

He stares at Roger, nods his head slowly.

"We're looking for a place to get some lunch."

"Not McDonald's," I say. "Someplace *local*. Where we can sample the cuisine native to this region. Where we can meet—"

Roger claps his hand over my mouth. I mumble, *"real* people, men of the West—" and then bite his hand.

"There's a place down the road," he says. "The Bluebird's on the left."

"Hey, thanks a lot," Roger says.

"He thought we were visitors from outer space—" I say.

"He thought *you* were a visitor from outer space."

The Bluebird is charmingly seedy. Roger leads me to the counter: at a table, we would be alone, protected. Here we may strike up a conversation.

Roger orders a hamburger, french fries, and a Coke. Oh, no, McDonald's would never do.

"Ham and cheese," I say. "Whole wheat?"

The waitress shakes her head. Her name tag says, "Darlene." Roger is fascinated. This is what he has been looking for: the heart of America. Waitresses named Darlene. No whole wheat bread.

She takes a pre-formed, frozen burger off a stack of other pre-formed, frozen burgers, flips it onto the grill.

"Mustard on that ham and cheese?" she asks, then slathers French's onto Wonder Bread.

Roger is getting high on the authenticity of it all.

"Where're you folks from?"

"California," says Roger.

"Berkeley," I say.

"Berkeley? They used to have riots there, didn't they?"

"Yeah," says Roger, "that's all over now."

"We live on the street that Patty Hearst lived on when she got kidnapped," I say.

"Oh, yeah?" says Darlene. She mops the counter. "Did you know her?"

"*Know* her? Patty and I were like *this*," I say, holding up two fingers together.

"No," Roger says, "we didn't know her."

"Yes or no?" Roger says. "Elizabeth. Make up your mind."

"Let go of my wrists!"

"If I let go of your wrists, will you answer me?"

"Yes. Let go."

He drops my hands.

"Roger," I say. "You have to have blood tests. They have to make sure we're not riddled with syphilis. There's a waiting period..."

"Yes or no?"

"I always wanted a real wedding. I promised Kate, when we were sixteen years old, that she could be my maid of honor. I want a white dress. And a ring bearer. A darling little blonde-haired boy. A ring bearer."

"Yes or no?"

"Maybe, Roger. Maybe."

"Get out."

"Roger—"

"If it isn't yes, it's no. We are through. Out of the car."

"Not in Heron, Montana. No."

"Out," Roger says.

I am immobile. I stare straight ahead. After five minutes of silence, Roger starts the car's engine.

North Dakota.

"You know what, Roger? At my first trial—"

"Elizabeth. It wasn't a trial. It was a hearing."

At my first trial, the social worker was a young man with a beard. He said, "We feel that it's important to keep the family unit together." He had studied family relationships at some of the best universities in the country. "Mr. Lafayette has agreed to take part in counseling."

The judge, who disappointed me by not wearing a black robe or carrying a gavel, looked at my father. My father stared him back, said, "I'm game."

"Mrs. Lafayette?"

"I'm—*game,*" my mother repeated, slowly and deliberately.

The judge returned me to my parents' custody, on the condition that we seek family therapy.

That night, my father packed the family unit into his car and drove us up to Oregon, away from understanding social workers and gavelless judges and probing counselors.

Pulling into gas stations, fill it up, please; then a plaintive look, a shrug to indicate the rest of the car, my father saying, "We don't have any money." *We.*

My second trial was in Florida. I was fourteen years old, sexually wayward. The social worker said I was 'acting out.'

"Acting up," my mother said. "She's always acting up."

They put me in the Children's Center for six weeks. Twice, for about ten minutes each time, I saw a psychiatric social worker, who told me that she understood my need for love.

At my third and final trial, the social worker patted me on the shoulder and said, "Don't be nervous." I knew enough to know that meant: act nervous, plaintive, shy. Sit in the chair, stare at the floor, look up for just a second, the voice barely above a whisper: "Yes, sir, I think I would be happier in a foster home."

"Kate."

"Elizabeth. I've been *worried* about you."

"You've been worried about me," I say. "God. I've been frantic about myself."

"Are you O.K.?"

"I don't want to marry him. I don't. I don't, I don't."

"Can't blame you."

"He's a pill," I say. "He's been good for me, but he's a pill."

"Come stay with me. I could wire you some money. I mean, probably. I'd have to borrow it from my sister."

"No. No. Not the money. But I might come stay with you. I might."

"My home is your home," Kate says.

"He has a *good* heart," I say. "He does, Kate. He does. He..." I hang up the phone.

Suddenly, we are in the Dakota badlands.

"The bad-lands," I say.

Crazy rock formations loom around us. They look like the sand castles Rachel and I used to build when we were kids, dripping wet sand into convoluted mounds.

"After God made the rest of the world, Saturday night, Saturday night, he got drunk."

"Shut up, Elizabeth."

"They left this part out of the Bible, Roger. Thought it detracted from the overall tone. Saturday night he got drunk. Cosmically sloshed. He reeled into North Dakota and made these rocks. He did, Roger."

"Your view of the landscape," Roger says, "is quite interesting. Primitive, bordering on the psychotic."

"Primitive, bordering on the psychotic," I mock.

"Kate—"

"Elizabeth Jane Lafayette. If you hang up on me one more time—"

"I won't. I promise."

"I've made up the hide-a-bed. I'm *expecting* you," she says.

"We're in North Dakota. We've just been through the badlands. I feel the way I felt when I turned eighteen and suddenly was no longer a ward of the state—I'm a helium balloon, let go of, headed for the stratosphere, or whatever the hell it is."

"You're not a helium balloon," Kate says. "You're a human being."

"You're so practical," I say. "I envy your practicality. I do."

"I'm *expecting* you," Kate repeats.

"The geography in this region fills me with existential despair. Don't laugh. It does. It's distorted. It's frightening—barren. It makes you realize that there's no big warm Daddy-God out there who made a nice little world for us all to live on."

"You get yourself here. I mean it. You get away from him. You don't need him anymore."

"I think I will."

"You better. I'll see you soon, Elizabeth. Real soon. Goodbye."

At the campground, I wander off while Roger pitches the tent. At the Trading Post, I spot a likely prospect: I judge him to be about twenty-two; the address written on his knapsack in laundry marker is a Boston University dorm.

"Hi-i," I say. "Hello."

I drive men wild with lust. I do. Don't ask me why: I have a square face, a peasant's body. My senior year in high school, in an unofficial poll, I was voted, "Girl We'd Most Like To..."

"Hello," he says, and blushes.

"God," I say, lifting my T-shirt away from my breasts and fluttering it, "it sure is hot. I feel like I've been in that hot old car for days. But this is a beautiful country. Where are you headed?" I ask casually.

"Boston," he says.

He's the one.

We sit on a nearby picnic table. His name is Ned. I am witty, charming, and then, by turns, unaccountably sad, staring into the distant sunset.

"Ned," I say, the words faltering out of my mouth, "Ned. I. Well. This may sound very odd, but I feel—I feel very—close. *Close*," I repeat, "to you."

"Oh, Elizabeth," Ned says.

I pour out the story of Roger and me, omitting details that might cause me to be viewed in an unfavorable light.

"That's a *shame*," Ned says. "He's a psychologist and he's crazy himself."

"Really," I say.

I pour out the story of my father, my crazy childhood, omitting details that might cause me to be viewed in an unfavorable light.

"If I could just get to my friend Kate. She lives in Boston..."

"*I* could take you there. I'm going East."

"You could?" I say, all delight and smiles. "You *could?*"

Sneaking away under cover of darkness. Under cover of darkness—I like that phrase. It sounds warm, comforting.

I rest my hand on Ned's leg. The black night hides the crazy rocks, the flat, free expanse of the Dakota plains. The car hurtles across the country, away from Roger, away, into some unknown freedom.

from Dead Languages

David Shields

I understand that whenever Demosthenes got a little tongue-tied he'd leave Athens to camp out on the Mediterranean coast where, with pebbles in his mouth, he'd rehearse his oration against the sound of the Aegean Sea until his rather unGreek diffidence ceased and words became waves within him. Then he'd return to Athens to deliver a very authoritative, unhesitant speech which always concerned the sanctity of the Greek city-state and never received anything less than unrestrained applause from the rude multitude. The trip to the Mediterranean, the swim at sea, the favorable reception in the senate: it's a delightful tale complete with moral in tow. And yet there are those—surely, Sandra, you are one of them—who will want to insist that Demosthenes, forced to flee Athens and lecture inattentive fish every time he was scheduled to speak about the city-state,

David Shields is the author of two novels, Dead Languages *and* Heroes; *a collection of linked stories,* A Handbook for Drowning; *and, most recently, a work of autobiographical nonfiction,* Remote. *His newest book is* Black Planet: Facing Race During an NBA Season. *He won the Phelan Award in 1981. "The Phelan prize was the first award I had ever received from my work, and it provided incalculable psychic—not to mention financial—sustenance at a crucial time." A Los Angeles native, he now lives in Seattle, where he teaches at the University of Washington.*

should have drowned himself at high tide, whereas I'd want to emphasize that Demosthenes never left the coast until he was speaking so loud he could no longer hear the Aegean arriving on the rocks.

The big city boy, who hates the city, leaves the city to perfect a speech in praise of the absolute supremacy of the city. The audience, impatient to applaud, doesn't perceive that the greatest orator in Western civilization often speaks with seaweed sliding out his mouth. Why would someone for whom talking was torture want to talk all the time before thousands of Athenians? Because otherwise he'd have drowned himself at high tide. My sister—so shy, so sincere—once wanted to be an actress. The best jazz drummer I've ever heard had only one arm. We all choose a calling that's the most radical contradiction of ourselves.

And what's my calling? I am not a postal clerk. All I've ever had are memories; metaphor is only an escape from error into elegance. No imagination, only memory. More specifically: Lido Isle the summer of 1960. I remember Father reading about the Rosenbergs in a wooden chair chained to a steel stake in the sand; Mother sitting at her black typewriter in her black swimsuit, inhaling Kents and exhaling black smoke while writing a retrospective on the Hollywood Ten for *The Nation* ("Perhaps the whole intent and purpose of the loyalty orders was merely to collect evidentiary leads—like a boy collecting wads of string in the hope that someday he will have enough for a noose"); Beth, too fat to have fun, never failing by lunch to complete the crossword puzzle; the hideous sand dunes in the distance, slime mold clinging to the four legs of the dock, the muddy shore at morning, but all that recedes and I see myself, absurdly small, seated in a white rowboat that later is to become much photographed by Father because it's the source of all mystery. It's the source of all mystery because, although it's without oars or owner and isn't moored, it never leaves the shore. Never. It's always there, always white, rusted, pure, austere.

The rowboat isn't only the Source of All Mystery and the Vehicle of the Voyage. It's also an Icon of My Own Isolation. *C'est moi.* I never leave the shore. I don't know how to swim. Tears lift the waves to high water. The horizon is Hong Kong. I decide to cross the Pacific so I can stop speaking English, with which I am having considerable difficulty, and learn Chinese, which seems so much faster, so much more natural. No pauses, just jabbering. I decide to row across but have no oars. I decide to swim across but don't know how to swim. I can't even float. Though I haven't yet heard of Demosthenes, I speak to the Pacific, love how dark it looks as night nears. I want from the waves what he wanted: a little bit of cruel constancy. I orate to the ocean what I've heard about all day—that neither of the Rosenbergs and none of the Hollywood Ten were guilty—and, all alone in the night, I become witty, jocular. I explain to the Pacific how helplessly attracted I am to Ruth Greenglass's red hair, how erotic her betrayal of the Rosenbergs is for me. My voice picks up power, I'm drowning out high tide, I can't hear it any more. The Pacific is puny. China is mere chimera. I start to stand in the boat, bellowing at the waves, but as I rise I lose my balance and fall overboard. I learn how to swim: the water is not warm.

I hope it's clear this is no mere tale of a four-year-old finding his first flippers, even if swimming is finally only swimming: an undertow here, a red tide there, a scorpion in the sand. And a family is only a family. My family was only a family. It wasn't a nightmare. It wasn't a concentration camp. Each of us isn't the sum total of all the faults of his family. That's impossible. That can't be who we are. So I suppose I selectively remember that Mother was writing an article, Father was reading a book, and Beth was completing crossword puzzles, while I wandered the island, wondering whether I should cut off my tongue or simply put a pistol to my head. My family was living in language whereas I was dying in it, and I understand such a situation is classical, not in the sense of Demosthenes but *Herr Doktor:* the opposite of success is suicide.

Beth had done so well in a high school course called Psychoanalysis and Literature that when the teacher—a handsome man who wore loud blazers and said such things as, "Have any of you ever seen a picture of Kafka? He looks like a criminal. Do you know why he looks like a criminal? Because he was an artist. Do you know why the artist is a criminal? Because he steals our secrets"—got tired, he'd let Beth lead the discussion. So well dressed, so seraphically smart, she'd stand up and say, "Did it occur to any of you that Gertrude's last words—'O my dear Hamlet'—are not without meaning for us?" Years later, of course, I wanted to do even better than Beth had done, but when Loud Blazer called on me I'd shake my head No, or maybe nod Yes, then after class he'd come up to me and say: "Are you sure your last name is Zorn?"

Place-Names: The Name. Zorn, Germany: Zorn. Three hundred years ago: "Are you Zorns from Zorn?" "Why, yes, of course, all Zorns are from Zorn." German; Jew. So the secret has been stolen, and not by Kafka. So I am not Demosthenes. Which is why it's curious to me that Mother often said she never trusted German-Jews because their loyalty was divided between culture and country and, in some of the last articles she wrote, attacked Kissinger, really quite viciously attacked him, for that very reason. Didn't she trust Father? Is that what this means? Who knows? Maybe that's why Father always insisted we were Russian. He liked to see himself as one of those who would have contradicted the Cossacks if he had had the chance. I can't believe Mother had any reason to mistrust Father or that, on the other hand, Father would have listened to such a harangue against his lineage. If memory serves, though, that's precisely what happened. The discovery that I'm a descendant of the Zorns from Zorn was a recent product of my own research.

I've never been exactly sure what part of Europe Mother's people came from, but wasn't she always the Cossack and Father the cowering Jew? Wasn't this his chance to be tough and didn't he bow and scrape? It's fashionable these days to equate marriage and murder, and I don't mean to invoke such a simple formula, but it would be a lie to say Mother was ever anything less than a tyrant or Father anything more than a mole. Mother often gave dinner parties for the West Coast correspondents of other magazines—very lavish affairs at which they drank a lot, talked very loudly and learnedly about everything in the world, and told me Mother was a marvelous writer as well as a "great gal," but which were always being interrupted by a call from someone's copyeditor "back East" who wanted the entire article on Governor Reagan rewritten by midnight. It was all very exciting.

It's one party in particular I remember. I don't remember what year it was or what season. Instead, I remember those terrible gingham curtains drawn back so the picture window presented rather spectacularly: the Bay and the Bridge, with a Moon. On one wall was a Klee print, and on the other wall was a black-and-white photograph, mounted and framed, of two children kissing, which, if you looked at it in the wrong light or without, say, love in your heart, you might take for nothing more than two water glasses touching. The first time Father saw it he thought it was waves, dark waves at dawn.

Even now I cannot convince him those are lips. The party people were reading one another's articles in one another's magazines, as they spooned chocolate mousse, which Beth had been so good to make, and sipped coffee. They were praising one another extravagantly and meditating upon the power of the written word, the nature of attractive typography. Oh, I don't know, maybe a few candles flickered in the black wind.

Then Father found something offensive about one of the articles, and the moon dissolved. He read aloud the first paragraph of the story, which was written by an Englishman for Reuters:

> At a $100-a-plate dinner last night sponsored by the San Francisco Jewish Welfare Fund, Israeli Prime Minister Golda Meir called for Jewish-American men and women to contribute one percent of their paychecks to the war effort, and all Jewish-American boys over the age of eighteen to enlist in the Israeli Army. She assured the affluent audience that visa applications would be waived for all potential soldiers. Alluding to Egyptian President Gamal Abdel Nasser's boast that "our aim is to drive Israel into the Red Sea," Prime Minister Meir said, "The people of Israel have never had, do not now have, and shall never have any intention of residing underwater," drawing a sustained, standing ovation from this charming city's ethnic elite.

"'Affluent audience,'" Father said. "'Potential soldiers.' 'Ethnic elite.' You call this objective reporting?"

Reuters, who was tapping the ashes of a sophisticated cigarette into his empty mousse dish, said, "For godsakes, chap, cheer up, will you? We call it 'in-depth analysis.'"

On the few occasions Father became furious, I always had the sense thirty years were receding before my eyes, and this time was no exception: the voice a vibrato; the face, quite literally, crimson; those thin legs very suddenly tight and mighty. Father stood, spilling his mousse.

"Teddy, sit down," Mother said.

Teddy—Father—sat down, then said, "In-depth analysis? What, are you kidding? This is slander."

"I found it—as a lead paragraph—wonderfully terse, wonderfully, really quite wonderfully, to the point," someone said.

"It's a nice mixture, Taylor, of reportage and local color," Mother said. "It really is."

"Annette, how can you say that?" Father pleaded, tugging on the tablecloth. "It's subtly, or not so subtly, anti-Semitic. I demand an apology."

And then, amid all the West Coast correspondents, Father put his napkin down on the table and just started weeping. Huge convulsive heaves of the shoulders and slobbering gasps for breath. While the discussion returned to more civilized concerns (international politics and pay raises and that kind of thing), Father got up and left, taking his mousse and a bent metal spoon with him into the bedroom. I'd like to say I went with him, helped him eat his mousse, held his hand, and told him I thought they were wrong, all wrong, but Mother stared at me to sit perfectly still, so I stayed. The control she had over people was really rather extraordinary. Maybe Father was bored silly with the conversation and just wanted an excuse to leave the table so he could sit up in bed, scoop pudding, and read some more about Sing Sing, but I imagine he squeezed a pillow tightly and cried the night away. He used to be such an emotional man.

And yet I don't see how he could have been expecting anything terribly much more from Mother, as it was just not her way to rush to Father's defense. She didn't do that sort of thing. Father was so helpless he would have needed the Russian Army as a defense and, although Mother was the Russian Army, she was never especially prone to eliminating the enemy for him. Or, rather, she *was* the enemy for him. Why was she always so sweet to strangers and so tough on Father? I wish I knew. The more helpless he became the more unhelpful she became and then, when she finally needed some attention, Father was nowhere to be found.

I don't mean to imply the sheer agony of watching Mother and Father argue was the sole cause of my curse. Sometimes, though, when I'm playing tennis I'll know I can't quite reach the ball if I hit it with a backhand, so I'll shift the racquet and return the ball lefty— a maneuver I didn't so much learn from Father as inherit from him— or when hurriedly filling out a form I'll realize my "Z," with its wicked horizontal slash, might just as well have been written by Mother. It's times like these when I acknowledge that if my parents affected my tennis game and my penmanship they must have had some influence upon my mouth as well. I recently learned that Mother wasn't the first person ever to say: "The past is but prologue to the present," although probably no one ever said it as often as she did. It's a very nice if somewhat too alliterative axiom, and it might serve well as my emblem throughout these episodes. The past is but prologue. I suppose I should begin at the beginning.

Contemporary pathological theory—Sandra tells me—has it that "the stuttering problem begins in early childhood and develops as a negative reaction by the child to disfluencies while speaking." Right around age three, children find language for the first time. In their eagerness and anxiety to master the communicative process by morning, almost all little ones encounter considerable difficulty at one time or another with their diction. Every day they add dozens of new words to their vocabularies and, impatient for progress, they trip over this *t*, fumble with that *f*. If just about every child babbles occasionally from age three to age five, only a very select one half of one percent go on to make a nasty adult habit out of it.

Why do some "develop a negative reaction to disfluencies" while others do not? Why is every stutterer I have ever met a man? And why are his eyes always rimmed with fear? The reason ninety percent of all impeded speakers are male is, according to Sandra, that little boys feel more pressure than little girls to perform verbal magic. In some ways it's an attractive theory, but I have my doubts. Beth claims she was already reading Nancy Drew mysteries when she was four, whereas I'd never pretend that at such an early age I was doing anything more ambitious than attempting to master the alphabet, that terrible catalogue of unspeakable sounds.

Still, I did always feel a certain subtle pressure to produce perfect speech, and for that I suppose I should blame Mother and Father, since Sandra is so convinced the origin of all stuttering is a scene in which one of the parents calls the child's attention to and scolds him for what is normal, everyday disfluency. The example Sandra uses is always the same: a boy and his mother lean out the second-floor window of a burning house, waiting for the boy's father to line up the ladder with the ledge of the window. The boy turns to his mother and says, "I-I-I'm afraid, Mommy." Sandra is certain that if the mother in such a situation says, "Don't worry, Melvin, Daddy will have us out of here in no time," Melvin will turn out all right, but if the mother says, "Don't say, 'I-I-I'm afraid,' Melvin, just 'I'm afraid,'" Melvin will try not to stutter on "I" the next time he says it. This, as we all know, is the beginning of the end. He will, as Sandra says, "develop a general orientation toward speech of 'what can I do not to stutter' instead of 'what can I do to talk.'" Poor little Melvin. I've always assumed his only hope was for the house to go up fast in flames.

There's no house on fire in my memory but, when Sandra insists that I must remember the origin of the disorder, I see a Pacific Palisades living room as the scene of the crime. Beth was away at a classical guitar lesson; Father, who had just returned from playing four sets of doubles at Rancho Park, was sprawled on the floor, bouncing a white tennis ball on the red Persian rug; Mother, who had to be in North Hollywood by noon to interview a screenwriter who'd been blacklisted and wanted to talk, was sitting in the Good Chair with her polished shoes on the stool and the puppy in her lap. The dog was named Bruin, in honor of Mother's alma mater, but it should have been called CIA, since it looked like nothing so much as the black-coated specter in *Mad's* "Spy vs. Spy." This would have been an appropriate appellation, too, as its only desires in the world were to claw your bare ruined legs, curl up in Mother's soul, and look at you lugubriously. It was wounded half a dozen years later when I got upset one afternoon about my inability to talk, even to a dog, and neglected to latch the back gate. Bruin ran right into the grillwork of a Mustang convertible.

At the origin of the disorder, in the living room on Saturday morning, Bruin was still healthy and dreaming in Mother's lap. Mother was sitting in the Good Chair, Father was bouncing a tennis ball on the Persian rug, and I was lying down on the couch. Yes, lying down on the couch, and I suspect the symbolism was intentional, since Mother said I should put a pillow behind my head and my arms at my side, just relax, close my eyes, and talk very slowly. I tried to do what Mother said, I honestly tried, but I was five years old, it was the month of May, and all that morning sun waxed the bay window with quasi-religious light, with reasons to live. It was obvious to me that outside the window was what is known as life, and inside the window was what is commonly referred to as death. I wanted very much to be outside and got up to go, but Father stood, guarding the front door, playing the patrolman for probably the first and last time in his life. Mother said if she could be a little late for her interview, "well, then, you can come right back here and lie down on the couch and listen to me for a few minutes, Buster." My name wasn't Buster. The dog's name was Bruin or, to free-associating friends of Beth's borrowing our house between marches throughout the sixties, Brewin'. The dog leapt off Mother's lap, pranced across the Persian rug, and Father opened the door to let her go outside. Beth was strumming Segovia transcriptions and eating fancy cookies at a nice Italian lady's house in Bel-Air.

"Are you comfortable over there on the couch?" Mother asked.

"Yes," I said.

"Are you happy?" she asked.

Surely she meant this as an inquiry into the general state of my spiritual life—what sort of reconciliation I'd arrived at between death and desire. Father sat upright and Mother raised her eyebrows when I said, "No, I'm not happy." She thought she was onto something. She thought I was going to tell her what she wanted to hear.

"Why not?" she asked.

"Because I'd rather be outside, playing," I said.

"Oh, right," she said, nodding. She slumped back in the Good Chair. Father returned to his prone position on the floor.

This wasn't working out the way she wanted. She wasn't establishing the empathy she was famous for establishing between herself and her subject. I guess I wasn't giving a very good interview. Mother went into the den to call the screenwriter and say she'd be a little late, while Father went to take a shower because in twenty minutes he was supposed to pick up Beth at the nice Italian lady's house in the hills. As he was walking out of the room he squeezed my shoulder and said, "Just relax, Jeremy. Don't worry about what Mom is saying." So then, of course, waiting for Mother to get off the phone, lying face down on the scratchy couch, I couldn't do anything except worry. Mother had just given me a new watch to teach me responsibility and make me acutely aware of my own mortality. Studying its blue face, its white dial, I admired the ease with which the silver second hand made its rounds, the way it couldn't stop moving if it wanted to.

When Mother returned from the den, she pulled the stool next to the couch, pushed the hair off my forehead, and blew smoke in my face. She said this very softly and sympathetically, she said it while massaging my skull, but what she said was: "Do you realize, Jeremy, that sometimes you talk too fast? Sometimes you're in just such a hurry to say something the words trip you up. Have you ever noticed that, honey? Sometimes you'll want to say a word so fast you won't be able to say it at all or you'll say the first sound of the word over and over. I don't want this to become a habit for you. There's no need to be quite so anxious. People will wait to hear what you have to say."

"I don't do that," I said.

"Do what?"

"Talk too fast."

"Sometimes you do," Mother said. "Not a lot or even often, but now and then you try to rush your words and you'll stumble over one of them. Daddy has noticed it, I've noticed it, and Beth said she's noticed it."

"Beth said that?"

"Yes"

"When?"

"She said yesterday the two of you were looking at the map of the United States in the World Book and, when you were racing to see who could name all the capital cities first, you had some difficulty saying 'Philadelphia.'"

"I didn't," I said. "She's a liar." Beth was a liar, but she was also the winner of the map game when Harrisburg, of all places, rather than Philadelphia, proved to be the capital of Pennsylvania.

I listened to the shower running, to the expansion of the pipes. I watched Bruin press her black little nose to the window and beg to be let back in. I studied the threads in the couch. I computed the fantastic rate at which Mother was removing cigarettes from her pack. I did anything I could to miss what Mother was saying because the main theme of her monologue was: "I just want to show you how easily you can say 'Philadelphia' if you'll concentrate on saying it very slowly and carefully. Come on now, Jeremy, say it with me: Fill-a-dell-fee-a. You can do it. I know you can. Show me you can do it. Say 'Philadelphia' for me, honey."

I tried. God knows I tried. But "Philadelphia" lay like dead weight on my chest, like helium in my head, neither light nor heavy, and yet with definite gravity to it: with downward pull. Sandra says the only way to lose a fear of certain words is to treat them as utterly random and insignificant collocations of sounds; this has the added advantage of echoing a lot of fancy Frog philosophy about how everything, being language, is babble. I tried to visualize "Philadelphia" as "Fill-a-dell-fee-a," but all I could think was Philadelphia was too far away. It was clear across the country, the country was very wide, and I was too small, too weak, too afraid to make the trip. I was in the Palisades and Philadelphia was in Philadelphia. It was too far. It was definitely out of the question. It isn't even the capital of Pennsylvania, I kept telling myself, trying to weaken the enemy, but Philadelphia was Constitution City, Locus of Brotherly Love, Metropolis for men who had large yellow farms and long white wigs. Teeth on lips forever, and all I could come up with was an infinitely extended, infinitely painful *Fffffffff*. That's all. Only that. *Fffffffff*. Nothing more.

"I don't feel like saying that word right now," I said.

"What word?" Mother asked.

"That word."

"What word?"

"You know."

"Give it a try."

"No," I said. "Not now. Maybe later. Not right now."

Mother shook her head in sadness and disgust. She withdrew to the den to call the screenwriter, canceling the interview, and came back carrying six boxes of flash cards. She waited until Father left to pick up Beth, then kicked off her shoes, cozied up next to me on the couch, and told me to lay my head in her lap. I did what she advised. For what seemed like forever, she flipped flash cards in front of my face. I was supposed to say what each picture depicted, which was a sympathetic gesture on her part since it was a game we'd played before and I'd always enjoyed. She assumed it would restore confidence in my ability to communicate, but one by one the tangible things of the world vanished on me. I couldn't say a chair was a chair, or an umbrella was an umbrella, or a zebra was a zebra. As Sandra likes to point out, what you can't identify doesn't exist; no stutterer can say his own name. Mother must have flipped four hundred flash cards, and not one card could I call. I wanted to do what Mother called "caption the picture," but my mouth refused to open. The words weren't there.

Beth and Father returned sooner than I'd expected. When Beth walked in the back door humming the new notes she'd learned, the contrast—Beth the musician, Jeremy the mutation—was so striking I buried my head in Mother's lap and burst into tears. It was a wonderful feeling to produce such loud and continuous sound after I'd been silent for so long. A truly excellent cry redistributes the bones of the body; with the cessation of sobbing, I felt more completely cleaned out than I've ever felt before or since. It's a difficult emotion to explain, but it was as if the most complete emptiness had suddenly passed into purity. I thought the ugly language living in my soul had finally been killed. The future held in store only flashing phrases; perfect sentences; burning, noble words.

Father was so embarrassed by my behavior he changed back into his tennis clothes and left to go bang a white ball against a green backboard. He was never very good at the game but terribly devoted to it, and I can remember hardly a day when he didn't come back from the courts with a tin of balls in one hand, his Jack Kramer in the other, a sweaty smile on his face. Always attentive and eager to help, Beth stopped humming, marched straight into her room, closed the door, and played morose ballads for me on her guitar. She played well, though she always played well. She was a very gifted little girl. The dog had scooted inside when Father opened the back door on his way to Rancho Park; it was all over me now, scratching my neck and licking salt from the tears as they streamed down my face.

"You can go outside and play now," Mother said, sitting on the couch, handing me Kleenex, stroking my arm. "You still have some time to play before dinner, Jeremy. I'm sorry, I didn't mean to upset you. You know that, honey. I'm very sorry. Please don't let anything I said bother you, because you're going to be just fine. Most of the time you speak beautifully. Give me a smile, Jeremy. Don't you want to go outside and play?"

This was something of a first for me, to stay put rather than rush outdoors. When frolicking outside, it's fairly common for most children to experience what might be termed the opposite of the pathetic fallacy: to feel, after a few hours of fun, that the dirt, the grass, the trees, the sun, the sky are simply a part of them, are buried deep inside their bodies. But I'd never felt that way before about a living room. The scratchy couch, the Persian rug, the Good Chair, the

unsteady chandelier, all these supposedly inanimate objects suddenly took on a life of their own and started playing house in my heart.
For anyone to feel like a living room is a minor disaster, but for a boy-
child it's the worst feeling in the world. The late afternoon sun dissolved into the artificial light of the overhead lamp. No, Mother, I
didn't want to go outside and play. All I really wanted to do was close
the curtains, turn off the lights, put my head on a pillow, and ascend.
No such luck. "Come help me take out the garbage," Mother said,
"and I'll make whatever you want for dinner."

Maybe I'm deluding myself when I say this scene was the inception
of the problem, since it's not as if from that time forward the only
thing I've been aware of has been my disfluency. That's simply not
the case. But, until Mother mentioned it to me, I'd never heard those
hesitations that are now habit. Apparently, other people had. It
offended them, they felt compelled to tell Mother, and she felt compelled to tell me. Mother didn't create the catch in my voice. She
only heard that something was wrong and, like any good reporter,
went straight to the source.

    Sandra says I must have become aware of the impropriety of
my speech earlier than age four but have chosen not to remember
it. She says the "traumatic nexus surrounding disfluency is invariably established no later than three and a half." Maybe so. I couldn't
say. The tableau in the living room is the earliest trauma I can come
up with. Sandra's eyes light up and she gets giddy all over when I
tell her, though, how solid middle class we Zorns were, because a
disproportionate percentage of sputterers comes from the ambitious
bourgeoisie, the rising gentry who, in the considered opinion of our
finest historians, prompted the English Revolution. Mother would
like to have covered the beheading of Charles I and Father would
like to have fought at Philiphaugh, but I don't think either one of
them realized how unrevolutionary they were, how upwardly
mobile, how extremely middle class. The filthy rich are so rich they
hire a private tutor to instruct little Theodore in the elusive art of
elocution; the filthy poor are so poor they don't know where little
Leroy is, let alone care how he communicates; but the filthy middle
class are so middle class they call little Jeremy onto the couch and
ask him why he talks so fast.

"Look at the graph," Sandra will say, pointing to some piece of paper on the wall. "Statistics don't lie." I suppose they don't. They show most stammerers coming from families on the move, families that don't have a fireplace but are seeking fame and fortune. The new chairs in the breakfast room, the well-swept patio, the maid on Friday, the stuttering son: these, apparently, are the true totems of creeping capitalism. The rich will always be rich, the poor will always be poor, but the middle class is always in motion, is always in a state of suspended transformation, is not necessarily tomorrow what it is today. All that social sliding throws some children into a tizzy and their confusion comes out in strangled articulation.

The last thing I would want to do would be to ascribe this fascinating phenomenon to mere class conflict—titubation as the burden of the bourgeoisie—but I do want to acknowledge the cultural context of my disfluency. A voice from the burning bush commanded Moses to lead his people out of Egypt, but Moses was "slow of speech, and of a slow tongue." When the time came to inform the Israelites of God's command, Moses' brother, Aaron, "spake all the words which the Lord had spoken unto Moses." I always imagine Moses standing in the desert, trimming the bush, and pleading: "C-c-come on, Aaron, why d-d-don't *you* tell them?" From Moses on, Jews have worried about words.

"Don't you see?" Father would say. "Jews have always been in exile. We have had to be contemplative in order to survive."

"So they read books and looked for loopholes in the law," I'd say.

"Don't be silly. Kafka, Proust, Freud, Marx, Einstein: all Jews in one way or another. You should be proud they are a part of you."

"I am," I would say. "I really am."

But I'm not. I really am not. I'm tired of hearing that you can flee so many times before you start looking for more long-lasting shelter, that if you have been trampled by life you can triumph in language, that the only recourse to everything is to read and write yourself into existence. It's no longer romantic to me, this Hebraic hunger for words. I hear the ceaseless clickety-clack of Mother's typewriter at the beach; I see a photograph of Father hiking in the High Sierra with a biography of Alger Hiss sticking out of his hip pocket; I imagine Beth masturbating to the pictures in the middle of *Modern Drama Review.* I see, I hear, I imagine these things, and I'm depressed beyond despair.

from Fat City

Leonard Gardner

On the day before Ernie's first bout, he drove with Faye Murdock out of town and across the Calaveras River—brown and high from the rains—and turned down a lane that ran parallel to the levee. At a dirt turnoff used by lovers and fishermen, he drove up onto the levee and parked out of sight of housing tracts while dull-gray mud hens flapped away in the late afternoon, running over the water as they flew. Dark clouds extended to the horizon. Along the muddy banks of the river, redwing blackbirds sang in the cattails. His arms around Faye, as before on so many other untraveled roads, Ernie whispered and blew in her small bitter ear.

Faye was a solemn dark-haired girl with large attractive teeth, fair skin, and a short fleshy body that seemed to Ernie impervious to stimulation. He had begun taking her out because for a time she had

Leonard Gardner was born in Stockton, California, and now lives in Mill Valley. He won the Jackson Award in 1963, and the Phelan Award in 1966 and 1968. Perhaps no other novel has captured the lives of the down-and-out more accurately than his novel Fat City, which shuttles between the lives of two boxers, one on his way down, the other, on his way up. His screen adaptation of Fat City was eventually made into a film directed by John Huston. His work has also appeared in Esquire, The Paris Review, Southwest Review, and other magazines.

gone with Steve Bonomo, whose success with a previous girl Ernie had read about on the wall of a high school lavatory. His first time alone with Faye, Ernie had sensed a difference from the other crossed-legged girls he had dated. He felt in her lips and arms a lonely employment of him. Doggedly his campaign had gone on until he and Faye were among those who cruised under the lights of Main Street in predictable, faithful pairs, the dense one-way traffic proceeding slowly through yellow lights, blocking the street to cross traffic, the riders conversing from car to car while horns blared, the procession starting off again with squealing tires and rapping pipes only to brake, lurching, once again to a creeping mass. Yet, for all his fidelity, Ernie remained as frustrated as the young men who cruised alone or in groups as he had once cruised, looking for that mythical female pedestrian who would like to go for a ride.

The sky darkened, the liquid singing of the blackbirds diminished and ceased, mud hens swam back to shore, climbed up the banks and huddled in the willows. The lights of a farm came on in the brown distance where patches of tule fog lay on the barren muddy fields. A wind came with the darkness, rattling the license plate, and a low, honking flight of geese passed.

Later in the night it began to rain. To Ernie the first patters were like small sounds from Faye's mouth. Her lips had been against his so long that his mind was drifting among images of reeds wavering with the delicate movements of her tongue. When the roof began drumming, they sat up. Rain was pouring over the windshield, battering the ground, hissing into the invisible river. Ernie opened the window and the cold rain blew against his face. From his hunger he realized that many hours had gone by. In the light of a match, Faye's wan and tired face, the downward angle of the cigarette, her rumpled clothes, unpinned hair, and the slump of her neck renewed his hopes.

Within closed steamy windows an embrace went on like the same endless moment, broken only by an occasional digestive murmur and Faye's lighting of cigarettes. Finally, in his weariness, Ernie began to accept that once again he had been baffled. There was no consolation from having tried everything he could think of. To appear in a ring tomorrow without ever having won this other battle seemed presumptuous and dangerous. He alone in the Lido Gym carried a burden of silence and deceptive innuendo, and he wondered if this could mean the difference between victory and defeat. He was persevering with his repertory of foreplay, which nothing else ever followed, when Faye's fingers came to rest on his thigh, over the small tin box in his pocket.

"Aspirin?"

Alarmed, he gave no answer, and uncertain what he should do, he allowed her hand into the pocket. She withdrew the box and he heard it click open in the darkness. As the silence continued he sagged against the door. The box snapped shut and was replaced.

"Were you planning it all this time?"

"No."

"You always carry them?"

"It was just in case something came up."

"You mean if you couldn't use them on me you'd use them on whoever would let you?"

"I wouldn't want anybody but you."

"What made you think I'd do it?"

"I was just hoping."

"Is that all you think I am?"

"What do you mean? We haven't even done it."

"You want to, though. Is that all you think about?"

"I don't think about that at all."

"You just said that's what you were hoping."

He thought a moment. "I just want what we'd both enjoy."

"Oh, sure."

For a while neither spoke, and Ernie wondered if he had talked his way clear.

"Do you really care for me?" she asked at last.

There was a silence so heady that he began to tremble. "I guess I'm in love," he answered, and slumped lower in fear of what he had said. Had he committed himself for nothing, or had he only said the one thing he should have said all along? The rain beat on the roof. They were sitting apart; he did not know now if she would even let him touch her, but unable to think of anything else, afraid the opportune moment might be passing, he reached out to her and she moved into his arms. It was as if the air had been knocked out of him. She clung to him and he contorted, suffocating, kicking the door as he tried to maneuver, knowing beyond all doubt that the inevitable moment had at last arrived. He pulled at her clothing, pushed her down on the seat. He sprawled, he thrust a foot through the spokes of the steering wheel. There was a smack of flesh. As Ernie's eyes pinched shut he felt the pulse of ecstatic oblivion and the horn began to honk.

In a moment all was still. Collapsed, conscious again of the rain on the roof, he realized he had experienced the ultimate in pleasure.

"Was it good?" he asked.

"It was nice," whispered Faye.

Ernie was gratified, hearing that. Still he was uncertain. He wondered if everything had gone as it should. Was that all there was to it? Perhaps it had been celebrated out of proportion because there was nothing else to live for. He lay with his face in a split in the seat, his nose squashed against the stuffing.

"It must be getting late."

"Yeah."

"Are we all right here?"

"We better go," he murmured into the seat.

"Do you think we should?"

He abruptly sat up. "We better get out of here."

"Maybe we shouldn't have stayed so long."

The engine rumbled, the lights shone out into the rain, the wipers swept and clacked across the windshield. After a few yards the car stopped, wheels spinning in the mud. Ernie shifted from low to reverse, trying to rock free, but the tires dug in and settled firmly.

"What'll we do? I should have gone home," said Faye.

Glad to get away from her, he stepped out into the rain. Leaving her at the wheel, he grasped the rear bumper, his back to the car, his shoes gripped by mud. Shouting directions, he heaved forward. The car thrust backward. He leaped away, screaming above the whining wheels. She shifted and the engine died.

"I can't do it," she said and he was afraid she was going to cry. Face streaming, he got back in to start the engine. "I wish we hadn't come," she said. "I wish I'd stayed home."

Ernie returned to the rear bumper. While the tires sprayed mud, he grunted and pushed and yelled at her not to spin the wheels. Finally, feet sucking and splashing, he walked off in search of boards, crashing angrily through the bushes down the steep slope of the levee. He was close to the water now but could not see it. In front of him was a black expanse with a sound like escaping steam. As he felt around on the bank he heard Faye calling from the car and he bellowed back, disgusted that she thought he would run off in the rain and leave her. Whipped by twigs, he was pulling himself along the bank from willow to willow when a whirring of wings rushed up before him. Recoiling, he slipped, throwing out his hands, striking the ground on his side, and instantly he was in the icy shock of the river, up to his waist, disbelieving, tearing away chunks of bank in terror. Blindly he clambered out and stood quaking on the slick bank, his teeth chattering, water pouring from his pants and his shoes full. Clutching twigs, his mind assailed by that black immersion, by what had happened in the car, he felt that everything had passed out of his control. He had to get home, had to get warm and dry and rested for his fight, but he was out here, wet in the bushes, stuck miles from town with a girl he might now never be able to get rid of. Through the hissing rain his horn sounded. Ernie moved ahead along the bank, weighed down by his pants.

He returned to the car dragging a waterlogged board.

"Ernie? Is that you?"

"Who else? What's all the noise about?"

"I was afraid you got lost."

Cursing, he jammed the board under the rear tire. He pushed, the wheels spun, the board cracked, the car surged ahead and mired down, Ernie collapsing in the glow of the taillights. Wallowing on his knees, he dug at the mud, jammed the cracked board back under the tire, and heaved against the car while Faye raced the engine. When they at last reached firm ground near the point where the levee road turned down again to the paved lane, the car lurched and careened ahead. Ernie ran after it down the turnoff.

"Will you call me tomorrow?" Faye asked on the way back to town.

"What for?"

"Because I want to talk to you."

Feeling the obligations already beginning, he agreed.

Her street was submerged from curb to curb, the water roaring under the car as they approached her house. Her porch light was the only one on in the block.

A carload of boxers departed in the rain. They rode past the county hospital, past leafless vineyards, orchards and walnut groves, barns, chicken pens and puddle-covered fields. On the back seat, slumped between Wes Haynes and Buford Wills—both wearing small black hats with upturned brims—sat Ernie Munger. Ruben Luna was driving. Beside him Babe Azzolino rode with Bobby Burgos, a Filipino bantamweight, who was his only fighter of the night. While the two managers talked on and on, Ernie nodded, dozed and jerked awake.

"We got the winners," said Ruben. "What do you think?"

"I'd say we got the winners."

"We got four sure winners. You know what I'd like to do some day? I'd like to take these guys to England. They appreciate class over there. When I turn these boys pro I'd really like to make that trip."

In Salinas they had a dinner of chili burgers. "This guy can't fight," said Ruben, sitting across from Ernie in the booth. "You'll knock him out. How you feel? Hardly wait to get in there?"

"I'll give it all I got," said Ernie.

"You may have to go the four rounds, so don't punch yourself out. Don't lose your head."

"I won't. I'll pace myself."

"It goes fast, though, so don't hang back."

"I won't hang back. I'll give it everything I got."

"Yeah, but you want to pace yourself. Buford, your guy's been around so you don't want to let him get a good shot at you. But he's a boozer, you know how these soldiers are. He won't go the limit."

Fog was blowing above the roofs and trees when they reached Monterey. Del Monte Gardens was near the edge of town. Ruben Luna, leaning slightly backward, coat and sweater unbuttoned, shirt open at the throat, hat back and arms swinging, led the way in. Several boxers were already in the dressing room, resting on tables, undressing, moving nervously around amid a murmur of voices and tense clearing of noses. Lightheaded from hours on the road, Ernie listlessly took off his clothes. In new boxing shoes, leather cup and a pair of purple-trimmed gold trunks with an embroidered A, he shifted about while Ruben wrapped his hands, moving with him, winding the gauze and muttering to him to keep still. With narrow strips of adhesive, the bandages were taped down and anchored between each finger. The gloves Ruben pulled first onto his own hands, pounding and kneading the padding away from the knuckles before he removed them and, braced, held them for Ernie to work on. They were smaller than those Ernie had trained with, and he shuffled in his light shoes, swinging his arms while Ruben pursued him, smearing Vaseline around his eyes and down the bridge of his nose. Ruben then crossed the room to Wes Haynes, who was sitting in T-shirt and jockstrap on the edge of a table, his red straightened hair in a high mound.

"I just hope I didn't leave my fight in the bedroom," Ernie confided to Buford Wills. Buford, matched for the semi-windup, was still in his street clothes. "Don't tell Ruben this, but I was out getting a little last night."

"I was too. That don't make no difference. It don't matter if you dead drunk, you got two hands you can beat that motherfucker. I don't care who he is. It all in your mind."

"I hope so."

"Hoping never done nothing. It *wanting* that do it. You got to want to win so bad you can taste it. If you want to win bad enough you win. They no way in hell this dude going beat me. He too old. I be all over him. I kick his ass so bad, every time he take a bite of food tomorrow he going think of me. He be one sore son-of-a-bitch. He going *know* he been in a fight. I get him before he get me. I going hit him with everything. I won't just *beat* that motherfucker, I going *kill* him." Buford was small and thin. His hair, divided at one side with a razor-blade part, was cropped close. His nose turned up, his nostrils flared, his lips were soft and full and his hooded eyes were narrowed in a constant frown. The year before, only fourteen, he had lied about his age and won the Golden Gloves novice flyweight title in San Francisco. Tonight he was fighting the champion of Fort Ord. "You want to know what make a good fighter?"

"What's that?"

"It believing in yourself. That the will to win. The rest condition. You want to kick ass, you kick ass."

"I hope you're right."

"You don't want to kick ass, you get your own ass whipped."

"I want to kick ass. Don't worry about that."

"You just shit out of luck."

"I said I wanted to kick ass."

"You got to want to kick ass *bad*. They no manager or trainer or pill can do it for you."

"I want to kick ass as bad as you do."

"Then you go out and kick ass."

"All right." Ernie moved away, irritated with his deferring to a boy. Lethargically he bobbed and shuffled. When his name was called through the doorway, he began wildly shadowboxing.

"Hold off. You'll wear yourself out. We got to go on now," said Ruben. "Babe, get the towels, get the towels."

"I didn't get a chance to warm up," Ernie complained.

"That's okay, you're ready. Just stay loose. Where's the bucket?"

"I got the bucket in my hand," whispered Babe. He was dressed in russet slacks, a yellow knit shirt and a moss-green cardigan sweater with a towel over one shoulder.

"Got the bottle?"

"The bottle's right here in the bucket."

"You put the water in it?"

"I wouldn't bring an empty bottle."

"I'm just asking. I don't want to bring my kid out there without any water."

"I got the damn water. Take it easy. I told you I got the water."

The three went out into the crowd. The referee, a short, bald, heavy man in gray, was leaning back with outspread arms on the ropes. A towel around his shoulders, Ernie scuffed his shoes in the resin box under the blazing lights. When he went to his corner, Ruben gripped the back of his neck and tried to shove the teeth protector into his mouth. Resisting, Ernie broke away and spit out his gum.

The bell tolled in summons. Whistles, restive clapping, echoed in the arena. At last a Mexican in a brilliant red robe jogged down the aisle, followed by his handlers. Ducking through the ropes, he caught a foot, and his lunge into the ring was converted to prancing and shadowboxing, a second scurrying after him attempting to untie the robe.

"Good," said Ruben. "You got the reach."

His name was Manuel Rosales. At the scattered applause given its announcement, Ernie was uneasy; but at his own introduction there was the same tribute to his merely being here in trunks. Ruben and Babe were out of the ring now but their massaging hands were still on him. The house lights went off and Rosales faced him across the white canvas. Startled by the bell and a shove against his back, Ernie bounded forward. His opponent turned around in his corner, went down on one knee and crossed himself. He rose immediately, his hair, in a grown-out crew cut, standing up like a wild boar's bristles. The two touched gloves across the referee's arm. Ernie, embarrassed about hitting Rosales so soon after prayer, reached out to touch gloves again and was struck on the side of the head. Offended, he lashed out and felt the thrilling impact of bone through the light gloves. Stirred by shouts, amazed by his power over the crowd, he sprang in, punching, and was jolted by a flurry. He backed off. Chewing on the mouthpiece, he danced around the ring while Rosales charged after him, swinging and missing. The referee maneuvered his nimble bulk out of their way, and the opposing seconds shouted unheeded instructions.

"Jab! Throw the right! Throw the right! Jab! One-two!"

"Pégale! Tírale al cuerpo! Abajo! Abajo!"

Between rounds Ruben coached with a ruthless expression Ernie had never seen on him before, his arms sometimes punching out in demonstrations.

"Step in and nail him. Understand what I mean?"

"Hook," croaked Babe, leaning through the ropes with the tape-covered water bottle.

At the bell, Ruben's hands were at Ernie's buttocks, heaving him up off the stool, and when Ernie came back after a round of dancing and jabbing, he was hit in the face with a wet sponge. He was rubbed, patted, squeezed and kneaded. Cold water was poured into his trunks. He was harangued, he was reprimanded, and he listened to nothing at all. As he stood up, the towel passed under his nose and he recoiled from the fumes of ammonia.

His lead sent a shower flying from Rosales' hair. He stepped away and Rosales hurled himself into the ropes.

"Go in! He's tired, he's tired, he's tired!" Ruben yelled, and Ernie realized he was tired too. He struck out and moved away. Backed into a corner, he was attempting to clinch when a blinding blow crushed his nose. Bent over with his arms around Rosales' waist, he became aware of the referee tugging on him. Locked together, the three staggered about, blood spattering their legs, until Ernie's grasp was broken.

Blearily he saw a gush of blood down his chest. The referee was holding him, looking up at his eyes. "I'm okay, I'm okay," Ernie said through a throbbing nose and began to understand that something was wrong with him. Afraid the fight was going to be stopped, he pushed toward Rosales, there openmouthed behind the referee, his gleaming body splashed with blood. He was blocked. He lunged, but the referee, his face fat and red above the black bow tie, was pressing him back, his fingers fumbling for the mouthpiece. Ernie turned his head from side to side, dodging his hand and protesting through the rubber: "Shit, I'm okay. Shit, goddamn it, I'm okay." Then Ruben was in the ring, holding him by the shoulders.

"Tilt your head back. Breathe through your mouth."

He was being sponged in his corner when his opponent, now back in the red robe, came over, mumbling, to hang an arm briefly around his neck.

"Look to me like he butted you," whispered Babe after Rosales had gone back across the spotted canvas.

"I don't know what it was."

"Sure he butted you. Because he can't punch," said Ruben, and he went to the referee.

With his hand on the back of Ernie's neck, Ruben complained loudly up the aisle to the dressing room, where Buford Wills sat lost in the folds of a royal-blue robe and Wes Haynes stood waiting in gloves, white shoes and jockstrap.

"You lose, huh?"

"He wasn't hurt at all. It should never been stopped."

Ernie's gloves were pulled off and the handwraps cut away with hasty precision. A gray-haired manager came and peered at his nose.

"You want to get a note from the doctor before you leave. You can get that nose set tomorrow and it won't cost you nothing."

"He was butted. They should throw that kid out of the ring."

Ernie removed the trunks and cup and they were given to Wes Haynes. Grumbling, he put them on. "They all bloody," he objected to Ruben.

"That's all right. It's not your blood."

Ernie was left standing with his head tilted back. Blood still trickling over his lips, he went to a mirror. His nose looked like a boiled sausage about to burst. He went into the shower room and, feeling the pulse of splintered bone, stood with closed eyes under the spray.

I'm getting my share, Ernie Munger assured himself at the station on Center Street under floodlights besieged by moths. Still he felt an uneasiness, an indefinable lack. He would phone Faye, talking on sometimes after a car crossed the thin black hose between office and pumps, talking while it waited, and complaining at the departing ring that the customer had not given him a chance to get out there.

"Are you very busy tonight?" Faye would ask, and he, thinking he heard an impinging, possessive, matrimonial tone, would feel a deadening resentment. Other times her voice was cheerfully independent and he felt he was in love.

On his nights off, his arm around her in a movie, he waited impatiently for the evening's consummation in the car. But at its approach she became somber, and afterwards was tense, petulant, glum.

"What's the matter?" he asked late one night on a levee amid sounds of crickets and frogs and the close rustle of leaves.

"Nothing."

In the distance, dominating the lights of the town, the red neon crest of Stockton's twelve-story skyscraper flashed, a line at a time.

CALIFORNIA
WESTERN
STATES
LIFE
PROTECTION

"Don't you feel good?"

"I'm all right."

"Is anything wrong?"

"I said *nothing.*"

"Well, what you getting mad about then?"

"I'm not *mad.*"

"Okay."

"Can't I be quiet if I feel like it without everybody getting all worked up?"

"You're the only one getting worked up."

"Well, leave me alone then. I have a right to my moods."

"All right, I can take a hint. Don't think I don't know what's wrong. I'm not stupid. I know what it is. Maybe you need somebody that's got more to give you."

"That's not it."

"You're unfulfilled. I know, I'm sorry, I'm not blind."

"I'm fulfilled. I'm perfectly fulfilled. That's not it at all."

"You didn't get real fulfillment."

"I feel perfectly fine. I'm fulfilled. Now don't worry about it. That's not what's bothering me at all. I just feel out of touch sometimes."

"You mean you're mad."

"I'm not mad. I'm a little worried, that's all."

Ernie felt a dismal apprehension. "What about?"

"You know what."

"We've been pretty careful."

"You've been pretty careful. If I was careful I'd never come out here. You wouldn't marry me now, I know you wouldn't. Men just don't after they've slept with somebody."

"They do too. They do it all the time. What are you talking about?"

"You wouldn't."

Caught between prudence and expediency, afraid of committing himself and afraid of losing his rights to her, he replied despondently: "I would too."

"When?"

"Well, when it's right for us both. We don't want to rush into a mess when we've got each other anyway."

"Don't you want to be with me every night?"

"Sure I do. Maybe I could get a day job."

"That's not what I meant."

"I guess I don't feel ready yet. I feel I need a few more fights first," he heard himself saying. "I just don't feel I'm ready to get married."

"I wasn't proposing to you. That's a thing I certainly would never do. I wouldn't want anybody who didn't want me."

"I want you."

"That's up to you. I wouldn't force myself on anyone. If you don't want to get married you don't have to. I wasn't asking anything about that. I just meant what if, you know, you got drafted or something—how do I know where I stand? Would you want me to wait?"

"Well, sure," said Ernie, thinking there was no harm in that and piqued by the thought of someone else having her.

"I mean these are things I'm just asking for my own sake. I don't want you to feel I'm obligating you."

"I don't, I don't," he assured her.

"Like what would you want if you had some more fights? What's that got to do with it? Would that make a difference? What would you feel like doing after you had them?"

"Then I guess I'd want somebody so it'd seem worth getting my ass kicked…so I could…I don't know…have a home. But I want to get set up first," he said, unconvinced, afraid of what he was saying.

"I don't want to hold you back. I want to be good for you." She put her fingers on his cheek, her eyes only hollows in the dim starlight. "I want to cook for you."

It filled him with panic. To such devotion, such sacrifice, he felt rejection would be unbearable, that to quibble at all would be an unthinkable cruelty. Profoundly moved, he kissed the lax waiting mouth with exquisite unhappiness.

Later, on her front porch, she looked so lovely to him, so graceful, her full lips in a smile so gentle, that he could not turn and go home. So many obstacles, so much uncertainty lay ahead in consequence of what he had been forced to say in the car, that this time of intimacy had a transitory sweetness. He would not marry her, and so she would not be his much longer. Eventually there would be conditions he could not agree to. He must cherish the present like a memory. This would be the time of Faye, this would soon be over. Her presence, her voice, the taste of her mouth would be replaced by another's and lost forever. Or perhaps there would be no other after her and he would again be alone with his lust. He would not marry her, so felt a blissful freeing of his love, an elation that carried him after her through the doorway to a final kiss that became not the last but the first in a fevered goodbye with her skirt up and his little tin box out in the glove compartment of the car. Sitting on the carpeted stairs leading up to the room where he hoped her parents were asleep, he pulled her down onto his lap.

Afterwards Ernie was pensive. Through days of peat-dust storms he waited uneasily. When a month was up he drove Faye to a doctor and sat in the car knowing already what the answer would be and feeling a singular peace. He would quit fighting. Certainly now he could no longer take the risks. There was no decision to make. He had no thoughts of escape from her and was strangely unperturbed.

There seemed to him only one thing to do. They were married in the Little Chapel of the Wayfarer in Carmel, the bride wearing a white dress, the groom expressionless in sport coat and slacks. After a dinner of swordfish steak on the wharf in Monterey, they phoned the news to their parents and rented a motel room under cypress trees. Two nights later they were sleeping in Faye's room.

On Ernie's second night back at work, his employer, Mario Florestano, was waiting for him in the doorway of the station, the largeness of his alerted face accentuated by frontal baldness, long ears, a slight neck and narrow shoulders.

"You left the shitter open," he said.

Ernie, seeking an attitude, looked at him with puzzled eyes. "I did? I thought I locked it up."

"You certainly did not. Want me to tell you what I saw when I drove in this morning? A wino coming out putting toilet paper in his pocket."

"I'd swear I locked it."

"Listen, didn't you hear me? I said I saw him coming *out*. Now what I want to know is how he got in."

"I can't figure it." Ernie gravely pulled on the end of his nose. "I'd swear I remember checking the door before I left."

"You couldn't of checked that door. That door was open. How else did he get in there and get that toilet paper? Did he have a passkey?"

"I don't know, he might of had one. I sure don't remember leaving that door open."

"Forget it, forget I ever said anything about it. Don't go on any more. It's settled." Florestano paced off under dangling fan belts, turned abruptly and came back. "If you don't want to admit it, forget it. He got in there and he got the toilet paper and arguing won't bring it back. Now I'm not trying to accuse you if you don't want to admit it. I just want you to realize your mistake so it won't happen again."

"I'd admit it if I thought I did it."

"I'm sure you would."

"If you want to put the blame on me it's up to you."

"No, no, it's not a matter of blaming anyone. These things happen. It was just something I wanted to call your attention to. Nobody wants to sit on a toilet seat a wino's been on. You got to think of the public. It's public relations. Personally I couldn't care less. One man's as good as another as long as they pay their way. Only there's people around that don't feel that way. So if an undesirable asks you for the key, the shitter's out of order. So that door stays locked."

"I *keep* it locked."

Mario Florestano gave him a long look. "So how's married life treating you?"

Left in charge, Ernie scattered sawdust on the floor of the lube room, pushed it around with a long-handled broom, scooped it up blackened, and dumped it in a drum of empty oil cans. He wiped off the grease rack, wiped and hung up the tools and ambled out to cars, thumbs hooked in his pants pockets. When the streetlights came on he went to the switchbox and the night air quivered in the tall white beams of the floodlights.

Poetry

Jane Hirshfield

Studying Wu Wei, Muir Beach

There are days when you go
out into the bright spring fields
with the blue halter, the thick length
of rope with its sky-and-cloud braiding,
even the bucket of grain—
All corn-and-molasses sweetness,
the *maraca* sound of shaken seduction—
and the one you have gone for simply will not be caught.
It could be that the grass that day is too ripe.
It could be the mare who comes over, jutting her body
between his and yours. It could be
the wild-anise breeze that wanders in and out of his mane.
He might nip at the smallest mouthful,
but your hands' slightest rising—no matter how slow,
how cautious—breaks him away.
He doesn't have to run, though he knows he could.
Knows he is faster, stronger, less tied.
He knows he can take you or leave you in the dust.
But set aside purpose, leave the buckles and clasps

Jane Hirshfield, born Jewish and embracing Buddhism, is a living example of the citizen of the East finding fertile soil in the West—and looking even further into the Far East for spiritual replenishment. Since winning the Jackson Award in 1986, she has published four collections of poetry, including The October Palace, Of Gravity and Angels, *and the most recent,* The Lives of the Heart. *She has also translated the love poems of Ono no Komachi and Izumi Shikibu, women of the ancient court of Japan, in* The Ink Dark Moon. *She currently lives in Marin.*

of intention draped over the fence, come forward
with both hands fully exposed, and he greedily eats.
Allows you to fondle his ears, scratch his neck, pull out
the broken half-carrot his soft-folded lips accept
tenderly from your palm. The mare edges close, and he
lays back one ear; the other stays pricked toward you,
in utmost attention. Whatever you came for,
this is what you will get: at best, a tempered affection
while red-tails circle and lupine shifts in the wind.
It is hard not to want to coerce a world that
takes what it pleases and walks away, but *Do not-doing,*
proposed Lao-tsu—and this horse. Today the world is tired.
It wants to lie down in green grass and stain its grey shoulders.
It wants to be left to study the non-human field,
to hold its own hungers, not yours, between its teeth.
Not words, but the sweetness of fennel. Not thought,
but the placid rituals of horse-dung and flies.
Nuzzling the festive altars from plantain to mustard,
from budded thistle to bent-stemmed rye. Feasting and flowering
and sleeping in every muscle, every muzzle, every bone it has.

For What Binds Us

There are names for what binds us:
strong forces, weak forces.
Look around, you can see them:
the skin that forms in a half-empty cup,
nails rusting into the places they join,
joints dovetailed on their own weight.
The way things stay so solidly
wherever they've been set down—
and gravity, scientists say, is weak.

And see how the flesh grows back
across a wound, with a great vehemence,
more strong

than the simple, untested surface before.
There's a name for it on horses,
when it comes back darker and raised: proud flesh,

as all flesh
is proud of its wounds, wears them
as honors given out after battle,
small triumphs pinned to the chest—

And when two people have loved each other
see how it is like a
scar between their bodies,
stronger, darker, and proud;
how the black cord makes of them a single fabric
that nothing can tear or mend.

For a Wedding on Mount Tamalpais

July,
and the rich apples
once again falling.

You put them to your lips,
as you were meant to,
enter a sweetness
the earth wants to give.

Everything loves this way,
in gold honey,
in gold mountain grass
that carries lightly the shadow of hawks,
the shadow of clouds passing by.

And the dry grasses,
the live oaks and bays,
taste the apples' deep sweetness

because you taste it, as you were meant to,
tasting the life that is yours,

while below, the foghorns bend to their work,
bringing home what is coming home,
blessing what goes.

Narcissus: Tel Aviv, Baghdad, San Francisco; February 1991

And then the precise
opening everywhere of the flowers,
which live after all in their own time.
It seemed they were oblivious but they were not,
they included it all, the nameless explosions
and the oil fires in every cell, the white petals
like mirrors opening in a slow-motion coming-apart
and the stems, the stems rising like green-flaring missiles,
like smoke, like the small sounds shaken
from those who were beaten—like dust from a carpet—
into the wind and the spring-scented rain.
They opened because it was time and they had no choice,
as the children were born in that time and that place
and became what they would without choice, or with only
a little choice, perhaps, for the lucky, the foolish or brave.
But precise and in fact wholly peaceful the flowers opened,
and precise and peaceful the earth: opened because it was asked.
Again and again it was asked and earth opened—
flowered and fell—because what was falling had asked
and could not be refused, as the seabirds that ask the green surface
to open are not refused but are instantly welcomed,
that they may enter and eat—
As soon refuse, battered and soaking, the dark mahogany rain.

History as the Painter Bonnard

Because nothing is ever finished
the painter would shuffle, *bonnarding*,
into galleries, museums, even the homes of his patrons,
with hidden palette and brush:
overscribble drapery and table with milk jug or fattened pear,
the clabbered, ripening colors of second sight.

Though he knew with time the pentimenti rise—
half-visible, half brine-swept fish, their plunged shapes
pocking the mind—toward the end, only revision mattered:
to look again, more deeply, harder, clearer,
the one redemption granted us to ask.

This, we say, is what we meant to say. This. This.
—as the kiss, the sorrowful murmur,
may cover a child's bruises, if not retract the blow.
While a woman in Prague asks softly, in good English
for the camera, "But who will give us back these twenty years?"

Ah love, o history, forgive
the squandered light and flung-down rags of chances,
old choices drifted terribly awry.
And world, self-portrait never right, receive this gift—
shuffling, spattered, stubborn,
something nameless opens in the heart: to touch
with soft-bent sable, ground-earth pigment, seed-clear oil,
the rounding, bright-fleshed present, if not the past.

The kissed child puts his hand at last back into his mother's,
though it is not the same;
her fine face neither right nor wrong, only thoroughly his.

(November-December 1989)

Philip Levine

28

At 28 I was still faithless.
I had crossed the country in a green Ford,
sleeping one night almost 14 hours in a motel
above Salt Lake City. I discovered
I'd had a fever all that day and thus the animals
that dotted the road, the small black spots
that formed and unformed crows, the flying pieces
of slate that threatened to break through
the windshield...were whatever they were.
I took two aspirins and an allergy pill—that was all
I had—and got into bed although it was light out.
That was 28 years ago. Since then I have died
only twice, once in slow motion against
the steel blue driver's side of a Plymouth
station wagon. One moment before impact I said
to myself, seriously, "This is going to hurt."
The kids in the Plymouth's back seat gaped
wildly, shouted, leaped, and the father held firm

Since winning the Jackson Award in 1961, Philip Levine has published more than ten volumes of poetry. He has received many awards for his poetry, including the American Book Award, the National Book Critics Circle Award, the National Book Award, and the Pulitzer Prize. Born in 1928 in Detroit, educated at Wayne State University, he settled in Fresno, California, "after a succession of stupid jobs." His poetry often depends on a sense of place, whether it is Detroit or California or what he describes as the "country of memory." "To get west you go east," he writes. "None of it matters, so just keep going, forward or back, until you've found the place or the place doesn't matter."

to the steering wheel as I slipped through the space
that was theirs, untouched, skidding first
on the black field of asphalt and broken glass
that is California 168, Tollhouse Road, and over
the edge of the mountain, the motorcycle
tumbling off on its own through nettles and grass
to come to a broken rest as all bodies must.
Often when I shave before a late dinner, especially
on summer evenings, I notice the white lines
on my right shoulder like the smeared imprint
of a leaf on silk or the delicate tracings
on a whale's fins that the smaller sea animals carve
to test his virtue, and I reenter the wide blue eyes
of that family of five that passed on their way
up the mountain.   But at 28 I was still faithless.
I could rise before dawn from a bed drenched
with my own sweat, repack the green Ford
in the dark, my own breath steaming
in the high, clear air, and head for California.
I could spend the next night in Squaw Valley
writing a letter to my wife and kids asleep hours
behind me in Colorado, I could listen to Rexroth
reminiscing on a Berkeley FM station in the voice
God uses to lecture Jesus Christ and still believe
two aspirins, an allergy pill, and proper rest were proof
against the cold that leaps in one blind moment
from the heart to the farthest shore to shudder
through the small sea creatures I never knew existed.

It seems the sun passing back and forth behind clouds
this morning threatens to withdraw its affections
and the sky is as distant and pale as a bored child
in the wrong classroom or a man of 28
drilled so often on the names of fruit-bearing trees
that he forgets even the date palm. Here in New England,
no longer new or English, the first frost
has stained the elms and maples outside my window,
and the kids on their way hunch their shoulders

against the cold. One boy drops his lunch box
with a clatter and mysteriously leaves it there
on the pavement as a subtle rebuke
to his mother, to a father holding tight to a wheel,
to a blue Plymouth that long ago entered the heaven
brooding above Detroit. If only they had stopped
all those years ago and become a family of five
descending one after the other the stone ledges
of Sweet Potato Mountain and found me face down
among the thistles and shale and lifted me to my feet.
I weighed no more than feathers do or the wish
to become pure spirit. If I had not broken my glasses
I could have gone on my way with a thank you,
with a gap-toothed smile.
                    28 years ago, faithless, I
found the great bay of San Francisco where the map
said it would be and crossed the bridge from Oakland
singing "I Cover the Waterfront" into the cold winds
and the dense odor of coffee. Before I settled
in East Palo Alto among divorcees and appliance salesmen,
fifty yards from the Union Pacific tracks, I spent a long weekend
with Arthur, my mentor to be. In a voice ruined, he said,
by all-night draughts of whiskey and coffee, he praised
the nobility of his lemon and orange trees, the tang
of his loquats, the archaic power of his figs.
In a gambler's green visor and stiff Levis, he bowed
to his wounded tomatoes swelling into late summer.
Kneeling in the parched loam by the high fence
he bared the elusive strawberries, his blunt fingers
working the stiff leaves over and over. It was August.
He was almost happy.
                    Faithless, I had not found
the olive trees bursting on the hillsides west
of US 99. I knew only the bitter black fruit
that clings with all its life to the hard seed.
I had not wakened to mockers wrangling in my yard
at dawn in a riot of sexual splendor or heard
the sea roar at Bondy Bay, the long fingers
of ocean running underneath the house all night

to rinse off the pain of nightmare. I had not
seen my final child, though he was on the way.
I had not become a family of five nor opened
my arms to receive the black gifts of a mountain road,
of ground cinders, pebbles, rough grass.

                                 At twice my age
Arthur, too, was faithless, or so he insisted
through the long sober evenings in Los Altos, once
crowded with the cries of coyotes. His face
darkened and his fists shook when he spoke
of Nothing, what he would become in that waiting blaze
of final cold, a whiteness like no other.
At 56, more scared of me than I of him,
his right forefinger raised to keep the beat,
he gravelled out his two great gifts of truth:
"I'd rather die than reread the last novels
of Henry James," and, "Philip, we must never lie
or we shall lose our souls." All one winter afternoon
he chanted in Breton French the coarse poems of Tristan Corbière,
his voice reaching into unforeseen sweetness, both hands
rising toward the ceiling, the tears held back so long
still held back, for he was dying and he was ready.

By April I had crossed the Pacheco Pass and found
roosting in the dark branches of the Joshua tree
the fabled magpie— "Had a long tongue and a long tail;
He could both talk and do." This is a holy land,
I thought. At a Sonoco station the attendant,
wiry and dour, said in perfect Okie, "Be careful, son,
a whole family was wiped out right here
just yesterday." At Berenda the fields flooded
for miles in every direction. Arthur's blank sky
stared down at an unruffled inland sea and threatened
to let go. On the way home I cut lilacs
from the divider strip of El Camino Real.
My wife was pregnant. All night we hugged
each other in our narrow bed as the rain
came on in sheets. A family of five, and all
of us were out of work. The dawn was silent.

The black roses, battered, unclenched, the burned petals
floated on the pond beside the playhouse.
Beneath the surface the tiny stunned pike circled
no prey we could see. That was not another life.
I was 29 now and faithless, not the father of the man
I am but the same man who all this day
sat in a still house watching the low clouds massing
in the west, the new winds coming on.
By late afternoon the kids are home from school,
clambering on my front porch, though day
after day I beg them not to. When I go
to the window they race off in mock horror,
daring me to follow. The huge crows that wake
me every morning settle back on the rain spout
next door to caw to the season. I could put them
all in a poem, title it "The Basket of Memory"
as though each image were an Easter egg waiting to hatch,
as though I understood the present and the past
or even why the 8 year old with a cap of blond hair
falling to her shoulders waves to me as she darts
between parked cars and cartwheels into the early dusk.

Robert Vasquez

At the Rainbow
for Linda, Theresa, and Phyllis

At fifteen, shaving by then, I passed
for eighteen and got in, in where alcoves
breathed with ill-matched lovers—
my sisters among them—who massed
and spun out their jagged, other selves.
I saw the rhythmic dark, year over

year, discharge their flare: they scored
my memory, adrift now in the drifting place.
Often I watched a slow song empty
the tabled sidelines; even the old poured
out, some dragged by wives, and traced
odd box shapes their feet repeated. *Plenty*

and *poor:* thoughts that rose as the crowd
rose—my sisters too—in the smoked air.
They rise on....They say saxophones
still start up Friday nights, the loud,

Raised in Fresno, California, Robert Vasquez was a Wallace Stegner Fellow in Poetry at
Stanford University, and has won many honors for his work, including three Academy of
American Poets Prizes, three National Society of Arts and Letters Awards, and a National
Writers' Union Award. His collection of poems, At the Rainbow, part of which won him
the Phelan Award in 1991, was published by the University of New Mexico Press as part
of the Mary Burritt Poetry Series. He currently teaches at the College of the Sequoias in
Visalia, California.

troubled notes wafting out from where
I learned to lean close and groaned

into girls I chose—no, took—and meant it.
In the Rainbow Ballroom in Fresno
I sulked, held hands, and wheeled among
the deep-bodied ones who reinvented
steps and turns turned fast or slow,
and this body sang, man to woman, song to song.

California Sonnets: Night Sequence
for the baby doctor

1.

I look up at the night's broad back
gone crazy with tattoos of light, seasonal
signs almost beyond stoppage, and let
the unsayable build skyward. As it is
I've put off sleep, its gray tunnel
circular and face-filled, to take in
pulse-points that work the peninsular dark.
Last night, below the ridge that blocks
out the ocean's amplitude, a woman
called me to bed. And slow's the sprawl
of the almost-in-love, their wave and blur
charging their own amplitude. Yielding, we took
to the windowsill, like children almost, the curtains
blown wide as if calling the star-sprawl in, almost.

2.

Witness the Bear's stoked belly, his burning
stupor commanding the rooftops....Of course
this changes nothing: by morning the windows
are wing-sliced; all day the languid ladies
of the field and wild cowpeas still carry
hillsides into spring; the oak's true
posture of pain deepens. But I know,

due to celestial warp, some stars are black
cinders where they seem to blaze: scars
of light that survive the body. Dead suns
do that; they haunt with their ghost-lit patinas;
they reach us with their fixed and mapped
movements, like old lovers: pliable arcs of light,
they come on inarticulate, glassy, and sure.

3.

For the nightsky's vault issues insomnia,
someone said, those troubled hours withholding
the passage and balance good sleep drifts back to.
In Los Altos I join the bare-knuckled ones
who browse the neoprene bags and dumpster spillage.
And my nose swells with the road-smear of skunk, not
the living kind that will not scare, but a tire-
smashed stripe, creamy clear, almost afloat.
They say eternity's a channel in the sky.
—As if the skunk soul veers upward and drafts
like a kite. —As if the skunk angels
could spot this small jaywalker, stalled
like the number 1, beneath the intersections
of heaven. —As if I were in love.

4.

Out of the fissured dark, columbine will mount,
stiffer, and sustain acres of thistle and mud;
the high, plain shouts of children
half-heard a block away at recess will strive
to twine the day together. Bells and mission. But
before you rise from sleep's wash, think of raccoons arrogant on
Dixon Way, who palm chicken bones
before they rehouse the flood drains; think
of me hogging a whole street the way ladles
hog zones in the sky. Think how the wintered
and rolling earth reveals itself, how
everything the night holds out and clarifies,
like love, withdraws suddenly from the limbs
and organs of intake: hands, eyes, and heart.

James Schevill

Living in a Boxcar in San Francisco

When you get older, you kind of settle like a house,
Except in my case, it's a boxcar...Smoke down
The doubledeck freeway, take a quick look out your window
Before you hit the distance...You'll see me sticking up,
My big boxcar solid in backyard sun, challenging the freeway,
Fresh brown paint, white-lettered name on the side:
EL CABALLO, Spanish for horse, we used to go bumping
From ranch to ranch, endless grazing land, horses
Kicking against the boxcar walls, waiting to run...
When they started building the freeway, it took a lot
Of sitting to get my boxcar left smack at the end of the line
When they retired me along with the railroad's end.
They were bulldozing everything for the freeway, trees,
Hills, houses...You bet they didn't expect a boxcar!
You should have seen their eyes frost up when they looked
Down from their surveying gadgets and saw this silent
Old hulk of a witness watching them. How they screamed
Before they decided to go around a few yards
And leave me tight against the noise and smoke,

James Schevill was educated at Harvard University and taught English at Brown University, but his roots are all Californian. A native of Berkeley, where he now lives, he is both a poet and playwright. He has published several collections of poetry—but perhaps his finest work is The Complete American Fantasies, a life's work and a sequence of poetry on the American scene, arranged in sections on decades from the 1920s through the 1990s. He has won the Phelan Award twice—in 1954 and 1960.

Their damn cars smashing all day and night.
So we go on. Not that it's a war. They don't pay me
No attention except they got to slow down for the curve.
I've had her fitted with lights and I sleep in her now.
I'm kind of deaf, so those cars pounding up there,
Going where they have to go, don't bother me.
I pull into my boxcar, my lights shining at the
End of the line, maybe the last brakeman of the old,
Clicking western rails, train whistling to the desert stars,
Slow puff over tough mountains to the waiting sea...
When there's a frontier to remember, you got to live in it.

In the Japanese Tea Garden in San Francisco

To create an expert difficulty
That defeats destruction,
Build a Japanese bridge.
Arch the wood in a high curve—
Block it with steep, splintery steps,
Flow under it a clear stream
With red fish for contemplation,
Assemble families for the climb.
Vary ages, sizes, forms, minds,
Quiet, ugly, lazy, combative temperaments;
Children to scream, stare, giggle at danger;
Frantic, laughing parents to warn of falls,
Broken legs; grandparents to mutter "impossible,"
And watch with resigned pleasure
The high, difficult crossing.
Shouts of triumph should be an absolute joy
Aimed to clarify the air, not muddle the fog.
At night, let the aging, wooden bridge
Rest in the silence of its lofty curve,
Worn, mirrored in the moonlit water,
The wheel of life that turns,
Extending the invitation of difficulty.

The Watch of the Live Oaks

Across the street from my childhood summer house,
A twisted strand of live oaks rises in the sky,
Boughs locked high in a green vault. Beneath their watch
A neighbor boy was killed, shot through a window,
As he stood drunk and cursing on the lawn.
I think of Robert Louis Stevenson,
Walking in dark groves, who called the oaks
"Woods for murderers to crawl among."
Compelled, we blaze our images on trees.
They only watch us from their silent peaks,
And yet without their arch of greenness
Who would walk out singing in the morning?
As among a grove of live oaks in the mountains,
Father Serra ordered the bells unpacked
For his new mission, hung the bells
From the sinuous, gnarled grace of an oak.
Seized by his writhing search for peace,
He rang the bells exultantly, crying:
"Hear and come! Come to the Holy Church of God!"
And the heathen oak became a Christian church.

Neighbors in a Coastal Town

Next door
in a shingle-sliding house,
paint curling off like worms
            in their crawling pace,
lives the neighbor whose guts I hate
            with his miser-face.

His house
is a jungle of mice and junk,
and he means to cut my property value
            with his ugly mess
of broken furniture, decaying wood,

nothing to bless.

In the morning
he stakes out his property line
with a tall, imaginary fence;
      I feel barbed wire,
though he only hammers sticks in the ground
      with eyes of fire.

His little head
sits on his neck like a grape,
and the rags of his clothes fill with dirt.
      To treat him mean
I give laughing parties for my friends;
      he watches behind a screen.

I think he was born
to life a hermit's isolation
and serve himself with trembling hands,
      trapped in a shell
of darkness where cold air blows
      no saving church bell.

But every time
I look at him with hate he changes;
his shoulders sag, his head sinks,
      he decays with his house,
as I paint desperately to keep my house alive
      and set traps for any mouse.

The Distance of AIDS

Across the Russian River
where I spend summer time
lives a man dying of AIDS.
He sits in his chair on the dock,
absorbing the sun with quiet intent.

From a distance I watch him,
unknown to the core,
and he watches me,
abstract figure on my high deck
against the river's flooding,

and we watch the river's
current like a waiting crime—
while two white and black
butterflies flash over the
wild grass, disappearing
clash in summer's dying time.

Thomas Avena

Azazel
(walking with Ana Mercedes)

"What is that smell, like something almost fetid?"

"No...like dry grass."

"Or fresh-bleached laundry."

"It smells like Ceanothus. Pollen. The fragrance
of young men. It's like a bathhouse."

"I know that smell," she said. "When I lived in Berkeley,
in a house that was like a cathedral. It's Bay Laurel."

And then we had the evidence. Shiny red and green leaves.
And the oil bursting on our fingertips.

The winner of the 1994 Jackson Award, Thomas Avena credits the San Francisco Foundation for allowing him to complete Dream of Order, *published by Mercury House in 1997. He is the recipient of a 1995 American Book Award for editing and cowriting* Life Sentences: Writers, Artists, and AIDS. *The editor of "Project Face to Face," an AIDS oral history and arts installation, he served as the project's writer-in-residence during its exhibition at the Smithsonian Institution's Experimental Gallery in 1991. He is also the author, with Adam Klein, of* Jerome: After the Pageant. *He currently lives in San Francisco.*

"I painted my room cerulean blue or cerulean Persian
blue, and there was a little Modigliani nude, like a small
postcard, under the skylight. I felt like that—reposed
and angular, at once, which is *luxury*. I had Joshua
punch a hole into the ceiling. The room was so
cold, all the heat would rise up into the skylight.
It looked up to a redwood tree. There was a window
set in the blue wall. About now, in late summer,
in August, late in the day, the light would shoot
in from the north. The heat came in with terrible
force. It turned the Bay Laurel leaves fire green.

"I never wanted to leave that place. I wanted to live
there forever. There was a horse pasture on a half-
acre of land—in the middle of Berkeley. A hundred
and twenty five grand. I tried to get them to invest.
But they just laughed at me. And now, *well.*"
We glimpsed something, pale and glinting, through the trees,
and saw that it was terraced stone, obscured by leaves.

It was an amphitheater, with oaks shooting from the rock.
Or the oaks were contained as if in stone vessels.

We had found, on Mount Tamalpais, the WPA amphitheater
built of wide seats of granite—flat and grand, for the American
bottom. And built by the American bottom—the WPA.

Looking into the distance, we could hold the whole city,
like an ornament, in the palm of our hands—and turn it.

The long path down from the amphitheater was stepped
in stone. There were split-rails of cedar that had aged and
smoothed to a rubbed pewter. They shone in the late afternoon
light. And these flowers: Goldenrod-colored Indian paintbrush.
Larkspur—the color of the eyes of that intemperate actress.
Wild yellow poppies—or were they tiny crocuses—
veined in brown. Stalks of white yarrow.

Then Foxy Loxy darted into the path.

"On the radio today. This senator talked about the collapse
of our systems. When the double-digit based years will
return to 1900 and everything will grind to a halt. They
said keep a written record of all your stocks and bonds.

"Of course there's no real information for us," she said.

For us who have neither stocks nor bonds.

"Let me tell you something. I am sick,
sick to death of…hammered by this Millennium Bug.

"And look, the last of the wild azaleas—in July."
Elusive, so late in the season, as their fragrance.

"Why doesn't anyone ever name a child Azalea?"

"Because she would be a spinster."

We continued our descent. "Of course now.
They couldn't pay me to live in Berkeley."

"Oh yes. They could pay you."

"No. They could never pay me."

"This is how we'll survive the Millennium Bug.
We need to find a hacker…to dis-invent *something*."

That evening, I looked up *azalea* in Webster's:
fr. Gk, fem. of *azaleos,* dry;
akin to L *aridus* dry—more at ARDOR.

The next definition was for *azathioprine:*
a purine immunosuppressant.

Directly below was *Azazel:*
an evil spirit of the wilderness to which a scapegoat
was sent by the Hebrews in a ritual of atonement.

The goat of removal.

There was a teasing or scratching against my ear
like a thin wire...

"I am an insect of personification," said the voice
"an insect, a goat—

"everything about your kind...the way you live,
is *wrong."*

I saw the lights of the city—extinguished,
and I awakened

but it was only the computer—
asleep.

They stood, silhouetted in the bronze urn: the wild white
azaleas wrapped against branches of bay laurel, their stems
tied in a white kerchief. Urn that had seen ashes and wine.

There was a pale lick of yellow on the petal.
They were sweet, at first breath,
and then the perverse whiff of fox
(for those who dared approach their secret).

The Daisy

She is talking into the phone
and as she declaims
the sienna-orange daisy
bows down over the lip of its vase

a Meiji bronze
with its gilt abraded
that was still dusted over
with the ashes of my lover

The Dalkon shield
that scarred her womb

the adhesions to the womb
and their white-hot pain

she's fallen in the street again

I found her a cane
cut from bird's eye maple
it is just the right size

her staff and her rod
and she hits cars with it

when they cut her off
but this speech will not be

cut off
(besides) I have
only terrible things
to say   as well

What comfort
in terrible things

like watching
a movie

where a woman stands alone
(on a white set)
in the pouring rain

it is dark
but she is lit (from inside)
with the whitest light

a stranger comes
and offers her his umbrella

we cannot tell
that she is beautiful
(but he can)

still, she is mad

she runs with him
under the trees

and the trees are white
are pillars of light

What comfort
in terrible things

because it means
that I am her brother

brother of circumstance

And as she talks

the property will go
her hut

on its little land

will be taken from her hand

in the center of the valley
the soft carpet of needles

underfoot
that she will lose

carpet of red fir needles
that cushions her back

those city streets   that concrete
like sandpaper on the spine

she isn't strong

in this economy
everyone's thriving

but we're not

It is not tenuous
it makes no sound—
the daisy in its bed of ash
bows down

My lover once threw her
out of our house

for some crime
which was not imagined

she has accomplishments
and like anyone

is despised for them

they are distant
this needn't even be said

what she says
is undeniable

In the morning
they will put more chemo
into my spine

I will lie down
with an inflamed brain

in the silence of cars
skimming in the rain

His ash
seeps into the daisy

and the daisy bows down

Her speech
is exhausting her

all her old methods
have failed her

her efforts of will—
failed her

she navigates
with her cane

the codeine and pills

she never thought she'd take

those city streets   that concrete
like sandpaper on the nerves

On this table
we served her

a roasted pig
in a sauce of rue
and juniper

and she laughed
and told the joke

"why is this night
different from all other nights..."

she drank
a glass of Merlot

and a glass of...

and Bill drank several glasses
of Barbaresco

and roared with laughter

we talked about
the properties of gin

with its coriander
and citrus peels

and crushed black juniper

until our conversation was blackened
was invaded—

the scent of crushed juniper
was everywhere

Until we toasted
terrible things

It is not tenuous
it makes no sound—
the daisy in its iron bed
bows down

(until) its bright blood head
touches the table

(of black marble)

Al Young

One West Coast
for Gordon Lapides

Green is the color of everything
that isnt brown, the tones ranging
like mountains, the colors changing.

You look up toward the hills & fog—
the familiarity of it after so many years
   a resident tourist.

     A young man walks
toward you in vague streetcrossing denims
& pronounced boots. From the pallor of
   his gait, the orange splotch twin gobs of sunset
   in his shades, from the way he vibrates
   his surrounding air, you can tell, you can tell
    he's friendly, circulating,

Born in Ocean Spring, Mississippi, Al Young was raised in the South and in Detroit. He has written in practically every literary medium, including plays, screenplays, poetry, and novels. Recognized as one of the most distinctive of the southern-born black writers, he has received Wallace Stegner, Guggenheim, National Endowment for the Arts, and Fulbright fellowships, as well as the 1969 Jackson Award. He has written over twenty books, and his work has been translated into more than a dozen languages. He travels extensively—reading, lecturing, and performing his work—but makes his home in the San Francisco Bay Area.

223

             he's a Californian: comes to visit,
          stays for years, marries, moves a wife in,
      kids, wears out TV sets, gets stranded on
              loneliness,
           afternoon pharmaceutica,
       so that the sky's got moon in it by
        3 o'clock, is blooo, is blown—

                   The girls: theyre all
            winners reared by grandmothers & CBS.

         Luckier ones get in a few dances with
       mom, a few hours, before dad goes back
     in the slam, before "G'bye I'm off
         to be a singer!" & another runaway
          Miss American future drifts
            over the mountain &
             into the clouds.

            Still
    there's a beautifulness about California.
It's based on the way each eyeblink toward
the palms & into the orange grove leads backstage
          into the onionfields.

Unreachable, winter happens inside you.

Your unshaded eyes dilate at the spectacle.

You take trips to contain the mystery.

Lonesome in the Country

How much of me is sandwiches radio beer?
How much pizza traffic & neon messages?
I take thoughtful journeys to supermarkets,
philosophize about the newest good movie,

camp out at magazine racks & on floors,
catch humanity leering back in laundromats,
invent shortcuts by the quarter hour.

There's meaning to all this itemization
& I'd do well to look for it in woodpiles

& in hills & springs & trees in the woods
instead of staying in my shack all the time
thinking too much,
                    falling asleep in old chairs

All those childhood years spent in farmhouses
& I still cant tell one bush from another—
Straight wilderness would wipe me out
faster than cancer from smoking cigarettes

My country friends are out all day long
stomping thru the woods all big-eyed &
that's me walking the road afternoons,
head in some book,
                    all that hilly sweetness wasting

Late January
Sonoma Mountain Road
in the Year of the Dragon

Leaving Home for Home

Seattle's still behind me now, and yet
through the rain and clouds up ahead
I can make out the beginnings
of a Portland as visually improbable
as a night in Tunisia; slow, sloshing
mirage of a place kept wet and green
for a motor-footed runner like me

to come upon and see. It's somebody's
Jerusalem if not exactly mine. Me?
I'm determined to make it into Salem
then Eugene by a quarter to nine.
What's all this endless driving about?
Tell me, Ray Carver, this is your country,
your early gin of origins. So once
again, what's in Alaska? What is it about
Vancouver, Bellevue, Siskiyou, Bremerton
I'm beginning to feel? Or is that all
up to me to figure out on the fly?
And say, Lawson Inada, jazz poet of Ashland,
Oregon! You too live in this stratosphere.
What's all this about salmon and chips,
alderwood, the Cascades, bumbershoots,
Puget Sound and Mt. Rainier, green bridges,
Green Death, ale, Mt. Shasta, water, water?

Old, eternally dislocated and hungry, hugger
of earth that I am, I love it all. I love
the breezy wide-openness of Northwest
Passages; woody, wet hermetic passages,
brash and brassy with reed; axes chopping
the region smooth. Rejoicing, realizing
you don't go on being a slumbering lumberman
if you can't seed the forest for the trees.
Finally housing gets to be so high
the timber market sinks to legendary lows.
But it's this legend, it's those lows
that brought me up to this part of the world.
But where will these gullies carry me?
Where am I headed on my way back
to a California I've never seen before?
And why am I trembling at the wheel?

Even though I know the car's still
moving, I can't imagine where it'll be
taking me. And yet oil companies grow
rich whether I drive on or pull to a halt.

Salt is what my African ancestors
used to throw over their shoulders
to stop bad luck, but for me right now,
keen on gasoline and the idea of forward movement
toward a spot where there'll be
ice cream, a fire and warmth, it's this
life at the top of the map that freezes.

The Imitation Dance

Time is Berkeley
the place is now
where some unenlightened children
beyond the rim of my attention
are actively lollygagging
on the hard sidewalk
laid in
where trees once loved so informally,
or dribbling Ishmael Reed's zen basketballs
across the playground in windy spring light.
I make nothing of this until the din subsides
& I'm forced to account for the silence.

Orange juice a roll some lettuce banana/milk
the way we eat now, appearances
real enough
dissolving in the juices
of my hidden stomach.
Form is emptiness.
                    Objects clutter my vision:
books beads fern shoes machine-parts a table
a decoration squash a
chance scattering of oolong leaf
the 29¢ teacup & pencils
apple seed a fragrant picture of you
pinned against the wall
to mountains

a TV set that's never worked
some clocks,
a moment,
our plastic cubbyhole in Ha Ha Street.

Everything is supposed to have changed yet
flatulence & decline are still being discussed
with the same open passion
in all but the right places;
I manage to stay as poor as ever,
a part-Indian excavator of old inner cities
out here at the edge of the jungle,
but one day I'm going to move
even further from the so-called center
on into the heart of things.

Years may pass again
or only some hours before I dance out
the shape of another clear day,
eternal unit of forever

Big Sur
after a pastel by Vivian Torrence

Sometimes it's the look of love
along a coast like Big Sur's
that galvanizes even the wash
& splash of blueness foaming
into green upon the rock &
circumstance of cliffs & promontories.
The blush of blooming seaplant,
the bloom of abalone blows even
the minds of oldtime naturalists
when the tide pours in and Indian
souls rush out to fill the night.
But always it's that look, that
luscious, lingering look rolling

in & out of cloud & wave alike,
that spills onto the leaves of fog
journals, that changes in its sameness
century on top of century, glimpsed
in a watchful, wakeful moment
along such breathable stretches
of majesty & heartbeat in the rush
of oceanic sureness on the big coast
trafficked by foot & by motorcade
with no mist to ground love down.

Past Winners of the James D. Phelan Award

1935 Gladys Merrifield
      George Hand
1936 Edward Ramsay
1937 Howard Edminister
      Sidney Meller
1938 Ann Stanford
1939 John Berry
1940 Sidney Meller
1942 Barbara Gibbs
1945 Robert Gardiner
1946 James Broughton
1947 Eleanor Hesthal
1948 Homer L. Sutton
1952 James Gavin
      Daniel Wise
      James Hewelcke
1954 John Edwards
      James Schevill
      Arnold Schwab
1956 Gonzalo Estrada
      Frank Wattron, Jr.
      Catherine Hurley
1958 Varley McBeth
      Audrey Doughty
      Clayton Barbeau
      William Stine
      George Price, Jr.
      E. Leonard Nathan
      Robert Brotherson
      Helen Caswell
1960 Edward Franklin
      Allan Cayous
      Harold Witt
      Thor Svenson
      Harry Lawton
      Richard Dillon
      Elizabeth Berryhill
      James Schevill
1962 George Price
      Daniel Moore
      Edwin Fussell

1964 John van der Zee
      Theodore Labrenz, Jr.
      Paul Fussell, Jr.
      Albert Ujcic
1966 Henri Coulette
      John Deck
      Ann Jones
      Leonard Gardner
      Frank Chin
1968 Leonard Gardner
      Frederic Hunter
      Theodore Labrenz, Jr.
      Wesley Marx
1970 John Hart
      Thomas Schmidt
1972 Marc Reid Rubel
1973 Nels Hanson
1974 Lyn Hejinian
1976 David Carkeet
1977 Keith Spencer Felton
1978 Richard Street
1979 Roberta Spear
1980 David Marshall St. John
1981 David Shields
1982 Melissa Brown-Pritchard
1983 Gary Young
1984 Dagoberto Gilb
1985 Peter Fish
1986 Sallie Tisdale
1987 Mark Coovelis
1988 Lise Goett
1990 Catherine Ann French
1991 Robert Vasquez
1992 Thomas Rooney
1993 Anne Calcagno
1994 Priscilla Lee
1995 Christopher Sindt
1996 Emmy Perez
1997 Rebekah Edwards
1998 Amanda Kim
1999 Eleni Sikelianos

Past Winners of the Joseph Henry Jackson Award

1957 Dennis R. Murphy	1980 Wendy Bishop
1958 William G. Wiegand	1981 Stephanie Marlis
1959 Ernest J. Gaines	1982 Lucille Lang Day
1960 James Fetler	1983 Michael Covino
1961 Philip Levine	1984 Anne Finger
1962 James Leigh	1985 Carol Snow
1963 Leonard Gardner	1986 Jane Hirshfield
1964 Floyd F. Salas	1987 Fenton Johnson
1965 Frank Chin	1988 Fae Myenne Ng
1966 Louis Dell Logan	1989 Bo Caldwell
1967 James D. Houston	1990 Walter David Pavlich
1968 Stanley T. Rice, Jr.	1991 Caroline Patterson
1969 Al Young	1992 Joshua Weiner
1970 Ernest Brawley	1993 Bart Rawlinson
1971 Richard Lourie	1994 Thomas Avena
1972 Raymond J. Kingsley	1995 Nona Caspers
1973 Russell Brandon	1996 Luke Trent
1974 Mark Jarman	1997 Mike Padilla
1975 Fred Matteson	1998 Dana Lomax
1976 Stephen Matthew Tracy	1999 Matthew Iribarne
1977 Stephanie Mines	
1978 John Thomas Lescroart	
1979 Mindy Eunsoo Pennybacker	

Past Winners of the Joseph Henry Jackson Special Award in Nonficton

1987 William Neal Soiffer	1994 Susan Jacobowitz
1988 Wendy Lesser	1997 Lisa Michaels
1989 Sharman Apt Russell	1998 Brian Bouldrey
1991 Emily Moore	1999 Joelle Fraser
1992 Sarah M. Liu	

Permissions

The San Francisco Foundation

The San Francisco Foundation was founded in 1948 by a group of community-spirited civic leaders. The Foundation is now one of the largest community foundations in the United States, with assets of more than $600 million. In 1998, Foundation Trustees approved more than $47 million in grants.

Community foundations allow a wide range of donors—individuals, families, corporations, and organizations—to create charitable funds that will continue to benefit their communities for all time. With its experienced, knowledgeable staff, the Foundation is able to assess local needs to assure that these charitable gifts are used most effectively.

The San Francisco Foundation aims to mobilize resources and guide their use to promote vibrant, sustainable communities throughout the Bay Area. In service to the community, the Foundation partners with diverse organizations and donors to create new opportunities and to be a catalyst for change.

In keeping with this mission, the Special Awards Program recognizes individuals and organizations making exemplary contributions to the community. The program offers awards in community leadership and artistic or literary achievement. With each award given, The San Francisco Foundation honors those who have enriched the lives of all the people who live, work, and play in the Bay Area.

Proceeds from the sale of *Writing Home: Award-Winning Literature from the New West* will support the establishment of an additional literary award for Bay Area residents.

**The San Francisco
Foundation**

About the Editor

Brian Bouldrey is the author of the novels *The Genius of Desire* (Ballantine, 1993) and *Love, the Magician* (Haworth, 2000), and the editor of *Traveling Souls: Contemporary Pilgrimage Stories* (Whereabouts, 1999), *Wrestling with the Angel* (Riverhead, 1995), and the *Best American Gay Fiction* series (Little, Brown). His fiction and essays have appeared most recently in *TriQuarterly, Zyzzyva, Fourteen Hills, Flesh and the Word, Sewanee Review, Poets and Writers, The Harvard Review, Men on Men, The James White Review,* and *Speak.* He is also a frequent contributor to the *San Francisco Bay Guardian,* where he is Associate Editor of the "Lit." supplement.